SPECIAL MESSAGE TO READERS

This book is published by

THE ULVERSCROFT FOUNDATION,

a registered charity in the U.K., No. 264873

The Foundation was established in 1974 to provide funds to help towards research, diagnosis and treatment of eye diseases. Below are a few examples of contributions made by THE ULVERSCROFT FOUNDATION:

★ A new Children's Assessment Unit at Moorfield's Hospital, London.

★ Twin operating theatres at the Western Ophthalmic Hospital, London.

★ The Frederick Thorpe Ulverscroft Chair of Ophthalmology at the University of Leicester.

★ Eye Laser equipment to various eye hospitals.

If you would like to help further the work of the Foundation by making a donation or leaving a legacy, every contribution, no matter how small, is received with gratitude. Please write for details to:

THE ULVERSCROFT FOUNDATION,
The Green, Bradgate Road, Anstey,
Leicestershire, LE7 7FU. England.

Telephone: (0533) 364325

I've travelled the world twice over,
Met the famous: saints and sinners,
Poets and artists, kings and queens,
Old stars and hopeful beginners,
I've been where no-one's been before,
Learned secrets from writers and cooks
All with one library ticket
To the wonderful world of books.

QUESTIONS OF IDENTITY

Michael Wyman, ex-MI6, now Professor of Philosophy at the University of Rome, finds himself involved with the Red Brigades when Professor Scheib, a leading bacteriologist is kidnapped. The only line to the Brigade's leader, Francesco Ponti, is through one of Wyman's brightest and most radical pupils, Monica Venuti. But she is the daughter of one of Italy's most influential diplomats, and no-one dare touch her. No-one except the CIA: but why is Scheib's disappearance causing the CIA so much concern?

BOB COOK

QUESTIONS OF IDENTITY

Complete and Unabridged

ULVERSCROFT
Leicester

First published in Great Britain in 1987 by
Victor Gollancz Ltd.,
London

First Large Print Edition
published January 1989
by arrangement with
Victor Gollancz Ltd.,
London

British Library CIP Data

Cook, Bob
Questions of identity.—Large print ed.—
Ulverscroft large print series: mystery
I. Title
823'.914[F]

ISBN 0-7089-1927-8

Published by
F. A. Thorpe (Publishing) Ltd.
Anstey, Leicestershire
Set by Rowland Phototypesetting Ltd.
Bury St. Edmunds, Suffolk
Printed and bound in Great Britain by
T. J. Press (Padstow) Ltd., Padstow, Cornwall

To Dawn

"As for myself, I walk abroad o' nights
And kill sick people groaning under walls;
Sometimes I go about and poison wells."

Christopher Marlowe, *The Jew of Malta*

". . . the city of Rome, where all cruel and shameful practices cluster and thrive."

Tacitus, *Annals XV*

Prologue

IT was hot. In an arid field fifty kilometres north-east of Rome, two men stood by a grey Lancia. One was a man in his late twenties. The other was about fifty. Both wore overalls. They were sweating, and two dusty shovels on the ground bore witness to their exertions.

"He's late," said the younger man.

The older man nodded calmly.

"There's no hurry," he said.

He wiped a handkerchief across his brow and lit a cigarette.

A Fiat truck came across the field towards them, churning up clouds of dust. It drew to a halt by the Lancia, and a middle-aged farmer got out.

"Good morning, gentlemen," he said.

"Good morning," they replied.

The farmer went to the back of the truck and opened the door.

"Come on girl," he said.

A sheep hopped out on to the dry grass and stared at the three men inquisitively.

"Her name's Gina," said the farmer.

"Hello Gina," said the young man.

Gina gazed at him blankly.

"How old is she?" asked the older man.

"Two years old, Professor."

The older man nodded.

"As you can see, we've started work on the field. It seems to be exactly what we need."

"I'm sure it is," said the farmer. "It's lain fallow for over five years. It's too near the road, so I can't keep animals here."

"And you're sure you haven't touched it?" asked the "professor". "No insecticides, fertilizers, anything of that sort?"

"Nothing at all."

"Good. The experiment would be ruined if this field were contaminated with insecticides."

"I understand, Professor," said the farmer. "But you won't have any problems."

"I hope not," said the "professor". He drew some money from a pocket in his overalls. "This is what you asked for, and there's a little extra for your trouble."

"Thank you," the farmer smiled. "I hope your experiment is a success."

"I hope so too. After we've finished today, we'll be returning in a couple of weeks, though we probably won't be seeing you. If you leave the field alone for at least a month you can be sure we won't need it any longer."

"Good," said the farmer. "Well, I'd better not detain you any longer. Goodbye, gentlemen."

The farmer got into his van and drove off. The young man turned to the "professor" and said:

"'A little extra for your trouble', eh, Franco? I never thought of tipping as a particularly egalitarian activity."

"It's what he expects of a professor," Franco said tonelessly.

"What exactly did you tell him?"

"I said I was doing research at the university into animal decomposition. I told him we needed to conduct an experiment."

"He wasn't suspicious?"

"Of course not," Franco said. "Why should he be?"

"Okay, Franco, so why are we doing this? Isn't it time you told me?"

"No," Franco grinned. "If you can't work out what I'm doing, then nor can anyone else."

"I suppose you think I'm too stupid to work it out."

"I don't *suppose* you are," Franco smiled, "I *know*. All in good time, my dear Vito."

He looked down at the sheep, and Gina replied with an expression of boredom.

"Well," he said, "there's no sense in hanging about."

He drew out a Walther P38 pistol, fitted it with a silencer, and held it about eight inches away from Gina's head. He squeezed the trigger three times in rapid succession. Gina's head virtually exploded under the impact of the bullets. She collapsed, twitched and lay still.

"Messy," Vito observed.

Franco nodded and wiped the barrel of the gun across his sleeve.

"It gets even messier," he said, walking over to the back of the Lancia.

He opened the boot and pulled out a machete.

"It's a good thing I haven't eaten," Vito remarked, as Franco returned to the carcass and began hacking it apart. He took little care over his butchery—Gina came apart in ragged, bloody chunks.

When he had finished, he sorted the limbs, head and internal organs into six heaps. The blood already stank, and flies buzzed greedily about the dismembered limbs.

"She'll rot quickly in this heat," Franco said.

"Is that good?"

"It certainly is. Right, let's finish off."

Each man picked up a pile of limbs and innards and took it to one of six holes they had dug that morning in various parts of the field. When each of them had made three trips, they refilled the holes with soil.

Once they had finished, they returned to the car. Franco pulled a large black plastic bag out of the boot and put the shovels and machete into it. The men then took off their overalls and boots, and these too went into the bag. They washed the blood and soil off their hands with water from a can, and changed into casual summer clothes.

"An excellent morning's work," Franco said as they drove off.

"I'm glad you think so," said Vito. "But Franco . . ."

"Yes?"

"How *do* you start a revolution with a dead sheep?"

1

IT was a little after 11.30 p.m. in Rome on September 23. A portly, middle-aged gentleman strolled towards his hotel on the Via Due Macelli. It was warm, and he paused every now and then to pat his brow with a handkerchief. A few other people were also on the street, but none seemed to notice him. Had they done so, a glance at his cigar and check suit would have told them that he was yet another American visitor to the city.

A yellow Fiat drove past the American and stopped a few yards ahead of him. A man got out of the back and walked up to him.

"*Buona sera*," said the man, "You are Professor Theodore Scheib?"

"I am," said the American. "And who might you be?"

The man produced an automatic and pointed it at the American.

"I am your executioner," he said

genially. "Or at least I will be if you don't get into the car."

"Jesus Christ," exclaimed the professor. "Is this a mugging?"

The other man's face screwed up in distaste.

"Nothing so crude," he said. "Think of it as your introduction to another facet of Italian life."

"I don't get it."

"Don't worry. You will."

He pointed to the car. The American shrugged, threw away his cigar, and got in.

Professor Scheib's hotel did not notice his absence that night. It was not until the next morning that inquiries began. The professor was due to give a lecture at the 14th International Symposium on Microbiology at the University of Rome. His failure to attend resulted in phone calls to his hotel, and in turn to the police. It was established that the professor had eaten a late meal with some friends at a restaurant near his hotel. He had said he would walk home.

The professor's colleagues were understandably distressed. They told the police that the professor was a quiet, happily married man who had devoted most of his sixty-three years to scientific inquiry. He was not accustomed to vanishing without trace.

The police were unimpressed. They knew all about the habits of Americans in Rome, and they had their own theories about his disappearance. They suppressed their grins and suggested that the professor was probably just enjoying himself somewhere and would not wish to be disturbed.

The truth emerged that evening. At 7.30 a phone call was made to the offices of a national newspaper. It was revealed that Professor Theodore M. Scheib had been kidnapped by a cell of the Red Brigades, Italy's most notorious terrorist organization. He would be set free if thirty-two members of the Red Brigades were released from prison. Their names were read out and the caller rang off.

The Carabinieri, Italy's para-military police, were alerted. The American embassy on the Via Veneto was informed. Within three hours the news was broadcast on television and radio. Journalists at the *Stampa Estera*, Rome's Foreign Press

Club, made hurried telephone calls to the American Embassy, the university, and their newspapers.

The usual questions were asked, and the usual evasive replies were given. Why Scheib? Was he a political figure? Definitely not, they said. Was there a military connection? Not any more. When was he military? At least twenty years ago: he was in the Chemical Warfare Corps at Fort Detrick, Maryland. What kind of work did he do? Research. Into what? Listen, boy, I'm no scientist; how should I know? Is he rich—influential connections? No. So why kidnap him? You tell us.

Despite the slight question mark over the professor's career, the kidnapping seemed to be a straightforward affair. The Red Brigades wanted the release of their comrades. By kidnapping a foreigner, it was assumed, they hoped that international pressure could be applied to the Italian government.

And then a new rumour emerged. It was suspected that the Red Brigade column responsible was headed by Francesco Ponti. Authorities on Italian terrorism declared that this threw a new light on the topic; Franco Ponti was the last active member of the Red Brigades' founding generation. Whereas nearly all the veterans of 1968 were reformed, imprisoned or in exile, Ponti was still there.

To the new generation of Red Brigadists, Ponti was a legendary figure. He was remorseless and surgically efficient. Middle-age had not softened or tired him. He was as committed as ever.

To the Carabinieri, Ponti was a vicious criminal. He lacked the youthful naïvety which tripped up many of his younger accomplices. He was an experienced killer, and he understood his enemy well.

His position was extreme even by the standards of the Red Brigades; only a full-scale war would bring the State crashing down. The size and nature of the casualty list did not interest him. As one policeman put it, he was "a thoroughly evil bastard".

2

JULIAN HEPBURN was the CIA's Head of Station in Rome. It was generally agreed that he was the right sort of man for the job. His silver hair was elegantly styled. His suits were skilfully tailored. His nails were faultlessly manicured. His face was impeccably shaved each morning by a barber in the Via Orlando who told him what a magnificent fellow he was. Hepburn liked that.

He was appointed to his post because someone at CIA headquarters at Langley had decided that "a bit of class" was required in Rome. "Class" was something Hepburn had in abundance. He was the product of a Philadelphia family who had struggled for generations to emulate European gentility.

Hepburn had inherited all his family's snobbery and pretension, and he applied them to his job. In his thirty years with the CIA he had never soiled his hands with field work, and he referred to those menials who actually gathered intelligence as "artisans" or "plumbers".

His visitor that morning was a perfect example of the operative he despised so much. Edgar P. Rawls was a bland, dark-haired man in his mid-forties, with tinted spectacles and an air of breezy cynicism that set Hepburn's teeth on edge. Most of his career had been spent in clandestine work for the CIA. He specialized in unarmed combat and sabotage, as well as undercover operations in a variety of countries. Hepburn thought he was horribly vulgar.

"Good morning Rawls," he said, as the agent entered his office.

"Hi, Julie," Rawls said.

"Do take a seat," Hepburn said, wincing at the diminutive. "And what can we do for you?"

"Didn't they tell you why I'm here?"

"I got a garbled message from Langley. Apparently they want you to investigate the Scheib kidnapping. It all seems a little strange to me. Italy isn't your main specialty, and I fail to see what you can do that the Italians can't. I appreciate that Scheib is important, but—if you'll forgive me—

what can you do to help? Or am I underestimating your superhuman powers?"

"We've got one or two leads," Rawls said, ignoring the sarcasm. "Ever heard of a girl called Monica Venuti?"

Hepburn thought about it for a moment and shook his head.

"No. But the surname is familiar."

"It ought to be," Rawls said. "Vittorio Venuti is the Italian cultural attaché in London. Here in Italy he's a big guy."

"Yes indeed," Hepburn agreed. "What about this girl?"

"She's his daughter, and she keeps bad company. She's a philosophy student at the university here, and she's very political."

"What does that mean?"

"She hangs around with people who've got Red Brigade connections. There's a possible link with Francesco Ponti."

"I see," Hepburn said. "And if this lead is so good, why aren't the Italians doing something about it?"

"Because of her old man. Venuti is right-wing, he's powerful, and he's probably a freemason. He's also crazy about his daughter."

"So," Hepburn said, "any investigation into his daughter would open up a political can of worms. I think I feel a migraine coming on."

"How come?"

"What exactly do you intend to do about this girl?"

"Oh, I don't know. Follow her up, maybe squeeze her a little. That kind of thing."

Hepburn groaned in disgust.

"I knew it" he lamented. "I have definitely got a migraine coming on. 'Follow her up.' 'Squeeze her.' This is Rome, Rawls, not Chicago. Politics out here are complicated. I work very hard to keep all kinds of people happy, so we can do our job effectively. I go to lots of dinners, shake hands with lots of important people, and kiss thousands of diplomatic asses each year, just so we can blend peacefully into the scenery. And what does Langley do? It sends out some hood to tread on every political corn in Rome. I have definitely got a migraine coming on."

"Take it easy, Julie," Rawls laughed. "You've got a nice, comfortable set-up here. I won't screw it up for you."

"Too damned right you won't," Hepburn muttered darkly. "You won't go anywhere near the Venuti girl. You won't talk to her, you won't send her letters, you won't peep through her keyhole. Understand?"

"I've got to do my job, Julie."

"Sure," Hepburn said. "You do your job. Your instructions are to investigate leads into the Scheib case. That's all you're going to do: investigate. You have no authority to make contact with anybody, especially members of the Red Brigades, suspected or otherwise. Your orders are to report your findings back to Langley. If anybody has to make contact, we'll organize it, not you. You report, they evaluate, we act. Got it?"

"Maybe that message from Langley wasn't so garbled after all."

"Maybe it wasn't," Hepburn agreed. "Now are you going to behave like a good little plumber, or am I going to have to send telexes home?"

"Stay cool, Julie," Rawls said, getting up. "I won't make you do any work for your living. After all, this is Rome, isn't it?"

"It's the lowest form of wit, Rawls," Hepburn said. "And before you go, there's one more thing you ought to know."

"Yeah? What's that?"

"I hate being called Julie."

3

PROFESSOR MICHAEL WYMAN, MA, PhD strolled gently towards his faculty building in the University of Rome. Even by Italy's sultry standards, the morning of October 7 was unusually hot. The sky was cloudless, there was no breeze, and the parched white buildings glowed with reflected heat.

The Faculty of Literature and Philosophy lay at the south-east corner of the Piazzale della Minerva. Wyman went up the steps into the main entrance and said good morning to the man at the reception desk. The porter greeted him with friendly courtesy. When Wyman first came to the university, the staff had regarded him with some suspicion. It had taken twelve months for Wyman's fluent Italian and easy charm to win them over. Now he was simply known as "Il professore inglese", and they treated him with the same esteem they showed his Italian colleagues.

Few people knew precisely why Wyman

had come to Rome. It was understood that he was a philosopher with impeccable Oxbridge credentials, though much of his career had been spent at the British Foreign Office. It was assumed that Wyman's new job was a stepping-stone to a comfortable Mediterranean retirement.

The truth was more complicated. Wyman *had* been at the Foreign Office, but not as a diplomat. He had worked for MI6, Britain's intelligence-gathering organization.

A new government had come to power, and public spending came under attack. Hard-faced men at the Treasury exchanged their scalpels for cleavers, and the economizing began. Very soon Wyman was without work: MI6 made him redundant, and his college abolished his tenure.

Wyman's reaction to this humiliation was savage and gratifying. After a well-planned coup, MI6 unwittingly boosted Wyman's pension by two million pounds, and he left for Europe. By threatening to publicize his exploit, Wyman ensured his immunity from the wrath of his former employers.

A year later, Wyman took up his post

in Rome. He was no stranger to the city, having worked for a while at the MI6 Rome Station. The new job delighted him: originally, Wyman had been a mathematical logician, but his post now allowed him to work in less arid branches of philosophy. He was an entertaining lecturer, and his students were fond of him. His thinning white hair, shabby suits and air of bespectacled vagueness made him seem the embodiment of English scholarship.

That term, Wyman was due to deliver a course of seven lectures entitled "Personal Identity", and today's was the first. He entered the third-floor lecture room and greeted his students.

"Good morning, good morning. Did you have a good vacation? Work hard? Thought not. Now, are we all here? Splendid. My word, even Paolo made it out of bed this morning. I'm flattered, Paolo. There are seven of these lectures, you know, and they're all in the morning. Do you think you'll wake up in time for all of them?"

"Will they be worth it?"

"I hope so," Wyman replied gravely. "But I don't suppose that will make any difference. If Plato himself were giving these lectures you'd probably sleep through most of them."

"Probably," Paolo agreed, and the other students laughed.

"Never mind." Wyman opened his briefcase and drew out his lecture-notes. "Very well: to business. This course is entitled 'Personal Identity'. Today I will give you a quick explanation of what that means.

"I am fifty-nine years old. Believe it or not, I was once nine years old. Physically, Wyman at fifty-nine has little in common with Wyman at nine. I used to be very small, thin, with blue eyes and lots of dark hair. I am now tall, fat, with red eyes and a small amount of white hair."

Wyman took out a faded old photograph and showed it to the students. Some of them giggled as they saw the shy little boy in Bermuda shorts who was now their lecturer.

"You could be forgiven," Wyman went on, "for not believing that the boy you see there was Michael Wyman. As I have said, our appearances have virtually nothing in common. We're pretty different mentally as well. My opinions are not the same as the boy's. We have different tastes, interests and desires. I would also like to think that I'm more intelligent than that boy, though some of you would probably disagree.

"But the fact is, that boy and I *are* the same person: Michael Wyman. We have always been thought of as one person with one name.

"The question I want to tackle over the next few weeks is this: what is it that makes a person at two different times one and the same person? Presumably there is something that links me to the boy in the photograph, in a way that does not link me to some other boy in some other photograph. What is it?

"To answer this question, we need to establish what a person is. We can define a human being in the same way we define other creatures—a featherless biped, for example, or a rational animal. How do we define *individual* human beings? For example, how do we distinguish Paolo from Monica?"

"Monica's a lot prettier than Paolo," Enzo observed.

"So are most people," Wyman added, and he paused to let the laughter die down. "But that isn't a satisfactory criterion. We can't *define* Monica as 'the human being who is prettier than Paolo'; this might distinguish her from Paolo, but it doesn't distinguish her from, for example, Sophia Loren. No, we need something better than that. Suppose Monica was once a particularly ugly baby: she would now have almost as little in common with that baby as she has with Paolo. Nevertheless, that baby was Monica in a way that Paolo *isn't* Monica. What's the difference?"

Monica overcame her embarrassment at these references to her good looks, and offered a suggestion:

"The difference is surely mental," she said. "You might not look like the boy in the picture, but you have the same mind."

"What does that mean?" Wyman asked. "After all, I think very differently from that boy. As I said, my opinions have changed, as have my tastes and other mental characteristics."

"But you have the same memories," Monica insisted. "You remember the same things as that boy. The only difference is that in the last fifty years you've added to your store of memories."

"Very good," Wyman said approvingly.

He looked around at the other students.

"Does anyone have a reply to that?"

There was a pause.

"Very well," Wyman continued. "Consider this: you will accept that there is such a thing as forgetfulness. When that boy had his picture taken, he could remember what had happened to him the day before. Now, at the age of fifty-nine, I haven't the slightest recollection of what happened to me the day before that photograph was taken. In fact, I don't even remember having the photograph taken. That's at least two memories I don't share with the boy. He was still me though, wasn't he?"

There was another pause in the lecture room. Long silences are a regular feature of philosophical discussions. Wyman noted the furrowed brows and strained expressions of his students with some satisfaction. Monica was easily his best student, and he expected her to return to the fray before the others. He was not disappointed.

"There's a connection, isn't there?" she said. "Your thoughts and memories are connected with the boy's, even if it's not a direct connection."

Wyman smiled and looked around.

"Yes," he said. "I think there is a connection. Does everyone understand what Monica's getting at? No? Let me put it this way. I don't want us to get bogged down in the question of what a mind is, because it isn't necessary. All we have to say is that a person partially consists of a series of mental events.

"Take the boy in the picture: he woke up, he experienced hunger, he wanted to eat food, he wanted a glass of water, he wondered what he would do that day, and so on.

"All these are mental events, and they were all connected to each other in a chain. In the course of fifty years, there were millions of such events, leading up to the Michael Wyman you see now.

"Of course, some of these events are more strongly connected than others. The desires and pleasures I experience today are more closely related to those I had yesterday than to those I had fifty years ago. Nevertheless, today's mental events *are* connected with those of fifty years ago. Think of it as a long chain of events—new links are added to the chain every day. The links at the far end are old and rusty, but the chain is still intact. The chain may be so long that we've forgotten what the far end looks like, but we still know it's there.

"Of course, this isn't a complete description of what a person is. All these mental events usually happen inside a body. For a full definition, we'll need to take that into account. After all, my body may have changed beyond all recognition, but it's still my body, isn't it? Perhaps you disagree.

"I think we'd better stop here for now. For our next meeting perhaps you'd like to consider that physical side of the problem."

The students got to their feet and resumed the conversations which Wyman had interrupted with his talk. As he put away his notes, Wyman reflected that lectures were a bit like TV commercials:

short bursts of persuasion sandwiched between better forms of entertainment. As usual, most of the young men were gathered around Monica. Her long dark hair and Hollywood features were of more obvious interest than the problems of Personal Identity.

He left the lecture room and stepped back out into the bright morning sunshine. A few yards from the entrance to the Faculty, a man stood waiting for him. He was a nondescript fellow in his mid-forties, with dark hair and tinted spectacles. Despite his air of complete anonymity, Wyman recognized him at once.

4

"MY dear fellow," Wyman exclaimed. "How are you?"

Edgar Rawls grinned sheepishly as Wyman shook his hand.

"Okay, I guess," he said. "You're nicely fixed up here, I see."

"Yes, better than I had expected, I must say. And what brings you to these parts?"

"A job."

"Ah," Wyman said understandingly. "So you're still with the Company?"

"CIA pensions are lousy," Rawls said. "So yes, I'm still working for them."

Wyman's eyes narrowed in suspicion.

"There are three possible reasons why you've run into me," he said. "One is pure chance, and I don't believe in that. Another is that you're making a social call, and a third is that you want some professional assistance. The second is possible, but the third is more likely. Am I right?"

"I bet you get a real lift out of being so smart," Rawls said.

"In which case," Wyman continued, "you'd like somewhere quiet to talk."

"You're doing fine," Rawls said. "Keep it up."

"If you want to talk freely in Rome, the best place is outside a bar on a noisy street. Let's find one."

"Let's," Rawls agreed.

They walked down the Viale Castro Pretorio and sat outside a bar. Wyman ordered two coffees, and when the waiter had brought them he turned to Rawls and said:

"I'll hear what you have to say in confidence and without prejudice. But you must understand this: I'm retired. I no longer work for the Firm, and I have settled down as an academic. I'll need a great deal of persuasion before involving myself in any more of those silly espionage games. Understood?"

"Yeah, I get it," Rawls said, but he sounded unimpressed.

"Very well: proceed."

Rawls grinned and took a sip of his coffee.

"I guess you've heard all about the Scheib kidnapping?"

"Yes," Wyman said. "Most distressing."

"Well, I'm the poor sonofabitch they've sent to find him."

Wyman blinked at Rawls in surprise.

"You? Surely this is a matter for the FBI rather than . . ."

"No. Scheib is our business. Do you know what he does?"

"He's a microbiologist, I believe. The papers said that he spends half the year at his university, and he normally spends the other half on sabbatical leave elsewhere."

"Right. What they didn't say is that 'elsewhere' happens to be Langley."

Wyman lit a cigarette and leaned back in his chair.

"Fascinating," he said. "So what does he do for you?"

"Two years ago a Soviet military scientist called Ishutin defected in Paris. It was very discreet and nobody mentioned it. The Russians were silent because they weren't going to publicize the defection of a top man. We were silent because Ishutin was gold, and we wanted him all to ourselves.

"Ishutin's specialty was chemical warfare. His job was to gauge US development in chemical weapons, and to work on counter-weapons. The KGB fed him everything they had on our chemical warfare programme, and he processed the information.

"Naturally, when we got Ishutin, we also got the KGB's entire low-down on our own work. We now know how much they know that we know, if you get me."

"Yes, I'm with you," Wyman said. "The usual tortuous nonsense."

"Maybe. But we also know what they're doing about it. Ishutin's been giving us detailed descriptions of the Soviet counter-programme. It's so detailed that we had to call in a scientist to make sense of it all."

"And that's where Scheib comes in, I suppose."

"Exactly," said Rawls.

"And now your fellow's been kidnapped by the Red Brigades. Rather unfortunate, isn't it? Or do you think it isn't a coincidence?"

"Who knows? That's what I'm here to

find out. If you want my opinion, the Red Brigades have got no idea of what they're sitting on. Sure, they know he used to work at Detrick, but that was years ago. I'm willing to bet money they think he's just another distinguished egghead.

"But that's just my opinion. I have to find out for sure. It may be a million to one, but if the kidnappers do know, they'll torture every last piece of information out of the old bastard."

"I see your problem," Wyman said. "If that information were made public . . ."

"You get the point. That guy has to be freed."

Wyman frowned in concentration.

"Just suppose his kidnappers *do* know about Scheib's work. How could they have come by the information?"

"Christ knows," Rawls admitted. "That's why I think it's all a coincidence."

"So how would any of this involve me?" Wyman said. "It's a fascinating story, but I still don't understand why you're telling it to me."

Rawls nodded.

"I'm coming to that. Ten days ago I met up with a friend of mine in the FBI called

Schwarz. This guy was over here to take a close look at a student at your university. Apparently this kid was a cousin of some New York hood, and there was a rumour that the kid might be involved in something. Drugs, I think.

"Anyway, the lead was no good, the kid was clean—or, at least, as clean as any student can be these days—and Schwarz went home. But while he was here, he found out one or two things about this kid's friends. It was the kind of stuff that was no use to the Feds, but might help somebody else, so he gave it to me."

He paused to drink the last of his coffee.

"I still don't see where I might fit in," Wyman said.

"You know a girl called Monica Venuti?"

Wyman nodded. "She's one of my better students."

"She's also as red as a Cherokee's dick."

"Quite possibly," Wyman smiled. "My students' political affiliations have no bearing on—"

"Maybe not," Rawls interrupted. "But listen to this. She used to hang around with a guy called Claudio Prando. This guy was an active member of an outfit known as *I Volsci*, and it's no secret that those people have close links with the Red Brigades."

"Oh, come on," Wyman laughed, "that's a bit tenuous, isn't it?"

"Okay," Rawls said, "try this."

He took a photograph out of his wallet and gave it to Wyman.

"That was taken in Paris six years ago."

Wyman removed his glasses and examined the photograph. It was a poorly focused shot of two men standing in front of a church.

"Who are they?"

"The one on the left is Prando. Even though he's disguised, we know that the one on the right is Francesco Ponti. It's the most recent picture of him anyone's got."

"And this is the man they think is behind the Scheib kidnapping?"

"Right."

"So why don't they question Prando?"

"They'd love to," Rawls grinned. "But there's a small problem. Prando died in a car crash six months ago. The only lead we've got left is Monica Venuti."

"And why hasn't she been questioned?"

"She was. After Prando died, some cop picked her up and gave her a bit of routine questioning. Nothing heavy; nobody wanted to charge her. Inside a month that cop got fired. How well do you know her?"

"Fairly well," Wyman said. "But not as well as you do, it would seem."

"What do you know about her background?"

"She has spent much of her life in England, I believe. Her father is an official at the Italian embassy. Her English is perfect. She's intelligent and good at her work. She's also very temperamental. I think her political activities are some sort of reaction against her father, who is quite influential. In other words, she's a typical young student of respectable origins."

Rawls nodded.

"Yeah, her old man is influential. He's got a lot of political muscle. He's also a freemason."

"Indeed?"

"That's why that cop got busted. From what I understand, Monica told Daddy that the Law was interested in her. A couple of funny handshakes later, one cop was out of a job and any file they might have had on her was burned. I wish I had a Daddy like that. It seems old Venuti is just crazy about his daughter. She can do no wrong. Her politics are just a silly phase."

"I'm inclined to agree. With the last bit, I mean."

"If anyone in Italy—police, Carabinieri, army, you name it—checks out his daughter, Venuti would hear about it and somebody would lose their balls. The free-masons still pull a lot of strings in this country. Nobody wants to commit career suicide over some girl, so they leave her alone."

"Let me guess the rest," Wyman said. "Despite all this intrigue, you still don't want to let a good lead go unchecked. You can't operate with Italian co-operation, so you're looking for the unofficial back door. And when you found out that Michael Wyman, ex-MI6, was actually teaching this girl, you couldn't believe your good luck."

"Something like that. You could do it, Wyman."

"Do what, exactly?"

"Squeeze her. Nothing severe—just enough to make her talk."

"Talk to whom? The police?"

"Not necessarily. I think she knows about Ponti and what he's up to. If you softened her up, she might spill something. Even if she didn't give Ponti away, she might at least implicate herself enough to allow the authorities a decent excuse to pull her in, because that's what they need."

"And how exactly would I 'soften her up'?"

"Jesus Christ, Wyman," Rawls groaned, "don't give me a hard time. You know the kid, and you're no fool. You proved that to me when we first met. If you wanted to, you could find a way."

"Possibly."

Wyman looked up at the bright blue sky for a few moments of contemplation. Then he looked down again and shook his head.

"No," he decided.

"No?"

"No. This business does not concern me. Even if I were still involved with the Firm, it would still be none of my business. This isn't espionage, it's police work."

"If those guys had kidnapped anyone but Scheib, I'd agree with you. But he's our man, Wyman. Even the Italians don't know who he is. Oh sure, they know he's important to us, but we can't tell them what he does. This guy is a walking encyclopaedia of state secrets. Not just any secrets: this is some of the hottest shit going."

Wyman grinned at Rawls' delicate phraseology.

"I'm sure you're right," he said. "But it's still not my concern. I'm a full-time academic now. You're asking me to disregard professional ethics."

"Ethics didn't bother you much when I last saw you," Rawls observed drily. "Okay, so you've tossed away your allegiance to Britain. I don't blame you: it's a lousy country. But this is your new home, Wyman. These terrorists are *your enemy*. Ever thought about that?"

Wyman tried hard not to laugh. He failed.

"Look," Rawls persisted, "How would the Italians feel if they knew you had the chance to help them out, and you blew it?"

"Please Rawls," Wyman chortled. "Spare me. I'm still not convinced by your speculations about this girl. If she has nothing to do with these *Brigadisti*, then I will jeopardize my position in the university by meddling in her private life for no good reason. Her all-powerful father might have something to say about that, don't you think? And there's the other possibility. If she does have a terrorist connection . . ."

"Go on."

"I have a wife and child. One foreign academic has already been struck: why not a second?"

"So that's it," Rawls snapped. "You've lost your nerve."

Wyman looked up in exasperation.

"Think about it, Rawls. Unlike yourself, I no longer operate under the auspices of a rich and powerful organization. When I worked for the Firm I was happy to take risks: I felt I had some power behind me. This no longer holds. Given my peculiar history, there would be few tears shed for me in Britain if something unpleasant were to happen."

Rawls nodded.

"Maybe you're right," he relented. "I forgot about your kid. Is it a boy or a girl?"

"A girl, Catherine. Do you have one of. . . ?"

"No, I'm still single. If you had my job, would you marry?"

"I suppose not," Wyman smiled. "Look, I'm sorry I can't help you with this business, I really am. Obviously, I shan't repeat what you've told me, but I can't get involved. It would place—"

"Forget it," Rawls said. "I can't twist your arm on this one. Just forget what I said."

"I'll do that," Wyman said solemnly. "I'm sure there are other ways of finding what you want. Perhaps one of your colleagues at the US embassy can help. That fellow Hepburn likes to cultivate influential friends, doesn't he? If he knew someone . . ."

"Hepburn is a creep," Rawls said vehemently.

"You're very emphatic about that,"

Wyman observed. "Have you had a dispute with him about something?"

"We don't get on," Rawls grinned. "Hepburn thinks people like me ought to wear boiler suits and carry spanners around."

"Oh dear," Wyman sympathized. "But there's more to it than that, I suspect."

"Jesus, Wyman, what is this? I thought you wanted out."

"I beg your pardon," Wyman said hastily. "Curiosity got the better of me for a second."

"Take it easy," Rawls said, waving his hand. "You might as well know. Hepburn's got a nice thing going here in Rome. He knows all the top people, and they all get on fine. He wants everything kept nice and quiet, so he's ordered me not to talk to anybody who might give him trouble."

"Does that include Monica Venuti?"

"Of course it does. When I told him who she was and what I had in mind, he hit the roof. I'm not supposed to engage in direct communication with anyone involved or potentially involved in the kidnapping. Can you believe that?"

"So that's why you came to me," Wyman said. "It all makes sense now. If I spoke to her, you would still technically be obeying orders."

"Ten out of ten," Rawls grunted. "You want a medal?"

"So," Wyman continued, "I was supposed to assist you with what was little more than insubordination. Was that the idea?"

Rawls nodded sheepishly.

"You could put it like that, I guess. People like me are always fighting two enemies: the Reds and my own bosses. It's crazy, Wyman."

"It certainly is," Wyman agreed. "You have my sympathies."

"But you still don't want to help?"

"I'm afraid not," Wyman said. "I think I'd look terrible in a boiler suit. Care for another coffee?"

5

MONICA VENUTI stepped off her bus at the western end of Corso Vittorio Emanuele, just by the Piazza della Chiesa Nuova. She left the Corso, and walked through the labyrinth of streets that lie between the River Tiber and the Piazza Navona.

She lived in the Via della Vetrina, a sombre little alley where rusty old Fiats were parked carelessly and anonymous washing flapped from the windows. Her flat was on the second floor of Number 6. She had moved in here on the advice of her political friends: the landlord, Gennaro, was old, partially deaf, and lived elsewhere. He displayed no curiosity about Monica's visitors and guests, and he was only concerned about getting his rent on time.

Monica entered the main doorway of the building, collected her mail, and went up to her flat. The morning's lecture was still fresh in her mind: she found Wyman's style of teaching refreshing. Unlike her other lecturers, Wyman was able to inject a flamboyant personal note into whatever he did. Who else would have found that ridiculous childhood photo? Wyman reminded Monica of England, a time and place that now seemed very remote.

Of her twenty-two years, ten had been spent in England. Like many people who are the products of two countries, Monica felt she did not properly belong to either. Her childhood had been lonely. Being foreign is an unforgivable crime among English schoolchildren, and as they grew older, their open hostility to Monica gave way to quiet ostracism. Monica retreated into bookish solitude.

There were no obvious scars. Monica grew into a tall, slender woman, whose shyness only rarely gave way to bitter wrath. Like many attractive women, she seemed unaware of her own beauty. She did not use make-up and dressed carelessly. She chose friends who shared her failure to conform. To Monica, these people were innocent outcasts, like herself, shunned for their honesty and special understanding. Most people would have called them inadequates and misfits, but Monica had little use for majority opinions.

She was a bright student, and Wyman encouraged her enthusiasm. Occasionally he would invite her to his apartment on the Via Porta Pinciana for tea with his wife Margaret. They would talk in English about philosophy, beginning with Monica's syllabus work, and often moving on to other topics, such as Wyman's original specialist field of Modal Logic.

This puzzled Monica. She realized that at some point in Wyman's career there had been a major trauma: Wyman had not only changed his field of work, but had also changed his country of residence. It was clear that the Wymans were very wealthy, and Monica knew that such wealth could not have been achieved solely through academic work. Plainly, Wyman had done something else as well, but her casual inquiries on the subject were met with the wooliest of replies. Only the English could deflect unwanted questions so skilfully.

She sat down and examined her mail.

There was a postcard from a friend on holiday in Israel, and a letter from England postmarked "London SW1".

She opened the envelope to find a letter from her father and a cheque. Her father apologized for his delay in writing, offering his usual excuses of work pressure and his wife's illness. Monica's mother was a robust hypochondriac whose imaginary ailments cost Signor Venuti a fortune in Harley Street bills.

The letter continued with a long stomach-churning description of her mother's latest complaint, as well as the usual strictures about avoiding bad company and concentrating on her studies. When Monica had read as much as she could bear, she put the letter down and got up to make some coffee.

There was a knock on the door, and Monica went over to open it. Before her stood the gnarled grey figure of Signor Gennaro, her landlord.

"Good morning, *Signorina*," he said. "I was wondering if you had received any mail today."

Monica smiled, knowing full well that her landlord had seen this morning's mail.

Because of her father's delay in writing, Monica had been somewhat late with her rent payment. She had promised Gennaro that as soon as her father's letter arrived, he would have his money. As a result, the old man had walked out each day from his house in the Trastevere to examine the post, and his journeys had finally borne fruit.

"Yes," Monica said. Gennaro was hard of hearing, so she spoke loudly and slowly. "My father's letter arrived this morning. I will need a day or two for the cheque to clear, if you don't mind."

"I suppose not," Gennaro grunted. "If I come back on Thursday, perhaps I can have the rent then?"

"Of course, Signor Gennaro. I will have the cash waiting for you."

"Thank you," Gennaro said, and went downstairs.

Monica shut the door. It occurred to her that, although she had always thought of Gennaro as an old man, she could not say how old he was. His face was not especially lined, but his hair was short and grizzled, and there were no teeth in his mouth, resulting in the sagging, shapeless jawline one associates with the old. What Gennaro did, where he was from, whether he was married or single, she neither knew nor particularly cared. Gennaro only ever talked about rent payments, and Monica had no inclination to widen the conversation.

If Monica had been asked her opinion of Gennaro as a person, she would have shrugged and dismissed him as a boring old man. If, however, the question had been about Gennaro as a landlord, the reply would have been quite different.

As a landlord, Gennaro belonged to the class of property-owning capitalists. His income did not come from productive labour, but from the rent paid him by other people who toiled for their wage. As an individual, Gennaro was of no interest to Monica. As a principle, he was an obscenity.

Monica had strong views about people like Gennaro and how they should be dealt with. Had he known about those views, it was unlikely that even Gennaro would have agreed to Monica's tenancy. For Gennaro, few things were more important than rent payments, but self-preservation was one of them. Monica's views were very strong indeed.

6

THE Via Gaeta is a quiet street running north-east from the Baths of Diocletian to the Viale Castro Pretorio, near the university. Number 5 is a large mustard-coloured villa adorned by bushes and palm trees. On the roof is a neat row of white aerials. Around the building stands a tall green fence. Beside the main gate is an entryphone, above which a metal plaque declares this building to be the Soviet embassy in Rome.

On the top floor was the office of the KGB's Rome *Rezident*, Colonel Yuri Mazurov. A tall, slender man in his late forties, Mazurov was reputed to be something of a scholar. His posting in Rome gave him the opportunity to indulge his lifelong passion for Classical history. His office contained hundreds of neatly arranged books on the subject. He had everything from Gibbon's *Decline and Fall* to Mommsen's *History of Rome*, and any number of ancient writers, from Sallust to

Ammianus. Mazurov's leisure hours were spent writing a monograph on the works of Eutropius, a particularly obscure writer who had taken his perverse academic fancy.

Mazurov was not married, and this aroused some suspicion among his more vigorously heterosexual colleagues. Others had a simpler explanation for Mazurov's bachelorhood, and they were probably more correct: Mazurov's nickname in the KGB was "Old Toilet-Breath".

His guest on the morning of October 9 had been flown out from London at the suggestion of KGB headquarters in Moscow. Anatoli Bulgakov had met Mazurov on a few occasions, and he recalled Mazurov's halitosis with some distaste.

When he entered the office, Bulgakov shook Mazurov's hand with his own arm fully extended. Unfortunately, this did not prevent him from catching some of the colonel's well-fermented breath.

"My dear Anatoli," Mazurov smiled. "How is London treating you? Things are somewhat chaotic there, I hear."

"That's an understatement, Colonel,"

Bulgakov said. "We have just lost thirty colleagues, and there are more to go. Fortunately, the Chamber of Commerce remains untouched."

"You didn't work with Gordievsky, did you?"

"No, thank God. He knew very little about me."

A month earlier, Oleg Gordievsky, head of KGB operations in Britain, had defected. Twenty-five Soviet diplomats were expelled, and more followed later. Many KGB operations were blown, and most agents in Britain were waiting to be removed by one means or another. Although Bulgakov was a KGB major, he had worked without reference to Gordievsky. He ran an autonomous unit based at the British-Soviet Chamber of Commerce in Lowndes Street, which was solely answerable to KGB headquarters.

"Are you at all under suspicion?" Mazurov asked. To Bulgakov's relief, the colonel sat behind his desk and motioned Bulgakov to a comfortable chair six feet away.

"I have always been under suspicion," Bulgakov grinned. "But the British seem determined not to expel me until they find out exactly what I'm doing. That means I should be safe until the year 2000, at least."

Mazurov laughed, and opened a drawer in his desk.

"I suppose you're wondering why you were asked to come here," he said, taking a cardboard file out of the drawer. "You'll be relieved to hear it's nothing to do with Gordievsky. In fact, it's really quite trivial."

He opened the file, took out three black-and-white photographs, and passed them across his desk to Bulgakov.

"We could have sent these over to London," he said, "but we thought it better to bring you over, just in case. Can you identify this man?"

Bulgakov studied the photographs closely. They were poorly taken, he noted, and grainy, as if enlarged from a small negative. They showed a dark-haired, bespectacled man leaving a taxi, paying the driver, and walking away.

"He's not in good focus, is he?" Bulgakov observed. "But I think I know who this is. He's a CIA man. His name is Edgar Rawls."

Mazurov nodded.

"Thank you," he said.

There was a pause.

"Well?" Bulgakov said. "Perhaps I might have an explanation."

"Yes," Mazurov said slowly. "One of our people spotted him leaving the American embassy. Apparently he is asking questions."

"About what?"

"The Red Brigades. We think he's investigating the Scheib kidnapping. '

Bulgakov's eyes widened in surprise.

"Are you sure? That isn't the CIA's business. Properly speaking—"

"The FBI should be investigating," Mazurov interrupted. "I know. But Rawls has visited Scheib's hotel, and he's been seen looking around in one or two places Scheib visited before the kidnapping. As you say, the picture is poorly focused, but it bore some resemblance to other pictures of him. That's why we wanted confirmation from you. I hear you know him quite well."

Bulgakov shrugged.

"I've met him a few times. Firstly in Chile, during the Allende period, and then East Germany. He was involved in the Wyman affair."

"Really? Wyman's in Rome now, you know."

"So I hear. What's he doing?"

"He teaches at the university. I understand he lives like a gentleman of leisure."

"So he should," Bulgakov said. "With two million pounds in his pocket, he can afford to relax. I still think we should make him an honorary colonel. You know, he did more damage to MI6 than all my people put together."

Mazurov laughed.

"Wyman's retired now, unlike our friend in the photograph. Rawls is still very active, and that's why you're here."

"That's a bit elliptical for my taste, Colonel," Bulgakov grinned. "I still don't understand why you need me."

"We'll get to that," Mazurov said. "You are quite right to observe that the Scheib affair doesn't concern the CIA. To the best of our knowledge, it doesn't. Unless Scheib is somehow of special importance."

"What does that mean?"

"Either Scheib is himself a CIA man, or he is involved in something of concern to intelligence. We can discount the first possibility. I have read every available file on this man, and nothing suggests a CIA connection. About thirty years ago he carried out military research at Fort Detrick, but that was on behalf of the US army. Since then, as far as anyone knows, he has been a legitimate academic scientist."

"So what work has he done that might be of use to intelligence?"

"No one knows. It's all a mystery, but if Rawls is here, it's our business."

"What do you have in mind?"

"Firstly, Rawls must be eliminated. If we remove the threat of CIA interference, it will be much easier to pursue our own investigation. Later, if we get an opportunity, we should talk to Scheib."

Bulgakov gazed at Mazurov with new interest. He lit a cigarette and leaned back in his chair.

"That raises two questions," he said. "Who is going to dispose of Rawls? And how will we talk to Scheib? We didn't kidnap him."

Mazurov smiled coyly.

"We didn't," he agreed, "but we are on good terms with those who did. And they will dispose of Rawls."

"I see." Bulgakov calmly inhaled a deep puff of smoke. "What is the nature of our relationship with these people?"

"Very cordial. You sound as if you disapprove."

"I do" Bulgakov said drily. "They're crude, stupid amateurs. I know the official line is to encourage them, but . . ."

"But what?"

"One of my men is worth a hundred Red Brigadists, Colonel. We both know that. They're inept and fickle. It doesn't matter how much you give them by way of arms or money, you can never be sure they'll do what you want. Links with them can be a public embarrassment. Look at Kovich."

"Kovich was a fool," Mazurov snapped.

"He was obeying orders," Bulgakov said.

In July 1978, the Spanish intelligence service witnessed a meeting in the South of France between Vitali Kovich, a KGB agent posing as an *Izvestia* correspondent, and Eugenio Arizgura, a leading member of the Basque ETA terrorists. The story made front-page headlines in Spain. The Russians replied with a frosty denial, but the truth was out: Russia had been caught dealing with European terrorists.

As a result, there was a growing body of feeling in the KGB that such direct links with terrorists were both risky and unnecessary. Better by far, it was argued, to give the arms and explosives legitimately to someone like Colonel Gaddafi, the Libyan leader, and allow him to take the risks. Bulgakov belonged to this school of thought, and he made no secret of his contempt for "amateurs", however well trained.

"So what are you planning, exactly?" Bulgakov asked.

"Now we are certain this is Rawls, we will hand him over to the Brigadists. Then we can try to establish who, or what, Scheib really is."

Bulgakov frowned.

"Do we know why they singled out Scheib for kidnapping?"

Mazurov gave a small, uneasy cough.

"I'm afraid we don't," he confessed.

"There's a limit to how frank these people are prepared to be with us."

Bulgakov smiled cynically.

"Then we don't know if the Red Brigades understand Scheib's importance? They might know who he is already."

"It's possible,' Mazurov conceded. "But I doubt it. Our own files are so inconclusive, I find it scarcely credible that they know more about him than we do. I think he was chosen more or less at random."

"In other words," Bulgakov said, "It's just possible that the Red Brigades are holding someone far more important than they realize. Rawls' presence does suggest that."

"Exactly. But I don't thing we can get to the bottom of all this until Rawls has been removed. How easy do you think that will be?"

"He's got an excellent record," Bulgakov said. "Vietnam, South America, Europe, even Moscow. But he's getting old. I noticed that during the Wyman episode. His reactions are slower, he makes occasional silly mistakes."

"So what's your verdict?"

"It's hard to say," Bulgakov shrugged.

"It depends on how good your amateur revolutionaries are. You know them better than I do."

Mazurov nodded thoughtfully.

"I see," he mused. "Well, we shall just have to watch what they do."

"We?"

"Yes, we. I have no work for you here at the moment, but I'd be grateful if you remained with us for a little while."

At once Bulgakov understood why he had been summoned to Rome. If the Red Brigades failed to remove Rawls, then Bulgakov's special knowledge would be brought into play.

"As you can see," Mazurov said, "the weather is particularly agreeable at the moment. You may regard your stay here as a short holiday. But do keep in touch."

7

"YOU will recall," Wyman said, "that we were trying to establish what a person is."

He looked over the group of students seated before him. Paolo had only just made it out of bed, and it showed. Enzo was chewing gum and thinking about his girlfriend. Giacomo was doodling on his notepaper, Giulio was gazing at Lucia, and Lucia was daydreaming. Only Monica showed any sign of interest.

"We were trying to explain why, despite all the differences between us, the boy in the photograph and I are one and the same person.

"So far, we have established that we share a unique combination of mental events—we have the same mental history, if you like.

"What about the physical aspect? Remember the photograph: a small, dark-haired boy. Fifty years later we have a large, white-haired man. Over the last five decades nearly all the cells in my body have been replaced by new cells.

"Hence, mine is a different, separate body from the boy's. Nevertheless, if we were to say 'Michael Wyman has several different bodies', it would sound rather absurd, wouldn't it?

"I asked you to consider this physical question before coming here. I am not such a naïve optimist as to suppose you have all done so, but it would be nice if somebody has. Does anyone have anything to offer? Paolo?"

Paolo shifted uncomfortably.

"Well, as a matter of fact . . ."

"Lucia?"

"I'm sorry, Professor . . ."

"Giulio?"

"I did think about it, Professor . . ."

"Indeed?"

"But I didn't come up with anything."

"Monica?"

"Yes," Monica said brightly. She opened her file and consulted some notes. "Why can't we just treat the physical question in the same way we describe the mental problem? We could say there is a long chain of physical events which lead to each other, just like the mental events."

"Splendid," Wyman beamed.

He looked around at the hesitant expressions on the faces of the other students.

"Let me explain," Wyman said. "We were trying to find the mental link between myself and the boy in the photograph. We decided it consisted of a chain of mental events. Monica suggests we can explain the physical link in the same way.

"For example: the boy's hair grew, and it was then cut. More hair appeared, and that was cut again. New cells were added to his bones, so the boy grew in size. *All the changes in this person's body can be described in terms of physical events.* Does that make sense?"

They all nodded, except for Enzo, who still looked unhappy.

"How does this tell us what a person is?" he asked.

"Look at it this way," Wyman said. "As a human *being* you, Enzo, are no different to Paolo. You are both examples of one species, like two identical footballs made in the same factory. As a *person*, however, you are very different to Paolo. The question is, what distinguishes you from him and everyone else? How do we explain your *identity* as Enzo?

"The answer seems to involve two things—a unique combination of mental events, as well as a unique combination of physical events. Does that answer your question?"

Enzo nodded.

"Excellent. Now, this leads on to a new question. We are trying to explain the nature of a person. We have two parallel chains of events—mental and physical. Do these give us a full explanation, or is something else required?

"Suppose we want to define the person commonly referred to as Michael Wyman. If I say 'Michael Wyman is defined as a series of mental and physical events which began in 1926, and which is still continuing sixty years later', is this enough?

"Of course, I could list all those events: the 'flu I caught in 1938, my desire to drink a glass of water in 1947, my first marriage in 1956, and so on. The list would be very long, but that doesn't matter; in theory, all these events could be recounted.

"But is all this enough to explain what is essentially *me*, rather than somebody else?

"Some people believe this *is* enough. They think that a person consists of no more than a series of intertwined mental and physical events. All these events can be described in an *impersonal* way—for example, one of the facts about me, that I caught 'flu in 1938, could be rephrased as 'an influenza virus entered a certain blood system in 1938'. All the facts which help to define me can be described without mentioning me at all.

"People who believe this are called Reductionists. They believe that the identity of a person *reduces* to no more than this combination of events.

"Not surprisingly, those who disagree with this view are called Non-Reductionists. They think that being a person involves more than just these chains of events. They believe there is something else besides, an extra ingredient of some kind.

"The Christian churches, for example, say that personal identity involves the possession of a soul. The soul is supposed to be distinct from anything physical, and it is said to survive death. If this is true, then Reductionists are wrong."

"Which do you believe?" Giulio asked.

"I suppose," Wyman said, "that if you thought I was a Reductionist, at least one of you would scuttle off to the University Church and denounce me as a heretic. I therefore won't tell you what I think: at least, not for the time being.

"This much I will say: most people are Non-Reductionists, even if they haven't thought about the problem. So I think we should give Reductionists a fair hearing, in the same way we should listen to all minority views."

"*All* minority views?" Monica asked. "Even ones you hate?"

"Especially the ones you hate," Wyman grinned. "After all, you have to know why you hate them."

8

EDGAR RAWLS strolled under the arches of the Colosseum and went to the ticket booth. He paid the 3000 lire admission fee and climbed the steps leading to the upper terraces of Rome's most famous theatre of death. It was a sunny morning, and a small crowd of tourists were inspecting the lower terraces of the amphitheatre. Even at a height of over forty metres, Rawls could make out the nasal accents of the fellow-Americans below him.

He walked around to the eastern side of the elliptical upper terrace. Through an archway, he could see a man sitting on a marble slab. The man was reading a guide-book and smoking a cigarette. Rawls sat down beside him.

"Good morning," Rawls said. "Any particular reason for choosing this place, or are you just a born romantic?"

The other man looked up and smiled.

"I've never seen this place before," he

said. "It seemed like a good opportunity. Do you realize the circumference of this building is 527 metres?"

"Amazing."

"Yes. It's 57 metres high, and the main axis is 188 metres long."

"You don't say."

"Apparently, work began on it in 72 AD, under the Emperor Vespasian, and finished eight years later under his son Titus. It held up to 50,000 spectators."

"No kidding."

"They even flooded the arena to re-enact naval battles."

"What do you want, Bulgakov?"

The Major sighed and closed his guide-book.

"I can see why it was an American who declared that history is bunk," he complained. "You people really don't have any sense of tradition, do you? Is it because you genuinely don't care, or because you are embarrassed by your own short existence?"

"I can only speak for myself," Rawls said, "and I don't give a shit."

Bulgakov nodded wistfully.

"It's really very sad," he said. "We

Russians are highly aware of history. For example, the *Rezident* in Rome, Mazurov, is a keen student of ancient history. I believe he writes articles on the subject. You'd never catch a CIA man doing that, would you?"

"Too damned right," Rawls agreed.

"He called me over here, you know. He had some photographs of you on his desk. Apparently you're looking for Scheib. Care for a cigarette?"

Rawls shook his head.

"More to the point," Bulgakov went on, "the Red Brigades know about you. Are you aware of that?"

Rawls shrugged.

"They had to hear, sooner or later. Are you guys feeding them?"

"We give them information."

"And other things."

"And other things," Bulgakov agreed. "They want to see you."

"When?"

"I don't know the full details. I'd really prefer not to know, but I've been dragged into this."

"Don't make me laugh," Rawls said.

"You sound like the woman who screamed rape during her third orgasm."

"No, really. I don't like those people, and I don't deal with them. Mazurov's in charge here, and he seems to approve of their activities."

"You don't?"

Bulgakov shook his head.

"No. You can't control people like that. Since they don't know what they're doing, that can be very awkward."

"So why tell me all this? In fact, why tell me anything?"

Bulgakov hesitated before replying.

"I'm not entirely sure," he said. "I think you're in danger. The Brigades might want to kill you."

"Would that make Mazurov happy?"

"Yes," Bulgakov said. "It would."

"So this is unofficial."

Bulgakov fell silent.

"In fact," Rawls went on, "you're putting your balls on the line by talking to me. Right?"

Bulgakov stood up and walked slowly over to the edge of the terrace. He glanced down at the happy tourists below and turned back to Rawls.

"I'm doing you a favour," he said finally. "I might need one in return. I also dislike the idea of you being killed by those overgrown schoolchildren."

Rawls frowned.

"Why should that bother you?"

"Good question," Bulgakov grinned. "Maybe I'm suffering from a touch of—dare I say it—professional ethics."

"There's no such thing," Rawls replied. "You need an analyst."

"In Russia, psychiatrists are controlled by the KGB. I'm not sure I want that kind of analysis. In America, however . . ."

Rawls gazed at Bulgakov with new understanding.

"So that's it," he said. "How are things in London nowadays? I hear it's pretty rough."

Bulgakov nodded.

"A little precarious," he said. "A bit like your own position, really."

"Who says I'm in trouble?" Rawls said. "So the Red Brigades want to talk to me. That's fine: I want to talk to them."

"What if they decide to kill you?"

Rawls shrugged.

"We'll have to see. I want Scheib."

"Why?"

"Orders, Bulgakov. Little guys behind desks at Langley, just like the little guys in Dzerzhinsky Square. They whistle, we jump."

"So you'll risk a meeting?"

"Why not?"

Bulgakov nodded thoughtfully.

"In that case, I might as well tell you. You will be contacted some time in the next twenty-four hours. They will give you a meeting place and a time. That's all I know."

Rawls smiled.

"That's all I need. Thanks."

He stood up and joined Bulgakov at the edge of the terrace. The tourists below were being herded out by their guide, cameras clicking to the last.

"Don't thank me," Bulgakov said, "Just remember my warning. If you have an ounce of good sense, you'll avoid that meeting."

Rawls shook his head and grinned.

"Pity I'm such a moron, isn't it?"

9

WITH some difficulty Rawls parked his car between a Vespa and a small truck a few yards away from the entrance to his hotel. As he locked the door, he paused and looked around him. The Via in Arcione is a small but busy street tucked behind the Quirinal Palace, official residence of the Italian president. The Trevi fountain, where countless people each waste three of their coins, is only a few yards away, and the street is usually filled with tourists strolling towards it. Nothing seemed unusual or suspicious, but Rawls could not dispel the sensation of being watched.

Having locked the car, Rawls entered his hotel. The man at the desk gave him his key, and he went upstairs. The sensation grew stronger. Rawls looked under his bed, glanced inside the wardrobe, and examined his suitcase. There was nothing wrong. He sat down on the bed and paused for reflection.

Rawls was not a thinking man. Much of his career had been military, and had consisted of executing plans laid by others. When it came to implementing the ideas of his leaders, Rawls was in a class of his own.

His skill at devising such plans was another matter. He disliked intellectuals and academics: at best they were useful strategists, at worst they were desk-bound meddlers. His grudging respect for Wyman came from knowing that the aged professor understood both aspects of the profession. That was a rare quality.

Unfortunately, Rawls now had to carry out a plan of his own. He could not let Hepburn know of his intentions, since nobody in the CIA would sanction them. Direct contact with Scheib's kidnappers went well beyond Rawls' original brief. His instructions had simply been to investigate, report, and let the experts do the negotiating. Now he was on his own, and he found the situation most disagreeable.

The telephone shattered his train of thought. He lifted the receiver and heard the voice of the receptionist.

"Mr. Rawls? There is a call for you."

"Okay," Rawls said, "I'll take it."

There was a click, and a soft voice came through in accented English.

"Mr. Rawls?"

"Speaking."

"Please listen, and please say nothing. If you want to meet us, you will do as we say. Please take notes.

"The day after tomorrow—Friday—you will get into your car at exactly 9 p.m. Please make sure it is parked where it is now. You will drive up the Via Crispi, and continue until you get to the Porta Pinciana. You will turn into the Villa Borghese and drive directly to the Piazza Canestre. There you will turn left and drive up to the Piazzale dei Martiri. You will then stop, and we will meet you. There are other ways of getting to this spot, but you won't take them. You will go by this route and not deviate. Naturally, you will go alone.

"If you do not follow these instructions precisely, you will not meet us. If you are wondering how we will follow your movements, bear this in mind: you are driving a white AlfaSud, registration number

W81947, which you hired yesterday morning. Do you have any questions?"

"I bet you know what colour underpants I'm wearing, don't you?"

There was a pause, and the voice resumed.

"Do you agree to this meeting?"

"Are we going to talk about Scheib?"

"Of course."

"See you on Friday."

The anonymous caller rang off, and Rawls put the phone down. He opened his street map of Rome and traced out the route he had just been given. It led directly from his hotel to the Villa Borghese. It also went directly past the home of Michael Wyman.

10

MICHAEL WYMAN lived with his wife Margaret and their year-old daughter at Number 36, Via Porta Pinciana. They owned a fifth-floor apartment of an elegant golden-brown building overlooking the Villa Borghese's riding-course, the Galoppatoio. On the evening of October 17, the Wymans had just finished their evening meal when their entryphone proclaimed an impromptu visit by Edgar Rawls.

"Evening ma'am," Rawls said, as Margaret showed him in. "Hope I'm not disturbing you."

"Of course not, Mr. Rawls," Margaret said affably. "Do come in."

He was shown into the Wymans' living room.

"Hello, Rawls," Wyman said. "And what can we do for you?"

"Perhaps you'd like coffee?" Margaret suggested.

"No thanks, ma'am."

"In that case, I'll leave you both alone," Margaret smiled. "Somehow, I don't think you've come to talk about analytical philosophy with Michael."

"Very astute of you ma'am," Rawls grinned, and Margaret left the room. "Things have happened since we spoke. You'd never guess who's in town."

"Go on," Wyman said drily. "Shock me."

"Bulgakov."

"Indeed? Have they finally thrown him out of London?"

"Not yet. They wanted him to identify me. It seems the Russians are feeding the Red Brigades."

"That isn't news," Wyman yawned. "It's an unpleasant fact of life. Have you seen Bulgakov?"

"He saw me. He gave me a tip-off that the Brigades want to arrange a meeting. He thinks I should keep clear."

"Really," Wyman said. "Why is Bulgakov so concerned for your welfare?"

"He doesn't like the arrangement. The KGB don't actually control the Brigades; they just help them along and hope for the best. Like you say, it isn't news. But it means they've got no control over the Scheib kidnapping. It's a risky set-up."

"It certainly is," Wyman agreed. "But it still doesn't explain why Bulgakov should play the Dutch uncle with you."

"The Brigades don't want to kill me—they just want a meeting. It's the Russians who want to see me out of action. They'd like to persuade the Brigades to do the job for them, but like I said, they can't give orders. Bulgakov told me the Brigades wanted a meeting, and he was right. I got a call yesterday with an appointment."

"Most intriguing," Wyman said. "Bulgakov tells you the Red Brigades want a meeting. He also tells you his colleagues would like you killed. He therefore advises you to avoid the meeting. This raises a number of interesting questions."

"Such as?"

"Why do the KGB want to kill you? You're no threat to them at the moment."

"Maybe they realize that Scheib is more important than anyone thought. When we spoke the other day, you wanted to know why I was on this, and not some Fed. The Russians must have asked the same question, and the answer is—Scheib is big. But they don't know how big. If they get me out of the way, that leaves them free to start their own negotiation with the Brigades. I'm guessing, but I think I'm right."

Wyman nodded.

"I'm inclined to agree. Perhaps they already know who Scheib is."

"Maybe," Rawls said. "But even so, they'd still want me out of the way. Your question's answered."

"Very well," Wyman conceded. "So why is Bulgakov giving you the warning? If he is acting on his own initiative, he is guilty of treason. You might know him quite well, but he is still your official enemy. Why did he meet you?"

"Bulgakov is worried," Rawls said. "Right now, London is the KGB's biggest headache. Everybody's balls are on the line. Bulgakov's probably safer than most of his buddies there, but he can't be sure. So he wants to buy a favour."

Wyman removed his spectacles, and absently nibbled the arm of the frame.

"Mmm," he said. "It makes some sense. He would want to cultivate a few friends on our side before he ever contemplated anything risky. Cautious chap, our

Bulgakov. Are you going to follow his advice?"

"I'm meeting the Brigades tomorrow night."

"Do you have a plan?"

"Sort of."

"And I suppose it involves me?"

"If that's okay."

Wyman slumped back in his chair and moaned.

"Why?" he lamented. "Why do I have to be dragged into this? I tried to explain . . ."

"Listen," Rawls protested. "Just listen. Please."

"If it simply consisted of listening, I wouldn't mind. I suspect, however, that you want slightly more of me."

"Maybe," Rawls agreed. "But hear me out. I haven't told my people about this idea, and I don't want to. But I could still do with a professional opinion."

Wyman nodded gloomily.

"Like I said, I agreed to meet the Brigades tomorrow night. They fixed up a meeting place in the Villa Borghese, and they gave me a route to get there. It goes past your front door."

"So?"

"So maybe you can keep an eye on me. Go for a walk nearby, or something. Just in case."

"Anything else?"

"Yes, there's more. I've been talking to a guy in the Carabinieri called Castellano. He's a specialist in anti-terrorism. If anything happens, you've got to see him."

"And what will we have to talk about? The weather?"

"He's interested in Monica Venuti."

"Not that again," Wyman groaned. "I told you—"

"Just see him, will you? It won't cost you anything. But you'll need to know what the plan is."

"The plan, the plan," Wyman mocked. "What is this bloody plan of yours? Is this some sort of fall-back, in case the Red Brigades fail to show up tomorrow?"

"Something like that."

"And it involves Monica Venuti?"

"Yeah."

"I might have known. You really can't take no for an answer, can you Rawls?"

"It runs in the family," Rawls explained. "My old man was a salesman."

"I can do without your genealogy," Wyman shuddered. "Just tell me what you have in mind."

11

BETWEEN eight and eight-thirty on Friday evening, Rawls ate a light meal at a pizzeria on the Via delle Muratte. He walked back to his hotel and went inside, deliberately ignoring his car, which was parked just on the other side of the entrance.

Up in his room, Rawls lay down on his bed and tried to relax. He took off his spectacles and looked at his reflection in the mirror across the room. His expression had not changed from its usual combination of boredom and sardonic impassivity. This surprised Rawls; he expected the strain of the last few days to show. There were no obvious signs of stress: his plentiful hair contained no grey, his face was scarcely lined. He reflected that if the outer man were always a perfect expression of his inner counterpart, Rawls would probably be in a wheelchair by now.

At ten to nine he got up, replaced his spectacles and went to his suitcase. He opened it and drew out an automatic pistol, which he put on a dressing table. He put on a shoulder-holster. A loose-fitting cream-coloured blazer disguised the arrangement neatly.

It was exactly nine o'clock when he stepped outside the door of the hotel and turned right towards his car. He paused and looked around him. A few people were passing through the street, but his sensation of being watched had gone. He went over to his car. One minute later he was driving up the Via Crispi towards his rendezvous.

Just as Rawls was leaving his hotel, Michael Wyman stepped out of the main door of his apartment. He too paused on the street and looked around. Not surprisingly, no pedestrians were in sight. He lit a cigarette and crossed the road.

He walked under the Porta Pinciana, the great stone gateway built by Aurelian in the third century and fortified by Belisarius in the sixth. Once, this was the entrance to Rome; now it was the way into Rome's most celebrated park. The Villa Borghese is normally just a daylight attraction. At night, the gardens and paths are seldom lit. Nobody was around as Wyman strolled down the Viale San Paolo del Brasile, which led to Rawls' meeting-point.

He was about half-way down it when Rawls' AlfaSud drove past him towards the Piazza Canestre. The car was unlit, and Wyman almost lost sight of it as soon as it had passed him. He heard it reach the Piazza and slow down to take the left turning towards the Piazzale dei Martiri.

Just as Wyman lost sight of the car altogether, it reappeared in a blinding white explosion. For a long, painful second, Wyman could see the car silhouetted against a brilliant backdrop, as fragments flew in all directions.

Shock transfixed Wyman for a few moments. A string of images whirled through his mind: Rawls, the day before; Rawls smiling, talking, pleading for support and advice; Rawls with his lunatic plan, the meeting with Ponti, the rendezvous, the car, the explosion. Wyman turned around and walked quickly back to his apartment.

12

TERRORISM has flourished in Italy since the late 1960s. One of the main reasons for this has been the absence of a single, State anti-terrorist unit with enough powers to do its job properly. Instead, there have been a number of rival military, quasi-military and intelligence bodies. Those groups seldom worked in concert, and they achieved little except to add to Italy's political bureaucracy. They are remembered only as a string of silly titles: the SID, which led to the SISMI and the SISDE, who were controlled by the CESIS, as well as the UCIGOS, who ran the various DIGOS belonging to the PS.

The problem was partially solved in 1978 by the creation of a special anti-terrorist unit of the Carabinieri, under General Carlo della Chiesa. The Carabinieri are Italy's para-military police: there are over 90,000 of them, and of the many varieties of Italian police they are the most efficient. Their stations are often found in remote villages where there is no civilian police presence.

A small but vital feature of della Chiesa's anti-terrorist group is the *Nucleo Operativo Centrale di Sicurezza*, or NOCS. This unit has been modelled on Britain's SAS, and it specializes in rescuing the hostages of terrorists. Unlike the SAS, however, it also has an investigative function.

Its leader at the time of the Scheib kidnapping was Colonel Augusto Castellano, who preferred to keep its activities out of the public eye as much as possible. He transferred the headquarters of the NOCS to a small set of offices in an unmarked building on the Via delle Quattro Fontane.

Castellano was a short, bald man with a prickly grey moustache and several chins. Thanks to a lifetime of good eating and a wife who did not understand the difference between a snack and a four-course meal, Castellano weighed about sixteen stone and disliked rapid movement. The Carabinieri did not manufacture a uniform adapted to his needs, so Castellano usually wore large cream-coloured suits indelibly stained by coffee, wine and Bolognese sauce.

On the afternoon of October 19, Castellano sat behind his desk and read reports concerning the man he was about to meet. Castellano had been phoned by Michael Wyman three hours after Rawls' death. He had agreed to a meeting, and asked his staff to assemble a swift report on the Englishman.

The results ran to three pages of terse, hurried typescript. It was known that Wyman had once been the Section V controller of MI6's Rome Station. It was also known that Wyman had left MI6 under strange circumstances, but the details were not known. A telex to MI6 had proved inconclusive: London refused to give Wyman a security rating, but did not suggest he was any kind of a threat. Castellano's staff had looked up the phrase "don't touch him with a barge-pole" in the dictionary, but could find no satisfactory translation.

Wyman was shown into Castellano's office at 3 p.m. The Colonel stood up and shook Wyman's hand.

"Good afternoon, Professor," he said genially.

"Good afternoon, Colonel," Wyman said. "I hope I'm not dragging you away from vital work."

"Not at all," Castellano replied. "Do sit down. I understand you knew the American."

"Yes," Wyman said as he took a seat. "I spoke to Rawls only two days ago. As you know, he was working on the Scheib kidnapping. He told me he had been in touch with you, and that you understood what was going on. We talked about what should happen if his meeting went wrong, and it was agreed that I should contact you without delay."

"Quite right," Castellano said. "I would have seen you earlier but, as you can imagine, we've been somewhat busy. We had to deal with the Press, the Americans had to be kept informed—it was all a bit of a nightmare."

"How have the Americans reacted?"

"Badly. There was some talk of sending Rawls' body back to America, so I had to explain that this was out of the question, thanks to the intensity of the blast. They weren't pleased."

"What did you tell them?"

"Everything. Firstly, nothing can be moved until our forensic people have examined the scene of the blast, and secondly, there's nothing to send back. There was enough explosive in that car to blow up the Vatican. It's an old trick: you wrap some explosive around the exhaust pipe and when it gets hot enough it goes off.

"That alone would have been enough to kill Rawls. But they also stuffed explosive elsewhere in the car—some near the engine, some behind the wheel rims—all over the place. The machine virtually disintegrated."

"What did the Americans say to that?"

"What can they say? Fortunately, Rawls has no next of kin, and the only people who know he was a CIA agent want to keep quiet about it. The official line is that he was a tourist who was killed by mistake. The Americans have agreed to invent the details, and we will confirm everything they say."

Wyman nodded.

"I see. Are the Americans aware that Rawls was in touch with you?"

"No, they aren't. To be honest, I wasn't particularly interested in Rawls' plans. It all sounded a little too romantic for my taste. He was only giving me formal notice of his scheme in case an attempt was made on his life. Since his fears were confirmed, there is little else I can do. Our investigations will simply have to continue without the benefit of Rawls' work."

"I see," Wyman said. "Since I was involved with Rawls' plans, does this mean you have no use for me either?"

Castellano smiled.

"On the contrary, Professor. Rawls explained your position in this matter. I understand he had a 'lead' on one of your students."

"Yes, Monica Venuti."

"He thought she was somehow implicated in the Scheib kidnapping. Do you feel the same?"

"At first," Wyman said, "I treated Rawls' conjectures with some scepticism. I can't say my views have changed substantially since then. She certainly does have some connection, however oblique, with the Red Brigades. Whether it's merely an acquaintance or full-blooded membership, I do not know.

"Rawls wanted me to exert pressure on Monica to help him with his inquiries. I refused, on the grounds that this would be a gross breach of professional standards. I still hold that view. However, there might be an alternative—a more delicate approach. It might be possible to do a little gentle probing. Perhaps this is all Rawls really had in mind."

"I see," Castellano said. "And what would this 'probing' consist of?"

"This term I am delivering a series of lectures on a fairly general philosophical topic. I will use some specific issues to illustrate the theoretical work, and I see no reason why I couldn't use terrorism as a working example. My lectures tend to be more like seminars, and there's a lot of group discussion. Perhaps we could prompt Monica into giving something away."

Castellano frowned.

"With respect, it sounds a bit abstract, Professor. In a lecture-room, Miss Venuti will be only too happy to voice her support for the revolutionary left. Half the kids in Italy do the same. We are, after all, looking for fairly specific information . . ."

"That's not just what I had in mind," Wyman smiled. "You see, my wife and I often see Monica outside working hours. She knows England quite well, and she's rather fond of our Anglo-Saxon habits.

"She is also a keen student, and we often talk about her work when she visits us. If the subject matter happened to be Italian terrorism, that might provide an opportunity for questions of a more specific kind."

Castellano nodded thoughtfully, kneading one of his many chins between thumb and forefinger.

"I understand," he said. "It's an interesting idea. You see, I would also like to talk to Miss Venuti, but there are various obstacles. You know her father has some influence . . ."

"He's a freemason, I believe."

"That rumour hasn't been proven," Castellano said coyly. "But as I say, he has some influence."

"Enough influence to stop you carrying out your investigations?"

"Certainly. Even if some of her friends are terrorists, that isn't enough to let me question her. I need proof of active involvement before we can risk her father's wrath. The last policeman who tried to question her learned that lesson the hard way.

"There is no question that you are in a much better position than we are to establish the truth about Monica Venuti. How quickly could you get any results?"

"That's the problem, Colonel. I can't work to any deadlines. For that reason, you will have to assume I can produce nothing: any information I can gather will be a bonus."

"Of course," Castellano agreed. "And in return . . ."

"I would need to be kept closely informed of your investigation into the Scheib case."

"I thought so," Castellano sighed. "Will you really need that knowledge?"

"Definitely," Wyman said. "If anything new emerges which might further implicate Monica or one of her friends, I will have to know. I will also need all the available information on Scheib's kidnappers—

who they are, their past histories, their *modus operandi*."

Castellano slumped wearily back in his chair.

"Professor, do you realize what you're asking? You are a civilian, and a foreign national as well. If it became known that you had access to secret files, and knowledge of undercover security operations, the scandal would ruin us all. I'm too old to be reduced to the ranks. Too old, and too fat."

"I am quite accustomed to handling sensitive information," Wyman laughed. "As you must know, it was my job . . ."

"I've heard about that," Castellano grunted. "MI6 aren't very fond of you, for some reason. I don't know what that reason is, and I don't want to. They haven't accused you of being a traitor, but they won't give you a security rating either. You don't appear to have left many friends behind."

"No, Colonel," Wyman grinned. "It was a minor professional dispute, that's all. I raised a protest about certain departmental economies, and I lost the battle but won the war. That didn't endear me to my employers."

"A bureaucratic squabble," Castellano said understandingly. "We have those in Italy too."

"So I hear," Wyman said. "So if I promise not to squabble with your bureaucrats, will I be allowed to have this information?"

"Very well," Castellano said reluctantly. "You may have the files."

"And will you keep me informed about your investigations?"

"If you insist. But on one condition: you must keep me equally well informed about the Venuti girl."

"Naturally," Wyman said. "Perhaps we can meet over lunch from time to time and pool our information."

The word "lunch" had a soothing effect on Castellano.

"An excellent idea," he said. "There's just one more thing . . ."

"Yes?"

"We've had difficulty translating a certain English idiom. Perhaps you can help us."

“Of course.”

“What exactly is meant by the phrase ‘Don’t touch him with a barge-pole’?”

13

"IT'S a week since we last spoke," Wyman said. "So I expect you will have forgotten the difference between Reductionism and Non-Reductionism. Giulio will remind us."

Giulio favoured Wyman with a startled blink.

"Eh?" he said.

"Reductionism, Giulio. What is it?"

Giulio looked down at his notes and tried to make sense of the confused hieroglyphs before him.

"Reductionists," he began, "are people who think that you are an impersonal description. No . . . that can't be right . . ."

"Not exactly, Giulio. Lucia: can you help?"

Lucia's notes were in better order.

"Reductionism," she recited, "is the belief that a person consists of no more than a combination of physical and mental events."

"Excellent," Wyman said. "And therefore Non-Reductionism is . . . ?"

"The belief that a person consists of more than just these events; that an extra ingredient is involved."

"Just so." Wyman put his hands in his pockets and looked around at the other students. "Are we all clear on that? It might help if I reminded you that the nub of Reductionism is that all these events can be explained in impersonal terms. Remember my 'flu in 1938. It can be described in a way that doesn't mention me at all, or any other person."

Paolo frowned and raised his hand.

"Do Reductionists claim that persons don't exist?"

"Not at all," Wyman said. "A Reductionist doesn't dispute the existence of persons. He is merely saying they *reduce* to events.

"Let me offer you an analogy. Organizations exist, and they are distinct from the people who belong to them. Take a topical organization like a football team—or better still, an organization of terrorists."

From the corner of his eye, Wyman

could see Monica watching him intently, but he was careful not to meet her gaze.

"Yes," he continued. "Consider an organization of terrorists; the Red Brigades, for example. The Red Brigades consist of all their members. Over the space of a few years, all the membership could change—old terrorists might be killed or imprisoned, and new ones could take their place. But the organization we call the 'Red Brigades' would still exist. In that sense, the Red Brigades are distinct from their members.

"However, if *all* the members were to die, or renounce their membership, the Red Brigades would cease to exist. This is because the Red Brigades consist solely of their members. If nobody belonged to them, they wouldn't exist.

"A Reductionist takes the same view about persons: a person is distinct from all the physical and mental events that make him up, but he does not exist separately from these events."

Monica shook her head.

"I can't agree," she said. "The Red Brigades consist of people grouped together under one idea. If you took away all the people, the idea would still exist, so the Red Brigades wouldn't disappear."

"That," Wyman said, "is the Non-Reductionist view. People consist of more than just the events that make them up: take away all the bits and pieces, and you are still left with something else besides."

"Exactly," Monica said.

"But think about this, Monica: you describe the Red Brigades as people grouped together under one idea. Isn't there another way of saying that?"

"What do you mean?"

"Couldn't we just say the Red Brigades are a group of people, each of whom believes in one idea?"

"I suppose so," Monica said suspiciously. "What of it?"

"If all those people renounced their membership, wouldn't that mean they had all renounced the idea?"

Monica hesitated.

"Perhaps," she conceded.

"And if nobody else believed in that idea, there would be no more Red Brigades, would there?"

She did not reply.

"So," he continued, "We are justified in

saying that the Red Brigades can be reduced to their physical membership. Even though we may speak of the Red Brigades as something distinct from their members, the Brigades still consist of no more than those members, do they?"

Monica nodded thoughtfully.

"Good," Wyman said. "And the Reductionist is saying the same about persons. Of course, when you think about a person this way, it's much harder to accept.

"A Non-Reductionist says that personal identity is the most important thing about a person. To be Enzo, it doesn't matter if Enzo has one leg or two, or is blind, or has green hair. Being Enzo is something over and above Enzo's physical and mental features, and it's 'Being Enzo' which makes him distinct from other people.

"A Reductionist says that it's the other way around: 'Being Enzo' is just a label we attach to a collection of events. The only things that count are the events themselves. If the Reductionist is correct, then the divisions between persons are reduced. The Reductionist says it's all very well to group events together and put labels like 'Monica' and 'Enzo' on them, but these groupings are little more than convenient expressions.

"This is why the Reductionist claims the divisions between people are reduced. The events within a person are not sealed off from the events outside him—they are just more closely related to each other. It's as if I were to scatter a bagful of marbles across the floor; there would be marbles everywhere, but they wouldn't be spread evenly. Some would collect in groups, and we could give these groups names. But no group would be 'sealed off' from the rest of the marbles. The Reductionist says that persons are like these groups of marbles: they are groups of events, and these events happen to be closer to each other than they are to other events. Does that make sense?"

The students nodded.

"Good. I have said the Reductionist view brings people closer, but that's only if they are contemporaries. In this sense, I am closer to Mussolini than I am to Julius Caesar, because the events we call 'Mussolini' are closer than the events we call 'Caesar'. Remember the boy in the photograph: I am nearer to you now than I am to that boy, even though he too was Michael Wyman."

"It's as if he were a totally different person," Paolo said.

"And in a way, he is. But remember: on this view, being a different person doesn't mean so much. The important thing is how close the events are. It's the same with future events. I am more closely related to what will happen next week than to the events in twenty years' time.

"If the Reductionist view is correct, then we should also change our attitude towards a number of important things: death, for example. Can anyone suggest why?"

Monica offered a tentative reply:

"If we believe a person consists of something special, over and above his brain and body, then when he dies, we lose that special something. But if he doesn't . . ."

"Go on."

". . . then it doesn't mean so much."

"Then why do we fear death?" Lucia asked.

"That's why I said we are inclined to be Non-Reductionists. We like to think we contain that 'special something' Monica spoke of. But we might be wrong."

Wyman put his hands back in his pockets and gazed down at the floor.

"Three days ago a man was killed in the Villa Borghese. You probably read about it in the newspapers, or saw the report on television. A bomb was placed in his car by the Red Brigades. I understand he was a tourist, and they killed him in error.

"I don't know if he was married; let's assume he was. His wife was no doubt shocked by the news. She will feel that something very important to her has been taken away. She's right, of course."

Wyman looked up, and his gaze fell on Monica.

"Nevertheless," he went on, "there's another way of looking at this death. Suppose this man was no more than a collection of events: have these events finished? I think not.

"He may have written letters, or a book. He may have planted a garden, or painted pictures. Whatever he was, he doubtless did things that affect events after his death. Such events could consist of no more than somebody else remembering his name. As time goes on, of course, there will be less of those events, and they will occur less often. But the collection of events we label with this man's name will go on after we call him 'dead'.

"It's an interesting way of looking at death, isn't it? I think it offers us some comfort."

If there was any change in Monica's expression, Wyman failed to detect it.

"Of course," Wyman said, "none of this justifies killing the poor fellow in the first place. Next week, I'd like to begin thinking about how Reductionism might affect our views about what is right and wrong."

14

THE following Friday Anatoli Bulgakov returned to the Via Gaeta for a final meeting with Mazurov. He found the *Rezident* immersed in his study of Eutropius, surrounded by lexica, commentaries and handwritten notes.

"Good morning, Colonel," Bulgakov said, as he entered Mazurov's office.

"Good morning," Mazurov said. "You know, this fellow Eutropius really is quite extraordinary."

A burst of Mazurov's radioactive breath wafted up, but Bulgakov struggled bravely to ignore it.

"Is that so?" Bulgakov said.

"Yes. He manages to relate the entire reign of Constantine without any mention of his conversion to Christianity. What would you make of that?"

"I know almost nothing about ancient history," Bulgakov said cautiously. "But it would seem that he wasn't a very good historian."

Mazurov slammed his fist on the table.

"Precisely," he exclaimed. "That's just what everyone else believes—'Eutropius was an idiot', they say. But don't you see, that would be like discussing Pontius Pilate without mentioning Jesus Christ. No one would really be that stupid, would they?"

Bulgakov thought about the various forms of stupidity he had encountered, and concluded that it was all too possible. His reply was more diplomatic:

"I take it you have your own theory on this omission, Colonel."

"I certainly do," Mazurov said. "Unfortunately, it would take a little too long to explain it here. I am sure you are anxious to be getting back to London."

"Yes," Bulgakov said, with little feeling. He was enjoying his stay in Rome. "Now that the Rawls business is over, I assume you have no further need of me."

"Exactly," Mazurov said. "Fortunately, our revolutionary friends have removed the first obstacle. In fact, they needed little prompting from us to dispose of Rawls."

"Indeed?"

"Yes. We offered them help—those

photographs, some extra information, your assistance, if necessary. They refused it."

"Wasn't that odd?"

"Not at all. You see, Rawls hired his car from a co-operative firm which employs one or two people with Brigadist sympathies. He was even stupid enough to hire the car in his own name and give the address of his hotel. Most unprofessional, I must say. I suppose it never occurred to him that their contacts are so good."

"So that's how they were able to fix Rawls' car."

"Precisely," Mazurov smiled. "They didn't even need to know what he looked like. All they had to do was load the car with explosive, and in effect Rawls would kill himself. The contact in the car-hire firm even gave them spare keys for the car, so there would be no sign that the machine had been tampered with."

"What a fool," Bulgakov said. "Why did he give his real name at the car-hire firm?"

"A blunder. A simple, thoughtless blunder. It can happen to all of us, Bulgakov. The cleverest people often do the stupidest things."

"Like Eutropius, you mean?"

Mazurov waved his finger reprovingly at Bulgakov.

"Don't provoke me," he laughed. "You know, I half suspect you mourn the passing of our friend Rawls."

Bulgakov shrugged.

"I knew him reasonably well. He was around when I was just starting. One hates to be sentimental about these things, but it's as if a small part of one's own history had died with him."

Mazurov nodded:

"I understand. That's how the CIA treat their own people. Someone like Rawls should have been put behind a desk years ago. He was too old for field work—you said the same thing yourself. The Americans have no sense of loyalty towards their people. They take no pride in their successful agents; they just work them until they are of no further use, and throw them away. Quite disgusting, really."

"Yes. So, now Rawls is out of the way, what will be your next step?"

"It's hard to say," Mazurov replied. "We haven't mentioned our interest in Scheib to the *Brigadisti*, and we probably won't for some time yet. At this stage, I simply intend to cultivate the friendship of Ponti and his associates. They come to us for favours occasionally, and we will give them everything they want."

"Everything?"

"Within reason. Their latest request, for example, is really quite trivial, but it costs us nothing to grant it. About ten days ago they were contacted by a foreigner in need of help. He claims to be a Chilean—a veteran member of the MIR, on the run. He needs money, and he says he's prepared to work for it. The Brigades want us to confirm that he is who he claims to be. Of course, it's no trouble for us to do these things, and it all builds up goodwill."

The *Movimiento de la Izquierda Revolucionaria*, or MIR, is Chile's "Movement of the Revolutionary Left", a Castroite guerrilla group dedicated to the overthrow of General Pinochet. The "Miristas" were founded in 1965, and their fortunes have swung from one extreme to the other. Under Allende, they were virtually absorbed within legitimate government departments, but since his overthrow they have been a hunted organization.

"Who is the man?" Bulgakov said. "I used to know Chile quite well. I was there during the Allende period. Perhaps I know him."

"Perhaps you do," Mazurov smiled. He took a small collection of passport photographs out of his desk and gave them to Bulgakov. A look of surprise appeared on the Major's face.

"It's impossible," he exclaimed. "This man is dead—he was killed twelve years ago."

"You know him, then?"

"Of course I do," Bulgakov said. "This is Pedro Torres. He was quite a well-known figure in Santiago. His hair's grey now, and it used to be longer, but it's unmistakably him. I was sure he had been killed."

Mazurov grinned.

"In that case you were wrong. These photographs were taken yesterday, by one of Ponti's friends. I think I can explain your surprise. It's now clear that this man is Torres: he gave the Brigades a list of five names of our people who knew him at the Santiago embassy. I knew if he was genuine, you would be able to identify him. His story is fascinating.

"As you know, Torres was thought to have been killed by Pinochet's forces in September 1973. In fact, he managed to bribe his executioners into releasing him, on the understanding that Pedro would never be heard of again. Torres stuck to the deal: he 'lost' his identity, and went to work as an ordinary labourer in a village in the Andes.

"Not surprisingly, he grew bored with his exile. A few years later, when he thought he had been forgotten, Torres rejoined the MIR at a base in Neltume, down south. Only a few of his colleagues knew who he was, and he was happy to keep it that way. He conducted many guerrilla operations, and enjoyed great success.

"Then in July '81 the army uncovered thirteen MIR camps in the Valdivia district, and Torres' was one of them. This time he had to flee the country. He drifted first to Argentina, then Cuba, France for a while, and finally here. As I said, he needs help to go home. He seems willing to work for his keep, and he's the sort of person Ponti and co. like having around."

"Yes," Bulgakov sneered. "Like all cheap hoodlums, they like to have a genuine guerrilla around. It gives them a bit more confidence when their own morale wanes."

"You're a cynic, Bulgakov, but you're probably right. Anyway, for whatever reason, the *Brigadisti* seem anxious to play host to Torres, provided he's genuine. Your identification seems to confirm it."

"Poor devil," Bulgakov said sadly. "He doesn't deserve it. If I change my mind about the photos, will they leave him alone?"

Mazurov smiled.

"You really despise them, don't you?"

"They're children, Colonel. Torres is a grown man, a real fighter. Why inflict these infants upon him? Can't we help him out?"

"Not now," Mazurov said. "We want to keep these children happy, remember."

Bulgakov shook his head in disgust.

"You know best, Colonel, but . . ."

"But what?"

"Perhaps I don't like Rome as much as I thought I did, that's all."

15

THE district of Ostiense lies a couple of miles south of central Rome. It gets its name from the Via Ostiensis, a road built in the fourth century BC to connect the salt marshes of the Tiber estuary with the port of Ostia, about twenty miles south-west of the capital.

Although Ostiense is nowadays one of Rome's less glamorous districts, it still contains one or two impressive reminders of its past. The Porta San Paolo, a stone archway flanked by two massive towers, dates back to the third century AD. A few yards away lies one of Rome's most startling sights, the pyramid of Gaius Cestius, a funeral monument dating back to 12 BC.

Not far from this grandeur is an unremarkable street called the Via del Gazometro. On the morning of October 27, two men sat inside one of its bars sipping coffee and watching the residents of Ostiense bustle through the rain outside.

"So, Mario," said one of the men, "have you got the confirmation you need, or are you still waiting?"

He was a tall man, somewhere in his mid-forties, with blue eyes and greying crew-cut hair. He spoke Italian with an odd, foreign accent. His companion Mario was shorter, and almost twenty years younger.

"It's arrived," Mario said. There was no mistaking his accent—the slurred, careless consonants indicated a native of Rome. "You have to understand, Pedro, this wasn't for my benefit. I've never doubted you, but the others wanted to be absolutely certain. We have to be very careful, you must appreciate that."

"Of course," Pedro said understandingly. "Being careful is no crime. Still, I'm glad you've got what you need. What is going to happen now?"

"To be honest, I'm not entirely sure," Mario said. "We've been highly operational recently, and that means there isn't much spare cash lying around. If you'd come six months ago, we'd have fixed you up with fake papers and bought your plane ticket for home without delay. I'm not sure we can do that just yet."

"No?" There was a note of disappointment in Pedro's voice. "It doesn't matter. I can wait."

"Good," Mario said. "We'll take care of you; don't worry about that. In the meantime, we can put you up at one of our safe houses. I'll introduce you to some of the others."

"Perhaps I can help with your work," Pedro said. "I'd hate to think I was just sponging off you."

"There's no question of sponging," Mario said quickly. "We're delighted to have you as our guest. Your people are fighting a struggle that makes ours look puny by comparison. I've heard about your work, but I never thought I'd meet one of you. It's a privilege to have you with us."

"I'm flattered," Pedro smiled. "But I would still be a lot happier if I could help in some way."

"I understand your feelings," Mario said. "But all I can do is pass on your request. We do have a hierarchy here, and I'm afraid I'm at the bottom of it. All these decisions about you—whether you work with us, when we can help you with money, and so on—these have to be made by those in charge."

"Naturally," Pedro said. "Perhaps I can meet these people."

"I hope so," Mario said. "The leader of our column is an extraordinary man. Very gifted, highly experienced. I think you'd be quite impressed by him."

"Is that so? Perhaps I can persuade him that I could be of some use. I too have some experience . . ."

Mario laughed.

"You're too modest, Pedro. I'd consider it an honour to work with you, and I'd be surprised if the others thought differently. Come and stay at the safe house, and see what happens."

"I'll do that," Pedro said. "Who knows? Perhaps one day you will be my guest in Chile."

"I'd like that very much," Mario said, and they both smiled.

16

ON the same day, two men arrived at the US embassy to see Julian Hepburn. One was short, squat and garrulous. This was Jones A. The other was tall, quiet and extremely bulky. This was Jones P. Both men wore poorly fitting grey suits, and a casual observer might have supposed they were policemen. In fact, they were CIA men sent out from Langley after Rawls' death.

Hepburn showed them into his office with some despondency. One look at Jones P. confirmed that yet another set of artisans had been sent to cause him discomfort. It was Jones A., however, who did most of the talking. He spoke with a high-pitched, insistent voice, and most of his sibilants were slurred by a mouthful of chewing-gum.

"I guess you mushta heard from Langley by now, shir. We're here to shtraighten out the Rawlsh businesh."

"So I hear," Hepburn said gloomily. "What exactly do you propose to do?"

"Rawlsh wash looking for a kid named Monica Venuti. You know about that, shir?"

"Yes I do," Hepburn said, and his heart sank.

"I guesh that's why he got hit, so maybe we oughta have a word with her. We'll follow up all the leadsh and shee where they get ush."

"Gentlemen," Hepburn said. "There are one or two things I should explain to you before you begin. Venuti is the daughter of a high-ranking Italian diplomat who's got a great deal of political influence. Contact with this girl could prejudice a large amount of goodwill from the Italian authorities, and we have to keep those people happy.

"When Rawls came here, I told him I couldn't allow him to approach Venuti, since the risks would be too great. I'm afraid I have to say the same thing to you. I can't let you make direct contact with any suspected terrorists or their associates. If you need to make approaches of that kind, tell me and I'll see what I can do.

I'm sure you understand why I'm saying this."

Jones A. and Jones P. exchanged knowing glances and smiled. Jones A. removed the gum from his mouth and put it in the crystal ashtray on Hepburn's desk.

"I'm sorry, sir," he said. "I guess you don't understand. We're here to find Scheib. Our orders don't say anything about keeping the wops happy. Rawls was onto Venuti, and they killed him. That makes her our number one suspect, and we're going in there with both barrels. I bet those greaseballs are laughing their heads off about Rawls, poor bastard. I can tell you, those sonsabitches are going to scream through their assholes by the time we've finished with them. They've gotta learn you don't mess about with the CIA."

"Right," concurred Jones P.

"Oh my God," Hepburn said weakly. "You don't know what you're saying. These aren't petty criminals you're talking about. They train them in camps in Russia and Czechoslovakia. They're professional killers, for Christ's sake. Rawls was an experienced operative, and look what happened—"

"Rawls was over the hill," Jones A. said dismissively, "God rest his soul. A good man, sure, the best, but he was too old. We're different, sir. You don't mess about with us."

"Right" said Jones P.

"You still don't understand," Hepburn insisted. "If you start messing around with terrorists and set up your own private war, there'll be hell to pay. We've got nearly thirty operations set up in Rome, and we don't need any publicity. This could screw everything up. I'm sorry, but I can't let you go ahead with this. That's an order."

Jones A. gazed at Hepburn as if he were a rare species of cockroach.

"You can't do that, sir. We've got authority to do whatever we need to get Scheib back. If that means blowing the balls off any number of pinko fag greaseballs, we'll do it."

"Right," Jones P. agreed.

"This is monstrous," Hepburn shouted. "Where do they find people like you? Jesus, this is a civilized country. You can't just go around behaving like a bunch of trigger-happy mafiosi. I'm going to put in a complaint to the Director about this. In the meantime—"

"You better read this, sir."

Jones A. produced a document from his jacket and handed it to Hepburn.

"That's our authorization," he explained. "Look who signed it."

Hepburn read the signature and suddenly felt the need for a stiff drink.

"We're here on the personal instructions of the Director," Jones A. continued. "We're going to get Scheib back if it means tearing this burg apart. Sorry if you don't like it, sir."

"I thought Rawls was a cave man," Hepburn said. "But I take it all back. Compared to you, the man was a brain surgeon."

"He was out of date," Jones A. said. "All this pussy-footing conspiratorial crap, pissing around in dark alleys and pretending to be Sam Spade. You don't play it like that with terrorists. You gotta pull out their toenails first and ask questions later.

"You know something, I hate to speak badly of the dead, and Edgar P. Rawls was a good man, God rest his soul, but deep down I know what his problem was: he was a liberal. Well, no one can accuse us of that."

"I'm sure they can't," Hepburn shuddered.

"So anyway, we're looking for Venuti and any other suspects. If you've got any files on these guys, we'd appreciate them, if you don't want to help, that's OK by me. We'll get what we need, one way or another. Like I was saying to Jones P. here, those wops won't know what hit them. We'll be kicking ass all the way. They got an easy touch with Rawls, but this time they're gonna learn—"

"Let me guess," Hepburn said wearily. "You don't mess about with the CIA."

"Right," said Jones P.

17

PROFESSOR THEODORE SCHEIB finished his meal and put the tray on a sideboard. He reflected that one of the very few advantages of being kidnapped in Italy was the prisoner's diet: you wouldn't have got *Cotolette alla Milanese* if you were in South America.

But this was small recompense for the professor's discomfort. For over a month he had been imprisoned in a room about eight feet by ten, which was poorly ventilated, with no natural light. Nevertheless, the room was well prepared: it contained his bed, a wash-basin, a toilet and an armchair.

To compensate for his lack of company, Scheib's captors gave him a large pile of American magazines and books, but he was allowed no newspapers. Twice a day, his meals would be brought in by one of his kidnappers, who would say nothing. If Scheib had a reasonable request—for cigars, or an aspirin, for example—the man would listen, go away, and reappear with what was wanted. Whenever Scheib asked for anything more—such as an explanation of what was going on, or when he would be released—he was ignored.

Just after lunch on October 27, Scheib was visited by a new face. He recognized him as the man with the gun who had bundled him into the car on the Via Due Macelli.

"Good afternoon, Professor Scheib," the man said genially. "How are you feeling today?"

"Pretty lousy," said the professor. "Can't think why."

"Perhaps I should introduce myself," the man said. "My name is Franco Ponti. I am responsible for your stay with us. I'm sorry I couldn't visit you sooner, but we've been rather busy recently."

"Really?" Scheib said. "Who else have you been abducting?"

"That's not what I meant," Ponti laughed. "You are our only guest, Professor, and from now on you will have my undivided attention."

"Is that good?" Scheib asked.

"But of course. You must be wondering why you've been kept captive for so long."

"It had crossed my mind."

"I will explain. As you know, we are a column of the Red Brigades. After we abducted you, we made our official demand known: you would be released if our comrades in prison were set free.

"Not surprisingly, the authorities refused to bow to our demand. They suggested negotiations, but we said our terms were unconditional, so we seem to have reached an impasse."

"You don't sound very bothered by that."

"I'm not," Ponti smiled. "We know perfectly well that our colleagues won't be released. The demand was merely a pretext for keeping you."

"And the real reason is . . . ?"

Ponti shook his head.

"All in good time, Professor. I can't tell you just yet, but all will become clear eventually."

"Before or after you shoot me?"

"There is no question of executing you, Professor. You may be certain of that. We haven't suggested to anyone that you will be killed, because nothing could be further from our minds. You can rest assured that in due course you'll be released safe and sound."

"That ought to make me very happy," Scheib said. "For some reason it doesn't."

"In the meantime," Ponti continued, "If there is anything we can do to make you more comfortable, just ask."

"More cigars?"

"Certainly."

"A bottle of Scotch?"

"With pleasure."

Scheib scratched his head in bewilderment.

"What did you do before you became a terrorist—were you a hotelier or something?"

"You are a valued guest," Ponti said. "It won't be too long, I hope, before you realize why. In the meantime, just try to relax. Perhaps this evening you will join me for dinner?"

Scheib shrugged.

"Why not?" he said. "I wasn't doing anything."

18

WYMAN sat in an armchair at home on the Via Porta Pinciana. Scattered around him were files, dossiers and reports, some of them dating back fifteen years. Colonel Castellano had kept to his side of the agreement, and provided Wyman with the Carabinieri's files on left-wing terrorism.

Of course, the documentation on the matter was so vast that even Wyman's capacious intellect could not be expected to digest it all. An obliging archivist had helped him gather enough information to gain a reasonable understanding of this massive, difficult subject.

Even with the help of the archivist, Wyman was still left with a great deal to read. That evening he relaxed with a jug of coffee and two packets of cigarettes as he waded through entire forests of official documentation. At the end of it all, with luck, he would have a better insight into the people who had kidnapped Scheib and blown up Rawls' car. The story that emerged from these files was bizarre and fantastic, worthy of the most implausible novelist. Unfortunately, it was all true.

Italian terrorism, and its equivalents throughout Europe, were born in the events of the late 1960s. The economic miracle of the post-war decades began to fade, and the State seemed poorly equipped to handle the new problems.

The new-found wealth of the *dolce vita* years was unevenly distributed, and often went untaxed. Corruption and incompetence had crept into most areas of Italian government. Unemployment was chronic, and there was an appalling shortage of housing. The education system was outdated and inadequate. Worst of all, nobody seemed able to tackle the crisis.

It was an ideal breeding ground for extreme politics. The official Italian Communist Party had apparently "sold out", and could no longer be relied upon to represent the interests of the disaffected. A number of small Marxist groups emerged, with varying degrees of interest in open revolution. Some were merely outspoken academics who, for all their talk of armed insurrection, would never have dreamed of exchanging talk and chalk for bullet and bomb. Others had fewer qualms.

The most radical and influential of these parties was *Potere Operaio*, or "Workers' Power", commonly known as Potop. This group stood furthest to the left of the official Italian Communists; while most of its members preferred to keep within the law, one in five held the "red card" of an activist. At its peak in 1969, Potop boasted five thousand members. Its activities included demonstrations, student strikes, and various forms of industrial agitation.

There was no single mastermind behind Potop, or any of the similar organizations of the time, but there was a powerful patron in the form of Giangiacomo Feltrinelli. No man—not even Colonel Gaddafi of Libya—has ever done so much to help the cause of European terrorism.

Feltrinelli was an only child in one of Europe's wealthiest families. A number of theories have been advanced to explain his fanatical obsession with the revolutionary left: his lonely, over-disciplined childhood, his domineering aristocratic mother, and his notorious sexual inadequacy. Whatever the reason, Feltrinelli devoted his vast inherited fortune to the cause of revolution in Europe.

He was a weak, pathetic figure, but the power of his money made up for his physical and psychological frailty. His publishing house was a tremendous success: he secured the European rights for Pasternak's *Dr. Zhivago* and Lampedusa's *The Leopard*, and he was the first to publish Carlos Marighella's *Mini-Manual*, a standard text-book of guerrilla warfare.

But publishing was only one of Feltrinelli's activities. He travelled around the world, establishing contacts with all forms of Communism. He had a villa in Czechoslovakia, he made friends with Fidel Castro, he visited the Tupamaros in Uruguay, and he forged links with all the key agitators in Western Europe. He helped Andreas Baader and Ulrike Meinhof set up Germany's Red Army Faction, and he bought arms for the Palestinians in Beirut. Most notoriously, he set up account number 15385 in a Swiss bank under the name "Robinson Crusoe", to finance a central unit in Zurich which co-ordinated services for revolutionaries in South America, Palestine, Germany, Spain, France, Greece and Italy.

At home, Feltrinelli poured absurdly large sums of money into Potop, paying off all its debts and allowing it the use of his printing presses. The Feltrinelli publishing house became the main source of radical and "underground" literature. If you wanted to organize a demonstration or build a home-made grenade, a Feltrinelli bookshop would supply you with the required reading.

Feltrinelli urged Potop to discard its attachments to legality, and to become a fully fledged clandestine organization. He failed, because too many of Potop's members clung to some faith in the democratic system. Undeterred by this, Feltrinelli went underground in 1970 and set up his own organization, the Proletarian Action Group or GAP.

Based in Feltrinelli's home city of Milan, GAP was Italy's first left-wing armed terrorist band. Feltrinelli sent some of his disciples to a KGB-run military training-camp at Karlovy Vary in Czechoslovakia. Later, he brought in Palestinian instructors from the Lebanon, and established his own camps in the Piedmont mountains.

The astonishing career of Giangiacomo Feltrinelli ended in March 1972, with a plot to blow up Milan's electricity supply. Feltrinelli climbed five metres up a high-tension pylon on the outskirts of the city. He had taped forty-three sticks of dynamite to the pylon, and was in the process of adding one more, when the timing mechanism accidentally went off. Bits of Feltrinelli were scattered over a fifty-yard radius, to be found later by a farmer's dog.

GAP died with its founder, but its facilities, training-camps, arms and money were taken over by the other terrorist groups who had now emerged beside it. There was the Armed Proletarian Nucleus, or NAP, the Front Line, the RP, the PFR, the UCC, the FCC, and a small but rapidly growing group called the Red Brigades.

The founder of the Red Brigades, like so many of the most notorious Western terrorists, came from a secure, respectable background. Renato Curcio was born in

Rome, the illegitimate son of a maidservant to the wealthy Zampa family. He had a strict Catholic upbringing, and was privately educated at a number of excellent schools. Finally, he studied at Trento University in northern Italy, where he was introduced to the world of revolutionary politics.

His first activities as a revolutionary were unspectacular and rather sordid. With the help of some friends, he kidnapped a business executive and a right-wing trade union leader. After a mock trial before a "People's Court", these men were beaten up and released.

In 1970 Curcio married a 25-year-old fellow student at Trento University called Margarita Cagol. With her support and encouragement, he created what was to be Italy's most notorious terrorist network. The Red Brigades collected ransoms, robbed banks, and murdered those they described as "enemies of the people". In 1974 Curcio was captured by the police, but was rescued a few months later by an armed raid on his prison, led by Margarita.

The following year, the Red Brigades

abducted a member of the Gancias, the Italian wine family, and held him in a "People's Prison" in Piedmont. They were discovered by the Carabinieri, who stormed the building. Margarita threw explosives at the policemen, and was shot dead as her husband escaped through another exit.

Nearly twelve months later, Curcio himself was wounded and captured. His trial was repeatedly postponed thanks to threats and further acts of terrorism. When it opened in 1978, Curcio's colleagues tried once again to halt the proceedings by kidnapping the president of the Christian Democratic Party, Aldo Moro.

This was the most spectacular of the Red Brigades' exploits. Moro had been prime minister five times, and was a personal friend of the Pope. He was kidnapped from his car on the Via Fani, and his five bodyguards were killed.

The timing was perfect. The political situation had not been going well, from the terrorists' point of view. The official Communist party was about to form a coalition with the other main parties, offering the hope of some stability in central government. As far as the extreme left was concerned, this would be the Communists' final act of treachery, and would greatly damage the prospects of radical reform.

The Moro kidnapping changed all that. The government dithered and Moro was shot. There was international outrage, and a massive police investigation, but the Red Brigades achieved their aim: the government coalition crumbled, and Italy was plunged once more into political turmoil.

Curcio was finally convicted, and was sentenced to remain in prison until the next century, but the Red Brigades carried on without him. The Moro tragedy, however, provoked a new backlash from the authorities. General della Chiesa's anti-terrorist squad enjoyed new powers and new successes. By the summer of 1980 there were nearly a thousand left-wing terrorists in prison.

For a while, the Red Brigades had posed a genuine threat to the Italian state. Their terrorism had been conducted against a backdrop of nearly ten years of social unrest, strikes, demonstrations, civil disorder and governmental chaos. With the new decade came greater social and political stability, and a corresponding decline in urban terrorism.

As a result, the Red Brigades adopted a harder, more professional line. For all his viciousness, Curcio had been something of a romantic, a firm believer in "the People" and their need to rebel. Red Brigade theory in the 1970s reflected his view: if the machinery of the state were not only weakened, but shown to be inadequate, the last traces of popular faith in "the system" would evaporate, and there would be revolution.

The theory changed as the Red Brigades entered their second decade. It was no longer a question of merely leading the People into revolution: the People must also be persuaded—pushed, if necessary. The State must be thrown into confusion, a chaos so terrible that no authority could cope with it. Then the People would have to rebel.

Wyman came to the end of the last file but one. He looked up at the clock and blinked in surprise. It was 4 a.m. There was only one document left to read, and it would probably be the most fascinating of all.

Throughout all the events that Wyman had studied, one man's name continually reappeared in the files. This man had been involved with the revolutionary left since its infancy, sometimes as a main protagonist, elsewhere as a shadowy figure on the sidelines. He was linked with all the key figures and organizations, from Potop, Feltrinelli and GAP to Curcio and the Red Brigades. His name was Franco Ponti.

19

ON the morning of the 28th, Pedro Torres, the Chilean, returned to the bar on the Via del Gazometro. Waiting for him was his friend Mario, and another man he had not met before. The second man was about the same age as Mario, but slimmer and more expensively dressed.

"Hello, Pedro," Mario said. "This is Michele Rucci. Michele—Pedro Torres."

The two men shook hands.

"We have arranged that Michele will take you to his safe house for the time being," Mario said.

"Delighted to have you," Michele said.

"Thank you," Pedro smiled. "Have you heard any more from your column leader, Mario?"

"I'm afraid not," Mario said. "Michele has passed on your offer of help, but we haven't heard a decision. You appreciate that yours isn't the most pressing case . . ."

"Of course," Torres said. "I understand the problem. You told me you were operational. Does that mean an operation is about to happen? Or is one already taking place?"

The two Italians exchanged anxious glances.

"I'm sorry," Pedro said hastily. "That was a stupid question. Please ignore it."

"Don't worry," Michele said to Mario. "He's been cleared, hasn't he?"

"I suppose so," Mario said slowly. "It's just that . . . oh, hell, what difference does it make? Yes Pedro, as I said, we're operational. You have heard about the American professor?"

Torres' eyes widened in surprise.

"No!" he exclaimed. "Your column . . . ?"

"Yes," Mario nodded. "I really can't say any more than that, but it's probably best that you should know."

"Jesus," Torres breathed. "No wonder you have little time for me. I'm sorry, I should have—"

"Nonsense," Mario said affably. "You couldn't possibly have realized. But perhaps you now understand why we can't attend to you as soon as you would wish."

"Of course," Pedro said. "So you are the people who—"

"Not us, exactly," Michele said. "It was our column commanders who pulled it off."

"And a very neat job it was too," Torres said. "I'll be interested to see how that business ends."

"So shall we," Mario grinned. "Our column leader is playing the whole thing very close to his chest. Nobody else really knows what he has in mind."

"Is that so? In Chile we tend to be more communal about our decisions. Except in the field, of course, and then everybody's under orders."

"It's a bit different here," Michele said. "You Miristas are mainly rural fighters. In the urban situation there's no clear-cut distinction between field and base. Usually they amount to the same thing.

"Columns vary in policy, of course, but once an operation has started, we find it best to let the column leaders make the decisions, even during quiet periods such as now. As long as the broad strategy of the organization is being maintained, nobody minds."

"That sounds logical enough," Pedro said. "But what happens when you have disagreements?"

"We don't," Mario said simply. "We can't afford them. Too many of our people have ended up in prison because of internal disputes."

"It used to be different, of course," Michele said. "Back in the 'seventies, everything was put to the vote. Even the decision to execute Aldo Moro was made collectively. Nowadays we're more pragmatic."

"I understand," Torres said. "I'd like to hear more about your techniques. I'm sure there's much you could teach me."

"I doubt it," Mario laughed. "But we'd be delighted to talk."

"At my place," Michele added.

"Of course," Pedro said.

A few minutes later, they left the bar and drove off in Michele's ancient Volkswagen towards the river. They crossed over the Ponte dell'Industria and went up to the Trastevere district. Torres was shown into a small apartment at Number 4, Vicolo del Cedro.

"It's not luxurious," Michele admitted, "but you've got a room to yourself and you can do what you like."

"It's fine," Pedro said. "If you think this isn't luxurious, I suggest you try a peasant's cabin in the Andes."

"We don't know how long you'll be here," Mario said. "It depends on what the column leader decides. He might want to move you to somewhere less central."

"Tell me," Torres said, "you haven't given me the name of your column leader, but if you're the people who kidnapped the American, then he must be Franco Ponti. Or are the stories false?"

"No," Mario said. "They're quite true. Ponti is in charge of our column."

"Is it true what they say about him? I've been hearing stories about Ponti for years, that he's the most single-minded member of the Brigades—that even Curcio stood in awe of him."

"That's true up to a point," Mario smiled. "But the popular image is of a bloodthirsty savage. He's not like that at all: he's cultured, highly educated, very much an intellectual. He's probably the best man the Brigades ever had."

"You'd like him," Michele said. "You and he have two things in common. You both hate capitalists . . ."

"Sure."

"And you both hate the Americans."

"Definitely," Torres said. "It sounds like a good basis for a friendship."

The three men laughed. Even revolutionaries should still make room in their lives for the occasional joke.

20

"MOST people," Wyman said, "agree about one moral idea: that things should go as well as possible for everyone. When we try to decide how the world ought to be run, few of us would disagree with that aim.

"Of course, once we've agreed on this, our problems really begin. How do we ensure that things should go as well as possible for everyone? There are any number of ideas on the subject."

He removed his glasses and polished them before continuing.

"One of our biggest problems," he went on, "is how individuals ought to run their own lives. What should people be aiming for? What do you think, Enzo?"

"Money," Enzo said unhesitatingly.

"Indeed?" Wyman said. "Why money?"

"It's the best means for achieving happiness."

"Perhaps it is," Wyman said. "But then

it isn't your ultimate aim. What you're really after is happiness. Isn't money just a means, rather than an end?"

"I suppose so," Enzo said.

Wyman nodded.

"Can you see a possible clash between an individual's personal aim and our moral view about the world?"

"What do you mean?"

"Well, we agree that things ought to go as well as possible for everyone. But someone's personal aim might conflict with that: he might be aiming for something which caused misery for other people."

"Like a capitalist?" Monica suggested.

"Possibly," Wyman smiled. "But you understand what I'm getting at? Good. What I'm interested in are these clashes between personal aims and public aims, and how we should resolve them."

He turned round and wrote the words "Separateness of Persons" on the blackboard.

"Another thing we're probably all agreed on is this: we are all separate persons, and each of us has his or her own life to lead. How important is this? If this is *very* important, then the clash between personal aims and public aims is difficult to resolve. If it's *not* very important, then public aims should take priority."

"What do you mean by that?" Lucia asked.

"If we think that being separate from other people is very important, then our responsibilities to ourselves are just as important—perhaps more important—than our responsibilities to those around us, our communities.

"But if we don't think that separateness is very important, then our communal responsibilities should get more priority, shouldn't they?"

Lucia nodded.

"Now," Wyman said. "Our Non-Reductionist thinks that separateness is very important. He believes that being a person is a special thing: it involves more than just having a brain and body, remember?

"So a Non-Reductionist thinks that a person's responsibility to himself is very important. He believes you should give a high priority to your own personal aim. What do you think that aim should be?"

"Lots of sleep," Paolo said, and they all laughed.

"Power?" Lucia offered.

"But why should you aim for these?" Wyman said. "Aren't these like Enzo's suggestion of money: means to an end?"

"You mean happiness?"

"I think I do," Wyman said. "But we can put it this way: the Non-Reductionist believes that each person's aim should be for a life in which everything goes as well as possible for himself. Isn't that so? And because he attaches great weight to the separateness of persons, he thinks this is very important, doesn't he?"

Monica frowned.

"But what about our original moral aim, that things should go as well as possible for everyone?"

"That's our problem, isn't it?" Wyman agreed. "That's where we get our clashes. Lucia wants to have power so she can be happy: that might mean she needs to tyrannize other people, and reduce their chances of being happy. How do we get round this problem?

"Let's go back to that moral idea: things should go as well as possible for everyone.

What do we mean by this? It's often thought it means the greatest sum of happiness, minus all the misery. It's like an equation: if you could add up all the happiness in the world, and take away from that all the misery, you'd be left with a figure—call it *x*. What our moral idea says is that *x* should be as large as possible.

"That sounds fine, but there's a small problem. Take Lucia's unholy quest for power. She might make herself extremely happy if she could enslave a few thousand people.

"Let's suppose Lucia turns out to be a benevolent despot, and she doesn't want to hurt anybody. People aren't much less happy under her rule than if they were free, and she's delighted to be their ruler. We could say that the total amount of happiness has increased enormously, and the amount of misery has only increased by a small amount, so *x* is greater than it was. Something's wrong, surely?"

"Only if you say so," Lucia sniffed.

"It's not just a question of how much happiness there is," Monica said. "It also matters how you spread that happiness around."

"Exactly," Wyman said. "Some people think it doesn't matter how happiness is distributed, as long as there's more of it. Others, like Monica, disagree. They think we should care about how that happiness is shared out among different people.

"If you believe this, and I suspect most people do to some extent, you need to add an extra rule to our moral idea. We agree that things should go as well as possible for everyone. But remember, our Non-Reductionist says it's extremely important that we are separate people. If we are equally deserving, then each of our lives should go equally well. Even if this can't actually be achieved, we should at least aim for it.

"So let's add this rule, for example: that no one should be worse off than other people through no fault of his own.

"How does this affect Lucia's quest for power? The people she rules are now worse off through no fault of their own. Even though the total happiness is increased, our new rule doesn't allow Lucia to be a tyrant."

"Bad luck, Lucia," Giulio sympathized.

"It was nice while it lasted," Lucia replied wistfully.

"This new rule is called a principle of distributive justice. The idea is that we decide whether something is right, not just by how much benefit it brings, but also by how that benefit is spread out among people. Does that make sense? Good."

"Wait a minute," Monica said. "This is just the Non-Reductionist view, isn't it?"

"That's right," Wyman said.

"So what does the Reductionist believe?"

"Well, let's think it through. Is he going to disagree with our general moral aim?"

"No," Monica said. "He'll agree with that."

"So he thinks that, in general, things should go as well as possible for everyone?"

"Yes."

"Very well; what about personal aims? The Non-Reductionist puts a high premium on the separateness of persons, so he gives a great importance to personal aims. What would the Reductionist think?"

"He doesn't attach much weight to the

separateness of persons . . . so he won't be very interested in personal aims. He'll think the general aim is much more important."

"Yes," Wyman agreed. "The clash between personal aims and public aims is less of a problem for the Reductionist, isn't it? He'll put the public aim first. The most important thing for him will be that things go as well as possible for everyone.

"But what about our problem of distribution, Monica? What does the Reductionist think about weighing up happiness and suffering?"

Monica thought hard, and shook her head.

"I'm sorry," she said. "I don't know."

"Well, he gives less weight to separateness of persons," Wyman said. "So he'd have to give less weight to the principle of distributive justice. He'd be less worried about how happiness is shared. But that isn't the end of the matter. Consider this possibility: we have to decide if we should inflict a certain amount of suffering on a man. If we do this, he will benefit later in life. Enzo: what would our Non-Reductionist say?"

"He'd say that was OK," Enzo said. "After all, he's aiming for his own greatest happiness."

"Very well. Suppose we are giving the same man this suffering, only this time we are doing it to benefit someone else. What would the Non-Reductionist say now?"

"He'd disagree," Enzo said. "The man doesn't benefit from his own suffering; it's not in his own best interest."

"Quite. He'd say we're distributing pain and suffering unfairly. In other words, the Non-Reductionist thinks it's fair to balance pain and happiness among different parts of a person's life, but not among different people.

"Now, what would the Reductionist think of giving the man suffering in order to benefit him later in life?"

"He'd think there was less justification for it," Monica said. "He's not the same man later on, is he? It would be like hurting one person to benefit another."

"Yes," Wyman agreed. "It *would* be like hurting one man to benefit another. Our Non-Reductionist doesn't believe in that at all, does he? But what does the Reductionist think?"

"He . . . doesn't mind," Monica said. "I don't understand. On the one hand, the Reductionist doesn't like that sort of compensation, but on the other hand he does. It doesn't make sense."

"Think of it this way," Wyman said. "The Reductionist thinks there's less justification for hurting someone to benefit them later on. But this doesn't mean there's *no* justification for it. And if there *is* a good reason for doing this between different parts of a person's life, then we should also do it between different people. He gives less weight to the distributive principle, but he gives it more scope.

"Remember: our Reductionist believes people are no more than the events which make them up. If this is so, then we should be worrying most of all about the quality of events, rather than 'whose' they are. Our aim should be to make sure that of all the experiences in the world, as many as possible should be good."

He paused to let this point sink in.

Giulio raised his hand with a question:

"Can't you use this argument to justify selfishness?"

"How would you do that?"

"Well, what about Lucia's aim? You said that if she took power over those people, the total sum of happiness would be increased. That means the sum total of good experiences would go up, and that's what the Reductionist wants, isn't it?"

"Does this mean I can be a tyrant again?" Lucia asked hopefully.

"I don't think so," Wyman laughed. "If you recall, the only reason Lucia wanted to be a tyrant in the first place was to fulfil her personal aim. What does the Reductionist think of personal aims, Lucia?"

"He doesn't think they're very important," Lucia admitted. "So I can't be a tyrant after all."

"I'm afraid not. But I agree that the Reductionist argument could be used to justify some interesting ideas."

"Some very strange ones, if you ask me," Giulio muttered.

"Perhaps," Wyman admitted. The gleam in Monica's eye told him she had caught his bait. "What do you think, Monica?"

"I agree with you," Monica said slowly. "I think you could use it in a very interesting way."

"Good," Wyman said. "Then perhaps you'd like to show us. For our next session, you might like to put forward a theory of some kind, using the Reductionist point of view."

"What would you like me to talk about?"

"Anything you want," Wyman smiled. "I suggest you pick the subject that most interests you, whatever that might be."

Monica thought about this for a moment, and a smile crept across her face.

"All right," she said softly. "I'll do that."

21

WYMAN left the faculty building and strolled through the Piazzale della Minerva on his way back to the car park. Just as he was passing the Physics faculty, he was accosted by two men in battered grey suits. One was short and stocky, but the other was very large indeed.

"You Wyman?" asked the smaller one.

"I am. And who might you be?"

"My name's Jones. We're with the Company. Understand you knew Rawls."

"I did," Wyman said. "A tragic business. What can I do for you?"

"We're taking over where Rawls left off. He was chasing one of your students, wasn't he?"

"What of it?"

"We're doing the same. You got anything to tell us about this kid Venuti?"

"Such as?"

"All those things you told Rawls and we never heard about. Where she lives, who her friends are, who she sleeps with, that kind of thing."

"I told Rawls nothing of the sort," Wyman snorted. "In fact, I told Rawls to go away. I don't discuss my students with other people. That applies to members of the CIA as well."

Jones A. and Jones P. exchanged glances.

"So you never said anything to Rawls about this girl?"

"I'm afraid not."

"Maybe you'd like to tell us."

Wyman shook his head.

"I don't think so," he said genially. "I suspect that if I gave you that sort of information, you might use it."

Jones A. and Jones P. exchanged further glances.

"A smart-ass," Jones A. said. "Listen, Wyman, you oughta know Venuti is our suspect number one. We need to get the information. Either we get it from you, the easy way . . ."

"Are you threatening me?" Wyman asked incredulously.

". . . or we get it from her. If you want to play daddy with this kid, you might stop to consider that. It could save her all kinds of hassle."

"Forgive me," Wyman laughed, "but you don't strike me as a couple of specialist trouble-shooters. In fact, you rather remind me of characters in a Hollywood gangster film I once saw. George Raft was in it, I think. Now who was the other fellow . . . ?"

"Cut the crap," Jones A. said impatiently. "We're here to find Scheib. We're also gonna find out who killed Rawls and blow his ass off. Are you going to help us or not?"

"Not," Wyman said.

"I don't think this guy takes us seriously," Jones A. said to Jones P.

"Very observant of you, Mr. Jones," Wyman said. "Now if that's all, I'm afraid I must leave you . . ."

"Hold on," Jones A. snapped. "Just you listen, Wyman. If you know something about that kid, we've got a right to hear it. Otherwise, we'll have to assume you're on the wrong side. Understand?"

"Perfectly," Wyman said. "Cheerio."

Wyman began to walk away.

"You've got a wife and kid, haven't you, Wyman?" Jones A. called out after him.

Wyman turned round, and his expression lost its good humour.

"Yes," Wyman said slowly. "I have a wife and child. If you go anywhere near them, you'll find out quickly enough whose side I'm on. You're a bore, Mr. Jones. A puffed-up little fool with delusions of grandeur. If you inflict your stupidity on me, or any of my family, the Red Brigades will be the least of your problems."

"Tell me about it," Jones A. jeered. "You've got no weight, Wyman. We know about you and MI6. They won't save you. Now listen to me: we are going to kick ass in this town. If you help, you're safe. If you don't, you're in the firing line. They killed one of our people, Wyman, and they're not gonna get away with it. You don't mess about with the CIA."

"Right," said Jones P.

"And that goes for you too."

Wyman gazed at the two men in stupefaction.

"You can't really exist," he said. "You

are a figment of somebody's imagination. A bad dream."

He walked away, shaking his head in disbelief.

Jones A. looked at Jones P. and grimaced.

"Damned intellectuals," he said. "They're all the same."

22

"WHAT exactly is the problem, Colonel?" Hepburn asked.

The moment he had been dreading finally arrived, as Colonel Augusto Castellano sat before him.

"You have two men in Rome. One of them is called Jones. I'm not sure which one; there is some confusion . . ."

"They're both called Jones," Hepburn said.

"Ah, so you know who I mean. Good. It appears these people are investigating the Scheib case."

"That's right," Hepburn said. "It's over a month since the professor was kidnapped, and since your people don't seem to be making too much progress, our headquarters sent these people out to investigate."

"I see," Castellano said. "The American who was killed, Rawls, he was doing the same, wasn't he?"

Hepburn nodded.

"So these people are here to replace him," Castellano said. "I understand. The problem, Mr. Hepburn, is their approach . . ."

"I know," Hepburn said. "They're about as subtle as a nuclear strike."

"Exactly," Castellano said. "They are not being at all discreet. They have threatened a number of people with violence . . ."

Hepburn moaned and buried his face in his hands.

". . . and it is only a question of time before they carry out their threats. This is quite alarming, don't you think?"

"Yes," Hepburn said feebly. "It's quite . . . alarming."

"The real problem concerns a girl called Monica Venuti, who is thought to be involved with the Ponti cell. At present, we still don't have enough evidence to implicate her with the terrorists, but we think this can be obtained, with a little patience.

"Unfortunately, your associates have little regard for legal niceties. Their inquiries are indiscreet, and they are jeopardizing our own investigations."

"I know, I know," Hepburn said. "Listen, Colonel, I assure you I had no hand in this. My authority has been overruled. If I had my way, these people would be put on the first plane home. I know what they're up to, but there's nothing I can do about it."

"Can't you communicate with your superiors? I'm sure if they knew what was going on . . ."

"Do you think I haven't tried? I've telexed the US continually since these hoodlums appeared. All the replies have amounted to one thing: leave them alone. What am I supposed to do?"

"I don't know, Mr. Hepburn," Castellano sighed. "It is all very unfortunate. You see, if these people carry out any of the threats they have been making so liberally, there might well be a formal complaint to the ambassador."

"Jesus," Hepburn breathed. "Is that what's going on?"

"I regret that it is. We really have no choice, Mr. Hepburn. These people cannot be allowed to continue behaving like this."

"Can't you just extradite them quietly? Arrest them, even?"

"Certainly," Castellano said. "How would your headquarters react to that?"

"Those idiots would probably lodge a complaint with the Italian police. That's the level of stupidity we're dealing with here. Still, if it removed the problem . . ."

"I'll bear it in mind," Castellano said. "At the moment, I have no solid case for extradition. There isn't much to arrest them for, either. But I have little doubt that in the next day or two they will do something to merit a swift reaction from my own people. Will I have your support if I take the necessary steps?"

"Support?" Hepburn said. "I'll pay you to do it."

"Excellent," Castellano beamed. "I'm delighted you've taken such a helpful attitude in this matter. It amazes me that men so unalike as yourself and the Jones men can be working for the same organization. Who are these people?"

Hepburn's face screwed up in distaste.

"They're artisans, Colonel. Plumbers."

23

"WHY don't you come over and meet him?" Mario said.

"I'd like to," Monica said uncertainly.

"But?"

"I don't know, Mario . . . I really should go to the library this morning. I'm supposed to be preparing a talk."

Mario replied with an exasperated snort.

It was about half-past nine on Tuesday morning. Mario, who had no permanent address of his own, had spent an uncomfortable night on Monica's floor. He planned to visit Michele's place in the Trastevere, in the hope of some news from Ponti and floor space for the coming night.

Though he hated to admit it, Mario was bored. Day after day passed, and there was no word from his column leader. Waiting for Ponti had become a little like waiting for Godot. His orders had been to do nothing until fresh instructions came, but for Mario this was the most difficult order to obey. He was impatient, and he wanted action. Matters were not helped by Ponti's stubborn refusal to explain his plans.

The previous evening, Mario had made a casual pass at Monica, and this had been curtly rebuffed. This didn't upset Mario, it merely baffled him. To be sure, Monica was what he termed "a stunner", and "stunners" did not hand out their favours liberally. He also realized that Monica was highly intelligent, and would not succumb to the usual clichés.

So Mario had done his best. As he later put it to Michele, he had "pulled all the stops out". He had been quiet, charming, and as modest as could reasonably be expected. He had toned down his praise for Monica's beauty, and stressed his respect for her as an individual. He expressed his delight that, despite such disparate origins, they should share the same convictions. Perhaps, he suggested, it would be possible for them to share even more than this.

Monica had listened to Mario's speech in silence. The only clue to her thoughts was a slight widening of the eyes indicating mild surprise. When he finished, she shook her head emphatically.

"No Mario," she said. "I think that would be a bad idea. Please don't raise the subject again."

It was unusual for Mario to take no for an answer, especially after just one attempt. But there was a note of determination in Monica's voice that precluded further discussion, so he shrugged and changed the subject.

It is seldom easy to sleep well after one's overtures have failed, and Mario's night on the floorboards was somewhat disagreeable. The next morning, however, he did his best to conceal his irritation.

Much of Mario's conversation concerned his new friend, the Chilean, Pedro Torres. Mario was impressed by the veteran's calmness and strength of character, and he spoke of Torres with something akin to hero-worship. He wanted Monica to meet the great man at Michele's house in the Trastevere. It was after this suggestion that Monica had raised the subject of her essay.

"I don't believe it," Mario said. "Right

now we are playing host to a great fighter, one of the finest people you could meet, and you'd rather prepare a talk. A talk! Are you serious? A piece of stale, dusty theory, in preference to a man like Torres? You students amaze me. Do you want to be an academic all your life, or do you want to see some hard reality? I know which I prefer."

"It's easy when you don't have the choice," Monica said crushingly. Mario had left school at seventeen.

"Very amusing," Mario said. "I was just trying to make the point that if you really want change—fundamental change—you get it with guns, not essays. You should have realized that by now. And the people who change things are men like Torres, not senile bourgeois pen-pushers like the man you write essays for."

He lit a cigarette and blew a provocative cloud of smoke at Monica.

"Professor Wyman isn't senile," she said. "He's a fine teacher, with a superb mind. And as I recall, Marx was an academic too. Does that make him a bourgeois pen-pusher?"

"You're comparing Wyman with Marx?" Mario said, and with mock awe he added: "I must meet this genius."

"Don't be ridiculous," Monica snapped. "Wyman is a bourgeois, and he's probably a reactionary too. That doesn't mean he has nothing to offer."

"All right," Mario said. "What's so useful about him?"

Monica paused.

"It's hard to explain," she said uneasily. "He knows how to look at things with detachment . . ."

"What things?"

"Right and wrong, how justice should work. He asks unusual questions about things which concern us."

"You've told him about us?"

"Of course not," Monica said irritably. "But I'd happily tell him where my sympathies lie. He'd treat it like an abstract problem, the way we would talk about the existence of God, or something like that. It's sometimes useful to see things that way."

"Meanwhile," Mario sneered, "millions are exploited, tortured and killed. People like your friend Wyman are happy to discuss any problem, as long as they're nowhere near it. I think it's time to stop talking and time to start doing."

"It helps if you know what you're doing," Monica said heavily. "Everybody works to a theory, Mario, including the Red Brigades. Even Curcio wrote pamphlets, debated and discussed. There's nothing wrong with that."

"Maybe," Mario conceded. "But at the end of the day, we've still got to fight. You too, Monica."

He put his cigarette out and went silent, knowing he had scored a point. There was a pause, then Monica said:

"Very well. Perhaps I should meet this friend of yours. I suppose the talk can wait."

"I'm sure it can," Mario grinned. "Believe me, you won't regret this."

He stood up and put on his leather jacket. A few minutes later they left Monica's flat and stepped into the sunny morning outside. Monica rode pillion on Mario's Vespa scooter as they drove off towards Michele's safe house in Trastevere. Across the street, in an old three-wheeled Piaggio van, a cine camera recorded their departure with a dispassionate gaze.

24

ON Tuesday evening Wyman had dinner with Colonel Castellano at a trattoria on the Via Cavour. The Colonel was in good spirits, and as he ploughed eagerly into a plate of *Spaghetti al Gorgonzola*, he told Wyman the latest news.

"We've discovered another of young Venuti's friends," he said. "A vicious little oaf called Mario Pagani. He's been on file for the last year or two, but it's only in the last eight months that he's been connected with the Red Brigades."

"How did you discover Monica knew him?"

"He went to her flat last night and they left together this morning. I'd love to know where they went."

"Weren't they followed?"

"We can't risk tailing Venuti just yet. The street the girl lives in is small and narrow. I suspect someone chose that address carefully, because it's too small for us to place a lookout there without being seen.

"All the buildings are fully occupied, so we couldn't put anybody in the flats opposite. The only thing we could do was set up a cine camera in a van parked outside. Stills are taken from the film and passed on to me. That's how we know about Pagani."

"I see," Wyman said. "I don't suppose there's any chance of my being able to . . ."

The Colonel's face sank in despondency, and he produced some photographs from his jacket pocket.

"I knew you'd ask," he sighed.

Wyman examined the photographs, and he looked at the Colonel in surprise.

"Is this Mario Pagani? I expected him to be a little younger."

"You're looking at the wrong one," Castellano said. "That's the girl's landlord, Salvatore Gennaro."

"Is he a suspect?"

Castellano laughed.

"No, Professor. Gennaro is a harmless old fool. He's half deaf, and he doesn't live on the premises, so he wouldn't have a clue about what goes on in the building. I suppose that's why they picked that flat."

"They?" Wyman asked. "You think that's a Red Brigade house?"

"It's possible. We found out who the previous occupants were. It appears there's been a high turnover of tenants. Three have been members of radical student organizations. Another one was arrested last year for possessing firearms, and four more are the subjects of other police investigations."

"My word," Wyman exclaimed. "Hasn't that place been raided yet?"

"No," Castellano said. "None of those crimes were committed while those people were living at that address. Furthermore, the same is true of dozens—perhaps hundreds—of addresses in Rome. If we were to raid every flat in town that had a bit of a history behind it, we'd treble our workload."

"I see," Wyman said. He found the pictures of Mario Pagani. They showed a short, stocky young man with dark, slicked-back hair and a leather jacket. "Typical young Roman, isn't he?"

"Only to look at," Castellano grunted.

"He's a karate enthusiast, and he likes inflicting it on other people. When this boy was doing his National Service, somebody got him into a fight. Pagani gave him two fractured legs and a severe head wound. Most of that National Service was spent in gaol. A thoroughly unpleasant kid."

"What do you propose to do about him?"

"We're following him," Castellano said, and he drew his napkin across his mouth. "I don't think Pagani's contacts would go very far up the Brigades' chain of command, but I could be wrong. Either way, he could still lead us to someone of greater interest."

"Such as Ponti?"

"Ah," Castellano sighed, "wouldn't that be wonderful? I would give a year's pay to find that bastard."

"I've read your file on him," Wyman said. "Quite an extraordinary fellow, isn't he?"

"That's one way of describing him; I can think of better ones. That file is useful, but it only gives an outline."

The Colonel emptied the rest of the Frascati into their glasses and called for the waiter. After they had ordered their main course, Wyman returned to the subject of Franco Ponti.

"I thought the file on Ponti was quite comprehensive," he said. "What do you know that isn't there?"

Castellano stroked his many chins pensively as he considered his reply.

"The thing you must understand about Ponti," he said slowly, "is that he's been around from the very beginning. He studied science at Padua University in the early 'sixties, and that's where he came into contact with Toni Negri, the guru of the extreme left. Negri had only recently become Professor of Political Science there, and he was looking for fresh converts. Later, when Negri was setting up Potop, Ponti was still at the university, doing his PhD.

"It was all good clean fun, up until then. Lots of hot air, no action. Then Ponti became a Potop hardliner, and things changed. He got to know Feltrinelli, and when *that* idiot wanted them all to become European Che Guevaras, Ponti agreed. He forgot his PhD, went underground, and joined GAP."

"The file became a little sparse after that," Wyman agreed.

"I'm not surprised," Castellano grinned. "That was in 1970, and our last decent photograph was taken of him three years after that. He's been the most elusive member of that bunch since they began. All these years later, he stages an operation in Rome, and we don't even know what he looks like. Extraordinary!"

"So what did happen when Ponti joined GAP? Or don't we know?"

"We have a fairly good idea," Castellano said. "A great deal emerged from the confessions of the *pentiti*, the ones we captured and who later had a change of heart. Most of what we know about Ponti comes from their accounts.

"After he joined GAP, Ponti trained in one of their camps in Piedmont. We know he went to Feltrinelli's villa in Prague on at least three occasions in 1971, and we can assume he trained at Karlovy Vary as well.

"After Feltrinelli died, Ponti joined Curcio's band of brothers, and he was responsible for a number of kidnappings. They said you could always tell when

Ponti was behind an abduction, because the victim never returned alive.

"And that was the problem. You see, even the Red Brigades had some kind of code of ethics. Even by their standards, Ponti was a maniac, and that made some of them feel uncomfortable."

"According to the file," Wyman said, "even Curcio was supposed to be a little frightened of Ponti. Is that true?"

"I'm sure of it," Castellano said. "You see, Curcio was an idealist, in spite of everything. He believed then—and still does, I'm sure—that revolution is just around the corner. His job was to set the fuse for it.

"He genuinely believed that the one thing stopping a mass uprising was fear of the State. His task was to dispel that fear by declaring war on the State, and exposing its weaknesses. That would generate spontaneous revolution.

"But Ponti didn't agree. He thinks of himself as a realist, and he knows perfectly well it would take more than just a few kidnappings and bank robberies to get people out on the streets. Ponti agreed with Curcio that people feared the State, but he thought you had to do more than just overcome the fear.

"No, Ponti's idea is that popular fear is here to stay, and that the Red Brigades should use that fear for their own ends."

"What does that mean?"

"It means you have to present people with something more terrifying than the power of the State—a nightmare that will force them to rebel."

"Such as?"

"The story is that in 1974, Ponti asked Curcio to consider making a small nuclear device, enough to create a one megaton explosion. This would be dangled in front of the country for long enough to demonstrate that the government was helpless to do anything about it."

"And then?"

"The bomb would be exploded, either here or in Milan. The State would disintegrate; then you would have revolution."

"Good heavens," Wyman exclaimed. "Was he serious?"

"Of course," Castellano said. "Ponti started his career as a scientist, remember.

He thought it would be well within his grasp."

"That doesn't sound right," Wyman frowned. "Ponti didn't do physics—as I recall, he studied biology."

Castellano shrugged.

"It doesn't matter. He certainly had the right connections, whatever his own qualifications may have been. The point is that Curcio was horrified by the suggestion, and he ordered Ponti never to mention it again. Indiscriminate mass killing simply wasn't Curcio's style."

"But Ponti likes the idea?"

"Only as a means to an end. He likes the idea as a quick route to revolution. The Red Brigades used to publish a bulletin called *ControInformazione* which was mostly propaganda. They would state their policy on one issue or another, and it was all fairly predictable.

"On one occasion, however, Ponti wrote an article for it. It was called 'Revolution with no strings attached', or something stupid like that. Like all the other Red Brigade writings, it was pompous, unintelligible gibberish; sentences that went on forever, obscure allusions, sociological jargon, that kind of thing.

"But if you read that article in the light of Ponti's known views, it began to make some sense. In general terms, he advocated the idea he put to Curcio: the one big operation that would be a short cut to a mass uprising."

"Was anyone impressed by this?"

"Not at the time," Castellano said. "After Curcio was imprisoned, Ponti went abroad. We think he went to Paris, but we can't be sure. He re-emerged in 1982, and then he found a more interested audience."

"What's changed?"

"The Red Brigades have changed, and Ponti probably has too. Nobody believes in spontaneous rebellion any more. They know you need a harsher approach, and Ponti certainly has that, even if he's given up the idea of mass murder.

"The new *Brigadisti* are a young crowd, Professor, and to them Ponti is something special. He's one of the originals, and he's *survived*. We've been after him for nearly fifteen years, but we've never got anywhere near him. They respect that.

Furthermore, he's a ruthless bastard, and they respect that even more."

"Strange people, the young," Wyman observed. "What about Professor Scheib? None of this explains why they should kidnap him. He's not a physicist, so he couldn't help make a nuclear weapon."

"I imagine Ponti's schemes are a lot less grand, nowadays," Castellano laughed. "I really don't think they've kidnapped Scheib for any reason to do with what he is. After all, what could they possibly want from a microbiologist?"

"With respect, Colonel," Wyman said, "Since neither of us knows anything at all about microbiology, we can't answer that question. But with a bit of luck, we might get an answer this weekend. I'm flying to England to see an old friend from my university, who knows Scheib quite well. They're in the same academic field. That might help."

"Possibly," Castellano shrugged. "Why are you so interested?"

"Why? For the same reason I corrected you about Ponti's degree a little while ago. It might be a complete coincidence, but . . ."

"Go on."

"Ponti took a degree in microbiology. His unfinished PhD was in Bacteriology."

"Really?" Castellano said. "Now that's interesting, isn't it?"

25

"MORE tea?" Wyman asked.

"No thank you," Monica said.

"Yes please," said Margaret.

Wyman poured out another cup of his favourite blend of Earl Grey and Darjeeling.

"We've run out, you know," he said to his wife. "Do remind me to get some more tomorrow."

"Where do you get it from?" Monica asked. "It's not easy to find good tea in Rome."

"It certainly isn't," Wyman agreed. "And I've given up trying. The Italians are splendid people, but they can only drink tea in a ratio of three tea-leaves to one gallon of water, and they insist on dipping pieces of lemon into it. Most peculiar."

"So where do you buy it from?" Monica repeated. "Or is that a secret?"

"Not at all," Wyman laughed. "I'm

flying to London tomorrow, and I shall buy it there."

"Are you going for long?"

"Just the weekend," Wyman said. "I need to pick up a few books I can't find in Rome, and I thought I'd say hello to one or two friends while I'm there."

"That sounds nice," Monica said. "Are you going as well, Margaret?"

"Of course not," Margaret said. "Michael would never let me spoil his fun."

"Quite right," Wyman growled playfully. "A woman's place, and all that."

"What about women philosophers?" Monica said.

"There are always honourable exceptions," Wyman conceded. "And how is your little talk shaping up?"

"Fine," Monica said, with some hesitancy.

"Is there a problem?"

"I don't know . . . I'm not sure if it's what you really want."

Wyman put his teacup down and lit a cigarette.

"All I want," he said, "is that you put the Reductionist theory to some use. I don't care what that is, as long as the Reductionist part of it makes sense. Does that help?"

"I'm not sure. I think you might dislike my conclusions."

"So what?" Wyman said simply.

Monica shifted uncomfortably.

"Perhaps you'd like to tell me what you're doing," Wyman suggested.

The ever-tactful Margaret got to her feet.

"I think Catherine needs some attention," she said. "Would you excuse me?"

"Of course," Wyman said, bestowing on her a surreptitious wink.

When Margaret had closed the door behind her, Monica began.

"I think Reductionism can provide a case for popular revolution. No, that's not right; there's already a case for revolution. The problem isn't *why* it should happen, but *how*."

"That's your starting point, is it?"

Monica nodded.

"Yes. Our country, like most others, protects itself against revolution in two ways. It does so by physically arming itself, which means a strong police force and judiciary. It also protects itself against the *idea* of revolution, and that's what I'm concerned with."

If Monica expected Wyman to greet her opinion with horror, she was disappointed.

"That's quite interesting," Wyman said calmly. "So how does a country protect itself against the idea?"

"By calling the agents of revolution 'terrorists'. That seals them off from the rest of the population: it makes them seem like public enemies, which they're not, and it suggests that terror is their only aim, which it isn't."

She stopped, expecting Wyman to comment. His only reply was to blow a long contemplative stream of smoke at the ceiling, so she went on.

"Revolutions usually involve some suffering. It would be crazy not to admit that; some people suffer, some also die. But it has to happen, and it's justified by the amount of suffering and death you prevent for the majority of the people. The trouble is, people don't look beyond that suffering. They don't realize it's pain for a good purpose.

"Most people are like children who shy

away from the pain of an inoculation, without understanding why they must go through the discomfort. Because people can't see further than the pain, they call revolutionaries 'terrorists', and shut them out like lepers."

"So," Wyman said, "the people we call 'terrorists' are really benevolent doctors? They know what's best for us?"

"Why not?" Monica said. "Why do you laugh at the idea? Once upon a time, people called in witches, they believed the world was flat, and that the best way to cure sickness involved leeches. There were minorities who knew better, and they were often persecuted for it. But now we know who was right, don't we?"

"Point taken," Wyman smiled. "And you think you can justify this 'necessary suffering'?"

"Using Reductionism, yes."

Wyman stubbed out his cigarette and fell silent.

"That's what I want to talk about," Monica added. "Do you mind my doing so next week?"

"My dear lady," Wyman laughed, "as far as I'm concerned, you may use your talk to justify the killing of the first-born, if you think Reductionism will do it."

Monica smiled in relief.

"Thank you," she said.

"I do have one or two questions," Wyman said, "if you don't mind my asking. Do you really believe in all this?"

"Yes," Monica said.

"And you would be willing to help in bringing about a revolution?"

"I would think it a privilege."

"Indeed? From what I read in the newspapers, one has plenty of opportunity to become involved in such activities. Have you ever been tempted . . . ?"

Monica laughed.

"How do you know I'm not involved already? You make me sound like the worst kind of armchair revolutionary."

"I didn't mean to," Wyman said. "But I wouldn't say that was such a bad thing to be. I'm a bit of an armchair man myself, you know."

"For all you know," Monica said, "I might already be working for the Red Brigades."

If you were, Wyman thought, you certainly wouldn't be telling me about it.

"Well of course, I don't know," he said. "But I think you'd like us all to *believe* you were. Isn't that so?"

Monica flushed with embarrassment.

"I don't know what you mean," she said lamely.

"I think you do," Wyman smiled.

Monica shook her head and looked at her watch.

"I'm afraid I have to go," she said quickly. "Thank you for inviting me here."

"My pleasure," Wyman said, getting to his feet.

Monica said goodbye to Margaret, and Wyman showed her out.

"Thank you for coming," he said. "I enjoyed our conversation very much, and I look forward to hearing the talk on Monday. And for heaven's sake, don't be put off by how you think I might react. All right?"

"Yes," Monica said. "I'll remember that."

Wyman closed the door behind her, and went back to the living room.

"What a strange girl," Margaret

observed. "Do you think she's really involved with all those terrorists?"

"She'd certainly like to be," Wyman said. "She has a vehement loathing for established opinions. Coupled with an active mind, that can make for one of two things. You will either get a radical philosopher who declares war on intellectual orthodoxy . . ."

"Or?"

"Or you'll get a violent revolutionary who declares war on the world. I do hope no one shows Monica how to use a gun."

26

WHILE the Wymans played host to Monica Venuti, Colonel Castellano sat in his office on the Via delle Quattro Fontane. On his desk was the National Service record of Mario Pagani. The Colonel had read the document again for further clues. He was having little luck.

Like most *Brigadisti*, Pagani came from a stable, comfortable background. His father was a motor mechanic, whose skill with cars had led to the ownership of a string of prosperous garages around Rome. Signor Pagani was a respectable gentleman: he had a large family, he went to church, and he voted for the Christian Democrats. He had even been known to pay his taxes occasionally. In other words, he was a typical Italian citizen.

Of his nine children, eight were equally unremarkable. Only Mario had been a little unusual. He had left school early, showing little inclination to get a job.

Eventually he was called up for National Service, where he distingushed himself by hospitalizing his sergeant.

Afterwards, Mario took a number of jobs, ranging from barman to bricklayer. None was successful. His family lost contact with him, and his present whereabouts were unknown to anyone.

Castellano read the last paragraphs with interest. Did Pagani's string of jobs indicate a drifter, or a man with a good reason for not wanting to be pinned down? It was standard technique for the *Brigadisti* to find themselves cover occupations as labourers or factory workers. If that applied to Pagani, it suggested he had been recruited just after his military service, in 1982.

By coincidence, the first reports of Franco Ponti's return to Rome emerged in 1982. The evidence was not conclusive, but it vindicated the Colonel's order to have Pagani traced. The first results arrived that morning. Pagani's most recent occupation had been as a bricklayer on a building site in Ostiense. The workmen usually took their coffee at a bar on the Via del Gazometro, and Pagani was often to be seen there. An officer had been detailed to keep an eye on the bar, and shortly after five o'clock the plan bore fruit. Castellano's telephone rang.

"Hello?"

"It's Soldani, Colonel, Pagani showed up. He met a friend, talked for a while, and left."

"Go on."

"I decided to leave Pagani and tail the friend. He drives an old Volkswagen Beetle."

"So do thousands of other people. Did you take down the number?"

"Of course, but I lost the car after he crossed the river."

"Cretin," Castellano said charitably. "Which way was he heading?"

"North, towards Trastevere."

"That could mean anything. Did you recognize him?"

"Sorry, Colonel. He was young, well dressed. Could be anybody."

"We'll see," Castellano said grimly. "Do you have any plans for this evening, Soldani?"

"Well, as a matter of fact . . ."

"Cancel them. You're going to go through the photographs."

"But Colonel, that could take all night . . ."

"It probably will," Castellano agreed. "And if that doesn't work, which it probably won't, you'll spend tomorrow looking for the owner of that Volkswagen. See you later, Soldani."

Castellano put the phone down and swore. On rare occasions, the Colonel derived satisfaction from his work, but this was not one of them. After thirty years in the Carabinieri, he realized that his chief priorities were comfort and a quiet life. This was seldom consistent with tackling frenzied revolutionaries.

The Colonel's secret ambition was to quit his job and open a pleasant little restaurant in a quiet corner of the city. His wife's cooking met the required standards, both in quality and quantity. Some years before, in an unaccustomed fit of optimism, he had suggested this to his spouse. Her reply was loud, vigorous and negative. Castellano never mentioned the idea again, but in moments of frustration, he would soothe himself with this culinary fantasy.

He took one last look at the Pagani file, and put it in his out tray. He wondered idly if the brave new world Pagani was seeking had any room for pleasant little restaurants in quiet corners of the city. Probably not, he decided. Terrorists had no idea about what really mattered; that was why they were terrorists. The Colonel leaned back in his chair and floated off into a pleasant daydream about the Ristorante Castellano.

27

ON the morning of Saturday, November 2, Wyman took an Alitalia flight from Fiumicino to London's Heathrow Airport. From there he went by taxi to central London. His hotel was a discreetly opulent establishment near Russell Square, offering Victorian decor, mediaeval staff and neolithic food. Wyman resolved not to dwell upon these horrors; he deposited his luggage and hurried out for a late lunch at a nearby restaurant.

Afterwards, he visited a tea shop in Covent Garden, where he replenished his supplies of Earl Grey and Darjeeling. The rest of his afternoon was spent in bookshops on the Charing Cross Road, where he bought a few second-hand introductions to various fields of scientific study.

The proprietors of these shops decided that Wyman was some sort of mature student in either medicine or biology, and they plagued him with a succession of "unrepeatable bargains". Wyman was offered a moth-eaten edition of Gray's *Anatomy* ("the pancreas is missing and the lungs are torn out, but otherwise it's perfect, sir"), a nauseating guide to tropical diseases ("you'll be amazed by the picture quality"), and a selection of works on pathology ("I'm sure the stains are only coffee, sir"). He politely refused all these magnificent offers, and returned to the hotel with his purchases.

He relaxed for an hour or so, and took a long, hot bath. Having emerged from the tub, he dressed and left the hotel again. A taxi took him to the Oxford and Cambridge Club on Pall Mall, where he was shown to a quiet room upstairs.

Waiting for him was a frail, bony individual in a tweed jacket and a pair of corduroy trousers made for someone several sizes larger. This was Professor Herbert Yeats, emeritus Professor of Biology at Wyman's university.

Wyman and Yeats had been friends from the time they were undergraduates at the same college. After graduating, they had gone their separate ways: Wyman remained at the college to do research into

Mathematical Logic, and Yeats had taken his PhD at an American university.

Later, when Wyman had left full-time academic work to join MI6, Yeats returned to their university to pursue a distinguished career, resulting in a professorship and a Nobel Prize nomination.

The two men kept in touch over the years, thanks to the two things they shared: a number of pleasant memories and an affection for Scotch whisky. Unfortunately, the latter had taken its toll of Yeats. His complexion was sallow and blotchy, and his speech had lost much of its lecture-room clarity. Wyman noted the slight tremor in Yeats' hand as he shook it.

"How are you, Bertie?" he said, as Yeats stood up to greet him.

"All right, I suppose," Yeats smiled. "How are you finding Rome?"

"It's a splendid post," Wyman said. "I have some excellent students, and the faculty lets me do as I please. What more could one want?"

"I don't know," Yeats observed, "but I suspect I'm about to find out. Your letter was a great surprise."

"I hope I haven't inconvenienced you too much," Wyman apologized. "It's all a little bizarre."

"I expect no less," Yeats smiled. "I didn't think you would content yourself with mere teaching work; not after all those years safeguarding our sceptred isle. I suppose you're now an employee of the Italian secret service—all Lugers and lasagne, eh?"

"Not exactly," Wyman laughed. "But I am vaguely involved in a police investigation. It's about this kidnapped American. You've read about that, I suppose?"

"I certainly have," Yeats said. "An appalling business. It's about two months now, isn't it? Do you think he's still alive?"

"I hope so," Wyman said. "The trouble is, no one seems to know why they kidnapped him. He wasn't rich, and he has no political significance whatsoever."

"Indeed," Yeats agreed. "So why are you involved in all this?"

"God knows, really," Wyman sighed. "These things just seem to happen to me. It's thought that one of my students might be connected with the kidnappers. For a number of reasons, the police are reluctant to deal with that student themselves, so I am giving them some assistance.

"Quite honestly, I don't think I can do very much for them. But now I've been dragged into this, I've decided to do a little investigation of my own. As you said yourself, Scheib was spirited away almost six weeks ago, and nobody has the slightest notion of where he is. At first I was reluctant to get involved—no, don't laugh, Bertie, I really was—but not any longer. So I've come to pick your brains for clues about Scheib."

"What sort of clues?"

"It seems to me," Wyman said, "that until we understand why they chose Scheib rather than anyone else, we won't know how to get him back. You see, I'm convinced Scheib has been abducted for a specific purpose. If they had wanted any old American, they could easily have found someone more famous, with better connections.

"These people thrive on publicity, and for the last four weeks they haven't received any. There's been no public pressure from the American government to get him back, so as a publicity stunt this business has been a dismal failure.

"In fact, if Scheib was kidnapped for any extrinsic reasons, they would have killed him by now. That's why I'm sure they got him for purely intrinsic reasons."

"And what might those be?" Yeats asked.

"That's why I wanted to see you tonight," Wyman said. "I believe you know about Scheib's career."

"I know Scheib personally," Yeats said. "We took our doctorates at the same university. I last saw him at a symposium in Switzerland twelve years ago. We both got stinking drunk and had a row about something. That reminds me: I've got some Scotch here. Fancy some?"

"Why not," Wyman said.

Yeats opened a canvas grip and produced a bottle of twelve-year-old Talisker.

"Never travel without it," he explained. "These clubs charge you the earth for blended Scotch that hardly deserves the name. Hang on a minute."

He left the room and reappeared a minute later with two glasses and a jug of water. He sat down again, poured two improbably large measures, and looked up at Wyman.

"I take it with water nowadays," he said. "How about you?"

"Neat, thanks," Wyman said. "This intrigues me, Bertie. I remember you once swore you'd never adulterate malt whisky with anything. What happened?"

"Two things," Yeats said. "Firstly, my doctor explained that if I carried on pouring neat alcohol into my system, my liver would end up looking like an old biscuit. As a professional biologist, I was obliged to agree.

"Secondly, I made an interesting discovery. A little water helps the stuff get into your bloodstream quicker. I find it gives life a pleasant blur. Cheers."

"Cheers," Wyman smiled.

"So," Yeats said, "what do you want to know about Scheib?"

"Let's begin with Scheib as an individual," Wyman said. "What do you know about him?"

Yeats leaned back in his chair and gazed ruminatively at his glass.

"He's so ordinary, he's downright

boring. Work's the number one thing in his life, and everything else plays second fiddle. That applies to his wife, his kids, and his bank account. As you know, he's not especially rich, and his vices are practically nonexistent. He likes his drink, I suppose, and he's got a passion for cigars.

"He's got very few outside interests—can't stand reading novels, as I recall—votes Republican, behaves like a Democrat, but really couldn't care less. If it doesn't come in a test tube, Scheib isn't interested in it."

Wyman nodded and lit a cigarette.

"It has to be Scheib the scientist," he said.

"I think you're right," Yeats agreed. "What do you want to know?"

"What's he done? What does he specialize in?"

"All sorts of things," Yeats said. "First and foremost, he's a bacteriologist. That term covers a lot of disciplines, of course, but he's worked in a number of them over the years."

"He worked at Fort Detrick, didn't he?"

"I thought you might raise that," Yeats

smiled. "As I recall, that's what the newspapers were trying to find out."

"They didn't get very far, though."

"I'm not surprised. There was nothing particularly sinister about what he did. Nearly all the papers he wrote there are publicly available nowadays. They're not newsworthy, which is why the Press gave up that line of inquiry."

"What did he work on?"

"Antitoxins for various poisons. He didn't break much new ground; the work largely consisted of devising large-scale production methods for a number of antisera. You see, it's one thing to produce a small sample of an antitoxin for research in a laboratory, but quite another to manufacture large amounts in a factory. Essentially, Scheib's work consisted of simplifying certain procedures for industrial purposes. Very dull, really."

"What has he done since then?"

"For a while he worked on bacteriophages. These are a kind of virus, usually found in soil or water, which can attack and neutralize colonies of bacteria. Every now and again, somebody tries to use these things for medical purposes, but they're really a waste of time, because the new drugs are much more effective.

"I don't think Scheib got very far, but he did publish a couple of papers on the subject. Is any of this useful to you?"

"Frankly, I don't know," Wyman admitted. "Look at it this way: is there anything Scheib is well known for—a standard text-book, or anything like that?"

Yeats downed the remainder of his Talisker and replenished his glass.

"There are a few papers," he said. "But they cover pretty obscure areas. Scheib is a clever chap, but he's not exactly a household name."

"Suppose I was a third-year undergraduate," Wyman said. "How would I know about Scheib?"

"There are a few old papers—very old, in fact—that might crop up on your reading list. He wrote a few things on how to prepare samples for experiments; the kind of basic reference work that you knock out in your spare time. They're really a throwback to his time at Detrick: quick, neat methods for producing toxins, for example."

"Toxins?" Wyman said. "I thought you said he worked on antitoxins."

"One implies the other," Yeats explained. "To experiment with an antitoxin, you need the original toxin to try it out on. Sometimes, the antitoxin is itself manufactured from the toxin. To produce one, you must know how to create a sample of the other."

"I see," Wyman said. "Could I get hold of these papers?"

"Of course. I've got a list of Scheib's published works in my bag. I'll underline the best-known items, and you can take it with you."

"Splendid," Wyman said. "You know, Bertie, this really is most confusing. I keep wishing they'd decided to kidnap a philosopher instead. Things would have been so much easier for me."

"Never mind," Yeats laughed. "Perhaps you'll have better luck next time."

28

"FOR the last four lectures, I have done most of the talking," Wyman said. "I hope it hasn't been too distressing for you."

He grinned impishly at his students, like a naughty schoolboy about to inflict a practical joke.

"We started off by talking about personal identity, and I told you about the Reductionist approaches.

"I then talked about morality. We agreed that we all want a world in which things go as well as possible for everyone. But there was a problem with personal aims. A Non-Reductionist thinks persons are special, so that a person's aims for himself should get high priority. This might clash with our public aim.

"The Reductionist disagrees: he thinks personal identity isn't what counts, and so personal aims should get less priority. He thinks that what really counts is the quality of events in the world. Because he's less interested in separate persons, he's not so worried about whose events these are. All that really matters, says the Reductionist, is that as many events as possible should be as good as possible.

"So, the Reductionist thinks there's less justification for arguments about compensation, but what justification there is should extend across the whole community.

"As I said last time, this could result in some interesting theories. Giulio thought such theories would be very strange."

Wyman glanced at Giulio in amusement.

"I wouldn't want to disappoint you, Giulio," he said. "I could produce a few ideas of my own, but I don't think they'd be nearly as outlandish as you suppose. And as I said, I've done most of the talking, and you must be frightfully bored by it all.

"So today I'll step down from my place and allow someone else to present you with their ideas. Monica has very kindly agreed to offer us her own theory, which relies on the Reductionist view about persons. I'd like you to give her a fair hearing, and then we'll talk about what she's said."

He beckoned Monica over to the front of the lecture room, and they changed places. It took a minute or two for Monica to arrange her notes, and then she began.

"Capitalism," she said, "is a system which prevents the majority of people from controlling a country's means of industrial production—"

She was interrupted by loud groans from Paolo and Enzo.

"I might have known," Giulio said.

Monica turned crimson with anger and embarrassment.

"Silence!" Wyman barked. His vehemence took the students aback. "Monica has taken a lot of trouble over her talk, and you'll do her the courtesy of listening in silence. Please continue, Monica."

There was an uneasy pause as Monica recovered her composure.

"As I said, Capitalism prevents most of a country's population from controlling the means of industrial production."

There was no interruption this time, so Monica took a deep breath and continued.

"Capitalism means that most people don't enjoy the full benefits of their own work. It's a system that requires people to work, but it can't provide work for everyone. It can't because it doesn't want to: high unemployment means a bigger scramble for jobs. It means people will put up with less pay and worse working conditions. If a worker knows he can be replaced easily, he'll feel less confident about pressing for higher wages.

"So Capitalism depends on misery. It depends on the acute misery of a minority of people, to ensure that the majority put up with their own 'ordinary' misery. Low wages mean low spending, bad housing, bad education, bad health, and crime."

She looked around her. The other students said nothing, and Wyman was listening intently to her words. Her confidence rose, and she went on: "So much for Capitalism. Now let's think about Democracy. This is supposed to be a free system. Most people think so, anyway. But we should ask ourselves this: if Democracy were truly a free system, where the majority got what they wanted, would they really put up with high unemployment, low wages, poor social conditions? Of course not. So what's wrong with this 'free' system?

"The answer is simple: it tolerates Capitalism. It doesn't matter how many political parties you have. It doesn't matter how free your elections are. If your system allows Capitalism to exist, it isn't really free. That's the paradox about Democracy: it's so free, it's a tyranny."

She noticed that Wyman was taking notes. The other students were exchanging knowing grins, but Monica still held their attention.

"The reasons for getting rid of Capitalism are obvious," she said. "We can see that this can only be achieved by getting rid of Democracy as well. I therefore propose a revolutionary programme to be rid of Democracy."

The grins vanished from the students' faces. They gazed at Monica as if she had landed from Mars.

"My programme has two main aims," she said. "Firstly, I must show the world that the so-called freedom of Democracy is an illusion. Secondly, I must wage war on the oppressors—the capitalists and the people who work on their behalf: judges, politicians, policemen, and so forth.

"I therefore suggest a campaign of bombings, shootings and kidnappings against these people. They will reply with a campaign of arrests, mass trials, and so on. Many of my colleagues will be arrested, but so will a lot of innocent people as well. This will help to show Democracy in its true colours: people will see what democratic 'freedom' really consists of.

"More importantly, the killing of politicians, policemen and others like them will weaken the machinery of the present system. When people in general realize how dishonest this system is, and how it has been undermined, they will rebel. This revolution will achieve the kind of society I am seeking."

"Good grief," Lucia breathed.

"Completely cracked," Paolo said, tapping his finger against his temple.

"Do be quiet," Wyman murmured.

"Of course," Monica said, "my programme seems open to a number of objections, and I'd now like to answer those.

"Firstly, you might say that I am acting

without consent of the majority of the population, and against their wishes. My answer is simple: I agree. Democracy is the most potent form of tyranny, precisely because it instils an illusion of freedom. Most people have been duped. The only way to make them realize they've been deceived is to do certain things they disapprove of, such as bombings and kidnappings.

"So I'm not impressed by this first objection: in essence, it accuses me of being undemocratic. Since I'm waging war on democracy, why should this bother me?

"The next objection is a graver one. You might say that I am causing suffering for some of the people whose interests I claim to represent. This charge could be put in two ways. You could say that a small minority is being made to suffer for the long-term benefit of a majority. You could say that an entire generation of people is being made to suffer for the benefit of many future generations. You could also accuse me of both these things."

Monica paused to rearrange her notes. She was more comfortable now, and her delivery was more fluent and relaxed.

"My reply to these charges rests on a Reductionist view of Personal Identity. Let me remind you of certain points I intend to use.

"I think that persons consist of no more than the mental and physical events that make them up. I think that we should worry less about persons, and more about these events. I think we should worry more about improving these events, and less about who they belong to.

"We should aim for the least possible suffering, however it is distributed. My aims as a revolutionary depend on all these ideas."

She noticed that Wyman was scribbling notes furiously on a notepad, and she paused again to let him catch up.

"If I were to sum up my aims as a revolutionary," Monica said, "it would be to achieve the least possible suffering for this generation and subsequent ones. If I achieve my revolution, the total suffering in my society will be reduced.

"To do this, I will need to *inflict* suffering, and sometimes death, on a relatively tiny fraction of the population. This will be justified by the huge quantities of suffering I will prevent for future people. Even if I bring suffering to an entire generation, the vast amount of suffering I will prevent for future generations will justify it."

Some of the other students began taking notes. Monica had moved away from general political beliefs, and was now using ideas they could tackle formally. It was here that they might trap her.

"That's the theory," Monica said. "And I suppose you'd now all like to tear it apart."

"That," Wyman smiled, "is Monica's way of asking if there are any questions. Are there any?"

Enzo raised his hand.

"Yes," he said. "Haven't you twisted things round? The Reductionist wants to reduce suffering; at least, he wants to reduce the *worst kinds* of suffering. You might reduce the overall amount of suffering—though I doubt it—but you're going to replace it with smaller amounts of a far worse kind of suffering. But the Reductionist doesn't want to *promote* any sort of suffering, and that's what you're doing. Haven't you perverted his aims?"

"I don't agree," Monica said. "I admit that I'm trying to alleviate one form of suffering by using another. I don't agree that my form is in any way worse. I can point to thousands of examples of social injustice—exploitation, unemployment, housing problems. Not only do these create acute suffering, but they also generate crimes such as mugging, assault, rape and murder, and these bring about the very worst forms of suffering.

"I agree that if there were a way of removing these injustices which required no infliction of suffering, it would be better than my way. But there's no such option. Mine is the *only* way to be rid of these injustices, and my way, regrettably, involves some suffering. But it doesn't worsen or increase the overall level of suffering, and it doesn't create new forms of suffering. Quite the opposite."

"How are you so sure that yours is the only way?" Lucia asked.

"By looking around me," Monica said. "Straightforward observation."

"Funny how the rest of us don't see things like that," Paolo observed.

"I said that Democracy deceives people.

It's not surprising you think the way you do."

"We've all been conned, have we?" Giulio asked.

"That's right," Monica said brightly.

"Hold on," Wyman broke in, "I can see a small problem here. Monica's theory depends on two things: firstly, the Reductionist theory about persons, and how we should concentrate on improving the quality of events by relieving suffering.

"Secondly, Monica's theory rests on her *empirical* view of the world: that is, the conclusions she's reached by day-to-day observation.

"So far, your objection to Monica's ideas has been empirical. She says Democracy has deceived people, you disagree. She says we already allow the worst kinds of suffering, you disagree.

"But none of you has asked about the theoretical part of her argument. Enzo hinted at it when he suggested that Monica has 'perverted' the Reductionist's aim. Monica has certainly used Reductionism in a special way. Do you think she's done it correctly? Do you agree with how she's put the theory to work?"

No one answered Wyman's question. The students frowned in concentration, but there were no instant replies.

"Enzo," Wyman said. "What do you believe?"

"I'm not sure," Enzo said. "I'm convinced she's wrong, but I'd need to think about it."

"Very well," Wyman said. "Do so. We'll stop here for now. Perhaps you'd like to think about a reply to Monica, Enzo, and we'll hear it next week."

"Sure," Enzo agreed. He looked at Monica curiously. "Do you really believe all that?" he asked her.

"I certainly do," Monica said calmly. "If you thought about it hard enough, you might too."

She smiled in satisfaction, and glanced at the professor. He did not return her smile. Wyman was reading his notes carefully. He wore a peculiar expression she had not seen before, which left her feeling puzzled and somewhat uneasy.

29

"THAT'S her," said Jones A.

"Right," breathed Jones P.

They were standing in the shadow of a doorway in the Vicolo delle Vacche, about twenty yards away from the junction with the Via della Vetrina. The front door of Number 6 was clearly visible as Monica unlocked it and went in.

After a suitable interval, Jones A. and Jones P. strolled into the Via della Vetrina, past Monica's front door. They saw her name on the entryphone, and noted the number of her flat.

"Now?" Jones P. whispered.

"No," said Jones A.

They walked on for a little while, turned into another street, and paused.

"Why not now?" Jones P. said. "She's alone."

"Sure, she's alone," Jones A. agreed. "But I've got something else in mind. We'll come back tomorrow."

"Yeah?" Jones P. seemed disappointed.

"Definitely. I want to nail that bitch properly."

"You know," Jones P. said, "maybe we oughta take it easy with the kid . . ."

Jones A. blinked up at him in surprise. "Is that a joke?"

"No," said Jones P. slowly. "I just thought—"

"You don't want to think," Jones A. said, shaking his head. "It'll only give you a headache. Why do you want to play it soft with her?"

An embarrassed grin spread across Jones P.'s face. "Well, she's kinda pretty . . ."

"Jesus H. Christ," exclaimed Jones A. "Can't you keep your dirty mind off it for one minute? Sometimes I think you're just an animal."

"Aw, come on," Jones P. protested. "I didn't mean anything. But she sure is pretty."

"Listen to me," Jones A. said sternly. "This isn't just any old broad we've got here, this is poison. Thanks to that little slut, Edgar P. Rawls got turned into corned beef three weeks ago.

"When I get my hands on that kid, I am going to cream her, and when I've finished, maybe she isn't going to be so pretty after all. You better get used to that idea. If you want a piece of tail, get yourself a nice whore instead. This kid is the enemy, understand?"

Jones P. lowered his head and nodded humbly.

"Right," he said.

30

WYMAN sat in his most comfortable armchair at home. On his lap was a selection of essays written by first-year undergraduates. Their struggles to master elementary logic were sometimes amusing, but more usually exasperating.

He had set them an essay title "What is the difference between false statements and misleading statements?". In theory, this question required a straightforward answer, but Wyman was an old hand, and expected anything but straightforwardness from his beginners.

The example he had given them was simple. Suppose a student was due to sit an exam, and at the last minute was told the paper was cancelled. He then went home, and his parents asked him how he had fared. "Very well indeed," the student replied, "I was able to answer all the questions." Would the student's reply be true or false?

Although Wyman went to pains to explain the difference between a false statement and one which was true but misleading, the essays in front of him displayed varying degrees of comprehension. "This student is a liar," one wrote, "and his parents should punish him severely." Wyman sighed in disgust and wrote a marginal comment of "This is supposed to be a logical problem, not a moral one."

Another essay declared the student to be "a model of honesty and correctness". Wyman's marginal note was caustic: "Suppose I said that yours was by far the best of these essays. If I omitted to tell you that they are all abysmal, would you think me a model of honesty?"

He put the essays down, reflecting that irony was often the last refuge of the desperate tutor. He lit a cigarette and picked up another file. This contained his own notes on Franco Ponti. For the fourth time that morning, Wyman decided to take a rest from his teaching work and look at what he called "the other matter".

Wyman was now convinced that Ponti had kidnapped Scheib because of the latter's career. The problem was that Wyman had no idea of what precise feature of Scheib's work interested the terrorist leader. Presumably, at some stage Ponti had come across an essay by Scheib which would be of some use to him. Wyman reasoned that this must have been when Ponti was a student at the University of Padua, twenty years before.

He returned to his own notes on the subject. Ponti first went to Padua in 1962, when he was twenty-one. He graduated four years later, having specialized in microbiology. The following year he embarked on his PhD course, abandoning it in 1968 to join Potop.

Wyman had phoned the University of Padua, and he asked if there were still copies of the prospectuses for science degrees in the years 1962 to 1966, as well as detailed information on the syllabuses. A helpful librarian found what Wyman wanted, and sent him some photocopies. He found most of the subject-matter unintelligible, but studied the reading-lists to see if anything by Scheib had cropped up.

To Wyman's intense delight, there were some entries. Students had been advised to read a number of translations of essays by Scheib, mostly concerned with bacteriophages.

Having got that far, Wyman resolved to press on and obtain translations. He found most of them in the Biochemistry faculty of his own university.

It was only when he had read through some of them that Wyman began to suspect he was chasing a red herring. All the articles were about antisera, antitoxins, and cures for infectious diseases. Why should any of that interest Franco Ponti? The terrorist surely wanted to inflict injury, rather than cure or prevent it. How could those articles help?

Nevertheless, Wyman ploughed on in the hope of further clues. At the end of each paper was a cluster of footnotes, referring the reader to related publications. In this respect, Scheib was something of an egomaniac: most of the references were to other works of his own.

Of course, Wyman reasoned, if Ponti had read one of those articles, he might well have read the other papers it referred to, even if those other publications were outside his syllabus. That increased

Wyman's workload considerably: another eight papers were added to his reading-list. Wyman wrote down their titles, resolving to read them at a later date.

He stubbed out his cigarette and paused for reflection. On a blank sheet of paper he wrote the words:

1. Scheib is a bacteriologist, specializing in antitoxins and antisera.
2. Ponti was a microbiologist, with a special interest in bacteriology.
3. Ponti knew about Scheib before he kidnapped him.
4. Why does Ponti need Scheib?

It occurred to Wyman that question 4 could be rephrased, so he added:

5. What could Scheib do for Ponti?

This put a new complexion on the problem. If Ponti was conversant with his subject, Scheib would only be needed for something Ponti could not do himself. What could that be? Presumably, it must be an advanced specialist piece of work. Only a specialist could know what that work might consist of; a layman could never guess. Wyman cursed his own ignorance, realizing that this whole line of inquiry would probably be fruitless.

Nothing peeved Wyman more than being confronted with the limits of his own knowledge. He was also irritated by his awareness that Colonel Castellano would have said "I told you so." The Colonel was not persuaded by Wyman's conjectures. He reminded Wyman that when Scheib's kidnappers had made their demands, they made no reference to his career. The demand was straightforward: it made no allusions to biochemistry in general, or bacteriology in particular.

Wyman read that demand again:

"Professor Theodore Scheib has been taken hostage by a column of the Red Brigades. If 32 imprisoned members of the Red Brigades are set free, we will release Scheib. Their names are . . ."

Wyman wondered what his first-year undergraduates would make of that statement. "These terrorists are liars," one would say, "and their parents should punish them severely." Another would insist that the terrorists "are a model of honesty and correctness".

So we return to logic, Wyman thought, relieved to be back on home ground. The statement was carefully worded: it wasn't false, but it wasn't honest either. It didn't tell the whole truth: if the convicts were released, they would release Scheib. The statement *suggested* that Scheib had been kidnapped to secure their release, but it did not *state* that. Like the hypothetical student who misled his parents about his exams, the Red Brigades' statement could present the truth with a dishonest intention.

"After all," Wyman muttered, "if I were a bold, bad terrorist, would honesty be at the top of my list of priorities?"

He lit another cigarette and reread the demand.

"Of course not," he chuckled.

31

THE sun was setting over Rome as Monica returned to her flat on the Via della Vetrina. She carried a number of textbooks that Wyman had recommended, and she planned to devote her evening to quiet study. This would not be easy; her thoughts continually strayed elsewhere.

Monica's commitment to her beliefs was absolute, but until now there had been no opportunity for her to put them into practice. Nothing had been asked of her except for help if and when it were required. Once upon a time, new members of the Brigades had immediately "dropped out" of their occupations to become full-time activists. Monica, however, was told to stay put and continue with her studies. Apparently this was what Ponti wanted, and though it frustrated her, his wish made some sense. Until Monica was given a specific task, there was no point in drawing attention to herself.

Monica had never met Ponti, or any other senior *Brigadisti*. It was explained to her that only when the time came for Monica to become an active member of the column would she meet Ponti and Vito Maresca, his deputy. For the time being she was, in effect, a reservist, and such a meeting would serve no purpose. Ponti's golden rule was that you should never know more than you needed, and that surplus knowledge was a liability. That rule was carefully observed. Monica was only in touch with the two junior members of the column, Mario and Michele. Orders from Ponti would be relayed through them, and so far the instructions had merely been to sit tight.

Pedro Torres was therefore the first veteran fighter that Monica had met, and he was something of a surprise. Whereas Mario and Michele made much of their ferocity and recklessness, Torres was calm and modest. It occurred to Monica that the braggadocio displayed by a fighter was inversely proportional to his experience. She wondered if Ponti was also like this.

The meeting with Torres left her feeling both exhilarated and humbled. She had read much about Chile and its sufferings. Torres made light of his hardships, but she could imagine what he had endured. Without realizing it, he threw Monica's inexperience and comfort into stark relief, making her feel like a spoilt, angry virgin. It was not a pleasant feeling.

But Monica was honest enough not to blame Torres for her discomfort. Indeed, she found him rather attractive, though she did not understand why. Torres was over twenty years her senior; his crew-cut hair and fine eyebrows were flecked with grey, and his face was lined by the sort of pain Monica had never understood. He was not a complex man, and his character was shaped more by practice than theory. None of this should have appealed to Monica, but her thoughts drifted back to him repeatedly.

She opened the door of Number 6 and went upstairs. To her surprise, the door of her flat swung open as she rested her hand against it. Monica frowned and went inside. The flat was unlit, and she could hear nothing. As she turned on the light, the door shut behind her. A large hand was clamped across her mouth, and another one pinned her arm back in a half-nelson.

Somebody else stepped in front of her and grinned.

"Hello, honey," said Jones A. "You got visitors. Now, when my friend takes his hand off your mouth, you're going to stay quiet. Okay?"

He nodded at the unseen man behind Monica, and the hand left Monica's mouth.

"*Cosa succede*?" she breathed, "*Non capisco* . . ."

"Don't give me that wop shit," Jones A. said impatiently. "We know you speak English."

Monica felt the grip on her arm tighten.

"All right," she said. "Who are you? What do you want?"

"That's better," Jones A. grinned. "We're looking for a guy called Scheib, and the word is you might be able to help. How does that sound?"

"I don't understand," Monica said.

"I think you do, honey. Scheib—the professor your buddies kidnapped. Remember him?"

Monica frowned.

"I have heard about this, of course. Why do you think—?"

"Oh, for Christ's sake," Jones A. said irritably. "We know who you are, honey. Remember Edgar Rawls, the poor bastard you blew up in the park? He was onto you, and we're here to finish off his job. We want to find Scheib, and that means finding Ponti. Ponti's your boss, isn't he? Start talking."

"You are mistaken," Monica said, doing her best to remain calm. "You have the wrong person. I'm a student—"

She was interrupted by the impact of Jones A.'s fist on her abdomen. The grip on her arm relaxed, and she crumpled on to the floor. Tears of pain welled in her eyes, blurring her first glimpse of Jones A.'s companion. He was a large man, much taller than Jones A., with the build of a heavyweight boxer.

"Get up, honey," Jones A. said.

Monica tried to get to her feet, but her legs would not support her. The hot ache throbbed in her stomach, and a vague nausea crept over her.

"You'll get more of that if you keep on playing dumb, honey," Jones A.

explained. "You tell us about Ponti and we'll leave you alone."

"Who are you?" Monica gasped.

"Like I said, we're from the same factory that produced Edgar Rawls, only we're meaner than him. A lot meaner."

Jones A. seemed to enjoy telling people what a terrible fellow he was.

"In fact," he continued, "you'd be amazed by just how mean we are. If you don't tell us what we want to hear, I'll give you a demonstration."

He produced a leather wallet, from which he drew out an ivory-handled cut-throat razor.

"I bet they tell you all about guns," he mused. "Bombs, grenades—you know it all, don't you honey? But did anyone ever tell you about these things?"

Monica's eyes bulged in dismay.

"You are mad," she hissed.

"You can really carve someone up with a razor," Jones A. continued. "I mean, who wants to look like a map of New York? I bet you don't."

He opened the razor and slashed playfully at Monica's face. She threw herself backwards, crashing into an armchair.

"I meant to miss that time," Jones A. smiled, as Jones P. picked Monica up and locked her arm again. "But next time, who knows? So, honey, where's Ponti?"

"I don't know what you're talking about," Monica panted. "You are insane."

Jones A. walked up and held the razor to Monica's throat.

"No, honey. You killed our man Rawls. Maybe you people think you can do what you like to American citizens, but you are going to have to understand one important point: you don't mess about with the CIA."

"Right," said Jones P.

"CIA?" Monica breathed. "In that case . . ."

A large dollop of Monica's spittle landed on the face of Jones A.

"Fascist," she said, by way of an explanation.

Jones A. stepped back and wiped the saliva from his eye. He nodded calmly, as if a suspicion had been confirmed, and glanced over Monica's head at the face of Jones P.

"You know something?" he said softly. "You're right. She is a pretty girl. We don't need to spoil her looks. Maybe you'd like to get a better look at her. Peel off the outer wrapper, know what I mean? And if you like the merchandise . . ."

Monica craned her neck to see the face of Jones P. His stupid grin explained everything.

"Oh, God," she said weakly.

There was a tap on the door, and all three looked at it in surprise. Jones A. pressed the razor back against Monica's throat and put his finger onto her lips.

There was another tap, and a voice called from outside.

"*Signorina*, may I come in?"

Monica sagged in disappointment. The voice belonged to old Gennaro, the landlord.

"Who's that?" Jones A. whispered.

"I know you're in there, *Signorina*," Gennaro called out, "but we're well into November now. I know you can hear me . . ."

Jones A. frowned.

"Is he going to piss off?" he muttered.

"No," Monica said. "Money is the only thing he cares about. You capitalists ought to approve of that."

"Cut the crap," Jones A. hissed. "Right. You let him in, you pay him the rent, you kick him out. I understand Italian, honey, so if anything else happens —*anything*—we'll kill you both. Dig?"

Monica nodded, and was released by Jones P. The two CIA men sat down on a sofa as Monica opened the door.

"Ah," Gennaro said. "I knew you were in there. I'm very sorry, *Signorina*, but I must insist you pay the rent."

He stepped into the room and nodded at the Americans, as Monica closed the door behind him.

"Good evening, gentlemen," he muttered. "I am sorry to disturb you, but this is most important."

Gennaro drew out a P38 automatic and fired several shots into Jones A. and Jones P. Large red wounds bloomed like flowers on their chests as they jerked back and died on Monica's sofa. Monica stood transfixed with shock as her landlord calmly stepped over to the bodies and examined their pulses.

Gennaro then turned to Monica and grinned. His next move was almost as surprising as his first: he drew a set of false teeth from his pocket and inserted them into his mouth. With his jawline restored, Gennaro at once looked much younger.

"I heard them talking when I arrived," he explained in a pleasant, cultured voice, quite unlike his usual slurred mumble. "I'm glad I wasn't too late. Are you all right?"

Monica replied by running out of the room to the toilet, where she was violently sick. A few minutes later she returned, looking somewhat the worse for wear.

"Who are you?" she said hoarsely.

"Your landlord," Gennaro smiled. "But my name isn't Gennaro. It's Francesco Ponti."

"You're Ponti? But . . ." Monica trailed off in stupefaction.

"I'd better explain," Ponti said briskly. "Mario advised you to live here. He did so on my instruction. This is one of our safe houses, though perhaps it isn't quite as safe as I supposed.

"Anyway, for the last five years, I have acted the part of Gennaro, the deaf old landlord of this address. The police haven't seen me for so long, they don't know what to look for—a man of about fifty, I suppose. Without my dentures I look at least ten years older, and they always forget that you turn grey eventually.

"Excellent cover, isn't it? If anyone ever tells you there's nothing to be gained from growing old, you'll know they're talking rubbish."

"Is there a real Gennaro?" Monica asked.

"No," Ponti said. "I created him. I'm sorry I couldn't tell you about this, but you know my rules. You would have learned eventually, of course."

"So why do you keep coming over here? If you're not really interested in the rent money . . ."

"On the contrary," Ponti laughed. "I am very interested in the rent. The people on the other floors are also my tenants, you know."

"They don't know about you?"

"Of course not. But you're right, there is another reason. The broom cupboards on the landings contain more than just cleaning equipment."

Monica shook her head in bewilderment.

"This is incredible," she said. "I never dreamed for one moment . . ."

"I'm glad you didn't. If you could have found out, then so could the police. Unfortunately, things have changed now."

Monica glanced at the bodies of the CIA men. Their faces still displayed the shock of seeing Ponti's gun.

"What are we going to do with these people?"

"We'll move them out tonight," Ponti said, "along with everything else that's hidden here."

"Will the police arrive?"

"I doubt it. These idiots were acting on their own initiative. They would never have got permission to come here like that. I'd be surprised if the police knew anything about it. Still, we can't be too careful, can we?"

"What about me?" Monica said. "Should I move out?"

"I don't see why," Ponti replied. "Provided there's no evidence here—and there won't be—I see no reason why you should move. If anyone else were keeping an eye on you, it would only attract their suspicion, wouldn't it?"

"I'm not sure I could stand being here any more," Monica said, "after what's happened . . . You know, I've never seen anyone killed before."

Ponti shrugged.

"Maybe not," he said brightly. "But you'll never be able to say that again, will you?"

32

ABOUT twenty minutes after he killed the CIA men, Ponti phoned Vito Maresca. They exchanged the usual passwords, and Ponti gave his orders:

"A small problem has arisen, and I could use your advice. When you have given our guest his evening meal, bring the van round to Angiolina's house."

"Angiolina?"

"That's right," Ponti said curtly.

"Okay," Vito said, and he hung up.

It was clear from Ponti's tone that the problem was not really small. Vito was surprised by the choice of meeting-place: "Angiolina" was their code-name for Monica Venuti. He assumed that Ponti had taken yet another decision without consulting anyone else. Such decisions annoyed Vito, as did Ponti's general unwillingness to divulge his plans, but he let it pass.

The "guest" Ponti mentioned was of

course Professor Scheib. Vito quickly prepared a steak and a salad for the captive, and gave him a flask of Chianti.

"Thank you," Scheib said as he received his meal. "Is the service included, or do you expect a tip?"

Vito scowled, but didn't reply. He locked the door of the professor's room and left the building. He walked down a couple of streets to where his van was parked, and drove away to the Via della Vetrina.

Once inside Monica's flat, he was confronted by a scene worthy of a Luis Buñuel film. Having shown Vito in, Monica sat in an armchair, still dazed by her earlier trauma. Ponti was leaning against the table, reading a magazine and calmly puffing on a cigarette. Around the room were several wooden crates. One contained a set of apple-green RGD-5 grenades, another contained ammunition-clips for Skorpion sub-machine guns. The rest contained similar items. In the middle of all this, stretched out on a sheet, were the bodies of the two CIA men, gazing stupidly at the ceiling.

"What the hell happened here?" Vito asked in astonishment.

Ponti looked up from his magazine and smiled.

"It would appear that the CIA are still interested in us," he said. "In fact, these gentlemen were explaining their interest to Monica when I arrived. This is Monica, by the way."

Vito nodded at the girl.

"Hello," Monica said.

"How did they find out about you?" Vito said.

"I don't know," she said helplessly, "I really don't. I've done nothing, but they seemed to think I've been involved all along. They thought I killed the other American."

Vito frowned.

"Why her?" he said to Ponti. "It doesn't make sense."

"Oh, I don't know," Ponti said. "Monica's quite outspoken about her views, aren't you, Monica?"

"I never told anyone—" Monica began.

"That's not what I meant," Ponti said soothingly. "All I'm saying is that people know where your allegiances lie. Why not?

Plenty of people support us without actually doing anything about it.

"Of course, there's more to it than that. We had a mutual friend in Claudio Prando. If he were still alive, I think these men would have been looking for him, not you."

"It's still bad news," Vito said. "If the CIA think this girl's with us, you can imagine what the Carabinieri are thinking."

"I don't agree," Ponti said. "It was the Americans who decided that Monica was a lead. I think that was largely because of the first agent we killed. These men were sent to replace Rawls. They must have known that Monica was Rawls' suspect, and concluded that he was killed to prevent him talking to her. It would have been a reasonable supposition. After all, we *did* kill Rawls for that reason, among others.

"But suppositions are one thing, and proof is quite another. Even the Carabinieri aren't allowed to behave like gangsters. Nobody has any evidence against Monica, simply because there isn't any. I know you dislike my policy about giving people minimal information, Vito. But you have to admit it's paid off here."

"I suppose so," Vito grunted. "But that doesn't apply any more, does it? These two men were killed in Monica's flat. She now knows what we use this building for, and she knows what you and I look like. Just suppose she was picked up by the police, for whatever reason. What would happen then?"

"I wouldn't say a word," Monica protested. "They couldn't make me talk."

"Oh no?" Vito said. "Have you ever been grilled by a cop? Suspected terrorists aren't exactly given VIP treatment, you know."

"I wouldn't worry about that," Ponti grinned. "I'd be surprised if anyone tried to pull Monica's fingernails out."

"I wouldn't care if they did," Monica said.

"I'm sure you wouldn't," Ponti said chivalrously. "But you have another reason to feel secure: your father."

"Who's that?" Vito asked.

"Why, none other than Vittorio Venuti," Ponti replied, "the pillar of the right-wing establishment. If anyone wanted to pull Monica's fingernails out, I think Signor Venuti might have something to say about it.

"You see, I think that's the main reason why nobody has pounced on Monica. The Carabinieri would need to feel very sure of their own evidence before arresting the daughter of one of our best-known diplomats."

"Maybe you're right," Vito said. "But what are we going to do about all this?"

He waved his arm at the bodies and the ammunition.

"That's why I asked you to bring the van," Ponti said. "*Rigor mortis* usually sets in two or three hours after death. I want to dump these bodies before that happens."

"And the arms?"

"After we've got rid of the bodies, we'll take the ammo to Rucci's house in Trastevere. Monica will stay behind, and there'll be nothing to suggest that anything happened here."

"What about the people upstairs?" Vito said. "Didn't anyone hear the shots?"

Ponti's face assumed a pained expression.

"Really, Vito," he sighed. "You do me less than justice."

He picked up his automatic and showed Vito the silencer.

"Okay," Vito said apologetically. "But what about the CIA? We've now killed three of their people. What happens if they send out more? Monica might not be so lucky next time."

"That could be a problem," Ponti conceded. "But I'm not very worried about it. I imagine the Carabinieri won't be too pleased when they find these bodies. That will be three deaths they have to explain away to the Press.

"I don't intend to hide these bodies. We'll just throw them into the Tiber. When they resurface, they'll get a fair amount of publicity; very embarrassing for the police, very embarrassing for the Americans. I think the CIA might decide to stay away after that."

A few minutes later, Vito went outside. Having made sure there was no one about, he went back upstairs and helped Ponti carry down two wooden crates, whose contents had been taken out to make room for Jones A. and Jones P.

They put the crates in the van and drove away. Half an hour later they came back for the arms and ammunition, which they took over to the safe house in the Trastevere. By the time they set off for home, it was nearly 11 p.m.

"I don't know about you," Vito said as they drove back, "but I'm exhausted."

"That's because you're out of shape," Ponti said. "You should take more exercise."

"And whose fault is that?" Vito replied indignantly. "For the last six weeks I've been doing nothing except cook meals for that idiot Scheib. When people talked about the qualities needed to be a Brigadist, I used to think they meant skill with guns and explosives. Now I know better: all you need is a diploma in *cordon bleu* cooking. I'm beginning to feel like a frustrated housewife."

Ponti laughed.

"Don't worry, Vito. You'll soon have plenty to do. Just be patient."

"Besides," Vito said, "you still haven't explained why we need Scheib. Is it anything to do with the Russians?"

"Why do you ask?"

"They seem very interested in him. As I recall, they even asked if they could speak to him. At the time, I thought they were just being cheeky, but now I'm beginning to wonder."

"It's quite simple," Ponti explained. "They know the CIA are trying to find Scheib. That suggests Scheib is of importance in some intelligence capacity. Naturally, the Russians would like to interrogate him."

"Is that true? Is Scheib really an intelligence man?"

"I've no idea," Ponti admitted. "He did once work as a military scientist, so he might well be connected with the CIA. That doesn't interest me at all, and I certainly won't let the Russians anywhere near him. That wouldn't fit in with our plans."

"It's generous of you to tell me all this," Vito said sarcastically. "While you're at it, perhaps you'd like to tell me what 'our' plans consist of."

"Not just yet," Ponti said. "For the time being, you only have to worry about one thing."

"What's that?"

"Your French bean salad."

"Eh?"

"Scheib's been complaining. Apparently, French beans should be served at room temperature, not chilled. He's very particular about these things, you know."

33

AT the Tiber end of the Corso Vittorio Emanuele, on its south side, is the Ristorante da Loreto. On warm days, its patrons dine outside and watch the groups of pedestrians strolling to and from the Vatican, just over the river. Wednesday, November 6, was not warm, however, and the outside tables were unattended. Inside the restaurant, at his own table, Colonel Castellano slurped leisurely at a bowl of *Pastina in Brodo*.

Italian restaurants cater for many kinds of patron. There are the young couples who dine in near silence, the large families who order everything on the menu, the groups of two or three local citizens holding vigorous seminars over their pasta, and the tourists who fill the establishment with their exotic babble.

Besides these, there is another species of diner, whose presence is the sign of a good restaurant: the Serious Eater. Such people are usually alone; they do not mind the company of others, but they regard it as a distraction from their top priority—the food. Serious Eaters often have a special relationship with the restaurant, and the waiters treat them with a respect and deference rarely conferred on other patrons. A special table is often kept aside for their use.

The Serious Eater is seldom young. He is usually fat, and his expression is one of dedication. Unlike the other diners, he tucks his napkin over his shirt collar, like a bib. This is the badge of his profession.

If the chef is a performing artist, then the Serious Eater is his true audience. The average patron may offer his appreciation of a good meal with a large tip and noisy compliments to the chef. No such ostentation is required of the Serious Eater; a satisfied nod will be quite enough to please the restaurant staff.

Castellano was a perfect specimen of the Serious Eater. He did not eat meals, so much as declare war on them. With an impetus worthy of a Panzer division, he ploughed through each course relentlessly, pausing only to wash the food down with glasses of house wine, or to break pieces of bread with his pink, stubby fingers. The *Pastina in Brodo* was quickly disposed of, as was the *Petto di Tacchino* which followed it.

Only when a cup of espresso was placed before him did the Colonel lean back in his chair. He lit a cigarette, and assumed an expression of profound contentment. At times like this, his recurring fantasy of opening the Ristorante Castellano grew more alluring than ever.

A young man entered the restaurant, looked around, and walked up to the Colonel.

"Good afternoon, sir," he said.

"Hello, Soldani," Castellano said affably. "Take a seat. Anything new?"

"I've found him," Soldani said.

He drew a chair away from another table and sat beside the Colonel.

"Go on," Castellano said.

"Michele Rucci. His car was spotted again in the Trastevere this morning, and we managed to tail him home. He lives at Number 4, Vicolo del Cedro."

"Very good," Castellano said approvingly. "Was anyone else there?"

"I only saw Rucci. He took some bags

of shopping inside, and left an hour later. That's a Brigade safe house, sir. I'm sure of it."

Castellano nodded thoughtfully, and took another sip of his coffee.

"Do you know who owns the building?" he asked.

"We're checking it," Soldani said. "Are we going to bust them?"

"Probably," Castellano said, after a pause. "He didn't see you, did he?"

"Definitely not. I've got a couple of people doing surveillance on the building, but nothing's emerged yet. As I said, Rucci left an hour ago, and we've seen nothing since."

A waiter appeared and put Castellano's bill on the table.

"Thank you," Castellano said. He reached inside his jacket and drew out some money. Having counted out what he owed, the Colonel left a reasonable tip and got to his feet.

"Doing anything this evening?" Castellano said softly.

Soldani recalled the last time the Colonel asked him this question, and he coughed uncomfortably.

"Well, sir . . ."

"Cancel it," Castellano said. "We're going to pay a visit to Signor Rucci."

34

MICHELE RUCCI returned home at 7 p.m. He was alone. After yesterday evening's panic, Michele's flat was now a warehouse of ammunition.

Mario and Pedro Torres had been out drinking together when Ponti arrived with the arms from Monica's flat. Ponti's instructions were swift and terse: the ammunition would be stored there until further notice. To minimize the risk, Michele's guests were to be evacuated as soon as possible. Michele must remain to keep an eye on the stores, but Mario and Pedro must find other accommodation without delay.

Michele suggested that Ponti might like to wait for the two men to return, so he could meet Pedro Torres. Ponti declined with regret, but he resolved to meet Pedro soon.

So early that morning, Mario and Pedro went out in search of fresh lodgings. It was agreed that if nothing turned up, Mario would stay with a former girlfriend in the Tuscolano district, and Pedro would return to Trastevere that evening.

Michele shut the door behind him and put the light on. He switched on the television, sat in an armchair, and lit a cigarette. As he tossed the spent match into an ashtray, the phone rang.

Michele got up again and turned off the television. There was a set procedure for phone calls: the caller would allow the phone to ring once, and he would hang up. Thirty seconds later he would call again.

This was not a call from one of Michele's comrades. The phone continued to ring, and Michele hesitated. Finally, he picked up the receiver.

"Hello?"

"Walk down the stairs slowly with your hands well above your head. If there is anyone with you, they should come too. The building is completely surrounded, and the street is blocked off. Once you are outside, lie face down on the ground with your hands behind your head. If you try anything else, we will shoot you. Is that clear?"

Michele slammed the phone down. He turned round and looked at the front window, about nine feet from him. The outside shutters were closed. Michele ran up to the window, opened it, and released the catch on the shutters. He went to one of the crates and drew out an RGD-5 grenade.

As he returned to the window, he recalled the advice of one of his trainers.

"Keep away from windows," the man had said. "If you're at least eight feet away, in an unlit room, you can shoot as well as you please, and they won't see you. Less than eight feet and you're a sitting duck."

Michele turned round again and switched off the light. He drew his gun out from a cupboard. The Czech-made Skorpion machine pistol is one of the most popular weapons in terrorism. It is only ten inches long, with a nine-inch steel-frame butt. Fully loaded, it weighs less than five pounds, and can deliver 840 rounds a minute. At close range, it can cut a man in two.

He loaded the Skorpion and put it down again. He picked up a cushion and threw it at one of the window shutters, knocking it open. Without pausing, he pulled the pin out of the RGD-5 and lobbed it through the window.

There was a sharp bang, and Michele could hear running footsteps at the end of the street. He picked up the Skorpion and listened out for further sounds. He could hear nothing.

For a full minute, silence reigned in the room. The phone rang again, and Michele lurched forward in surprise. He scowled at the machine, and ripped its cord out from the wall. Silence reigned once more.

Michele went over to the door and stood to one side of it. In one movement, he flung it open and fired down the stairway. Once again, he saw nothing, but could hear running footsteps. He swore angrily, and ran back towards the window. They would have to pass below him, he thought, and this time he would see the bastards.

He got to the window and began shooting. He could see them now, running back towards a group of cars. One turned round to reply to Michele's fire, but he was too late: Michele squeezed the trigger first, and the other man pitched forward.

"Got you," Michele shouted aloud, and he let off another triumphant hail of bullets.

And then something strange happened. Across the road, someone turned on a spotlight. It shone directly into Michele's face, blinding him. Once more he recalled his trainer's advice, but it was too late. Michele's head burst open like a ripe watermelon, and he toppled back on to the carpet.

Pedro Torres turned into the Vicolo del Cedro and stopped in surprise. Cameras flashed all over the street, as newsmen recorded the scene outside Michele's flat. A thirty-foot section of the street was cordoned off and surrounded by dark blue Carabinieri vans.

Pedro could see an ambulance outside Number 4. Two men emerged from the doorway, carrying someone on a stretcher. The sheet across the casualty's head told the rest of the story. Pedro turned round and walked away, trying not to look like a man whose landlord has just been killed.

35

THE next morning was sunny, but there was a chill in the air. Late in the year, Rome's colours lose a little of their warmth. The glowing umber buildings seem to pale, and the dominant colours are white and olive-blue. This gradual shift in hue is most noticeable by the river Tiber, where the bleached stone bridges stand out against the stagnant blue waters.

Wyman walked over the Ponte Umberto, towards the old Palace of Justice on the west bank. Over to his left, about a quarter of a mile away, was the drum turret of Castel Sant'Angelo, formerly the mausoleum of the Emperor Hadrian.

Wyman glanced down at the river and saw what he was looking for. At the end of the bridge, a set of steps led down to the river bank, where a group of men were standing. Some were uniformed Carabinieri, and another wore a diver's outfit. Wyman could also make out a familiar portly figure in a grimy, cream-coloured suit.

Wyman walked down the steps and went up to Castellano.

"Good morning, Professor," Castellano said. "I didn't just call to keep you informed. I think you might be able to help us."

"Indeed?" Wyman said. "What do you have in mind?"

"We have a corpse on our hands," Castellano said. "It floated up a couple of hours ago. Don't look alarmed, he wasn't a friend of yours."

Castellano pointed to a tarpaulin covering that morning's find. He leaned down to draw it back, then paused.

"Have you eaten recently?" he asked.

"I've had breakfast," Wyman admitted. "But don't worry."

"Very well," Castellano said drily. "Don't say you weren't warned. If you want to throw up, aim anywhere except the river. The diver's job is nasty enough already. He won't appreciate a surprise shampoo."

He drew back the tarpaulin, exposing a mangled, lacerated face.

"His name's Jones," Wyman said. "He was one of the CIA men who accosted me at the university."

Castellano nodded in satisfaction.

"Thought so," he said contentedly. "I think the other one is still down there. That's why we've brought the diver."

"Bit of a mess, isn't he?" Wyman observed.

"I've seen worse," Castellano said.

"How long do you think he's been in the water?"

"A good question. There's no *rigor mortis*, which means he's been dead for about two days, at least. It depends on how soon they threw him in."

"How soon after what?"

"After they killed him."

Wyman blinked in surprise.

"You mean he wasn't drowned?"

Castellano shrugged.

"I'm no forensic expert," he said, "and I look forward to hearing their report. But I can tell you right now, this man was killed before he went in."

He pulled the tarpaulin back a little further, exposing bullet holes on the throat and chest.

"Good grief," Wyman exclaimed.

"I think we'll see the same thing with his colleague."

Castellano covered the body once more, and lit a cigarette.

"They *have* been busy, haven't they?" Wyman remarked. "I wonder what happened."

"The same thought crossed my mind," Castellano said sourly. "It's all very irritating."

He jabbed a thumb at a couple of photographers up on the bridge.

"With every dead body, you get a swarm of parasites. And I've got to think of some answers for their questions."

"They're simply doing their job," Wyman said.

"I know," Castellano sighed. "But what am I supposed to say? 'That's three American tourists accidentally murdered, gentlemen. Nothing unusual. Not newsworthy. Please go away.'"

"I see your problem," Wyman sympathized.

"And then there's the CIA man—Hepburn. He'll want an explanation, of course. I will have to tell him that if his people insist on sending agents out here, they can expect the casualty list to grow. Very irritating."

There was a shout from the group of Carabinieri, as the diver resurfaced.

"He's found the other one," Castellano said.

The policemen threw a line out towards the diver, who made an affirmative gesture and went down again.

"What about yesterday evening?" Wyman asked. "I hear you had an interesting time."

"We were lucky," Castellano said. "That idiot was sitting on a munitions factory. If anything had gone off in there, the whole building would have exploded. Thank God he was on his own."

"Pity you couldn't get him alive," Wyman observed.

"He wasn't going to give us the pleasure. He made that quite clear when he threw the grenade into the street."

"Was anyone hurt?"

"Not by the grenade. He managed to shoot one of our people afterwards. The man's still in hospital, but he should be all right."

Wyman nodded. "You *were* lucky," he said. "What do you make of it all?"

"God knows," Castellano sighed. "None of this seems to get us any nearer to Scheib. There's no obvious connection between any of this and the American. Are you having any luck with the Venuti girl?"

"Not really," Wyman said. "She's happy to preach the theory of armed revolution to anyone who will listen. One would expect more discretion from a practising urban terrorist."

"That's right," Castellano said. "Those kids are always delighted to talk about it, as long as there's no obligation to put theory into practice. You'll know about it if she becomes actively involved: the first sign will be a sudden reluctance to make fresh converts. I wonder if she ever knew these people were after her."

Wyman frowned.

"Do we have a link between these deaths and yesterday evening's find?"

"Not yet. I'm hoping the forensic people might supply that."

"I don't know about you, Colonel," Wyman said, "but I find the whole business increasingly confusing."

"*You're* confused?" Castellano exclaimed. "How do you think I feel? Listen, Professor: Rucci's flat was stuffed with arms. There were boxes of bullets, plastic explosives, ammo clips and grenades. You could hardly walk in there. If you had that much illicit ammunition, would you store it in a tiny flat like Rucci's?"

"What are you suggesting?"

"It just doesn't make sense," Castellano said. "You keep arms hidden away, not lying around by the TV set. Those arms didn't belong in that flat."

"So where did they belong? And why were they moved away from there?"

There was another shout, as the diver resurfaced. He climbed on to the bank and gave the line to the waiting Carabinieri. A few minutes later, the bulky, rotting corpse of Jones P. was hauled ashore.

"I don't know where those arms came from," Castellano murmured. "But I wonder if those two knew."

"Now that's an interesting idea," Wyman said.

36

THROUGHOUT Sunday morning the bells of a thousand churches summoned the faithful to mass. For the first eighteen years of her life, Monica had gone to church every week with her parents. After she left home, however, she became true to her atheism. She made a point of never leaving her flat on Sundays, and she poured scorn on those who did.

Monica believed the Church was evil, a savage weapon in the armoury of a repressive system. She preached her atheism with evangelical fervour, damning the clergy and sending the faithful laity to political purgatory. At best, the Christian proletariat could be forgiven, for they knew not what they did. At worst, they were Judases, who had sold out to the worst kind of corruption. For the priests, there could be no salvation.

In England, a number of things had always puzzled Monica, and religion was one of them. Her fellow-students at Rome were often shocked by her opinions on the subject, but in England the reaction was very different. "Ah yes," they would say, "very interesting. Yes, you might well have a point there. Care for another coffee?" Nobody minded Monica's views, but nobody seemed particularly interested in them, either. She secretly envied their breezy indifference to the whole topic, but she could never share it. A true revolutionary could never condone any form of apathy.

So Monica spent November 10 as she did her previous Sundays, surrounded by secular reading matter in her flat. She had nearly finished Marx's *Grundrisse* when the entryphone rang.

Last Tuesday's encounter with Jones A. and Jones P. had taught her new vigilance: instead of answering the buzzer, she opened the window and glanced into the street. Below her stood the unexpected figure of Pedro Torres.

"Hello," she shouted happily. "Come upstairs."

She opened the door, and a few seconds later the Chilean entered the room.

"I hope I'm not disturbing you," he apologized.

"Of course not," she smiled. "It's good to see you. Do you know what's going on? Since Michele was killed I haven't heard anything."

"I'm not surprised," Torres said, as he sat down. "Mario's hiding. The last time I saw him, on Friday, he was staying with a girl in Tuscolano, but he wanted to move on."

"What about you?" Monica said. "I thought you might have been arrested."

"I was lucky," Torres said. "I was out that day with Mario, trying to find a new safe house. We couldn't get anything, but by the time I returned it was all over. I could see them bringing out Michele's body. If I'd got back there half an hour earlier, I would probably have joined him in the ambulance."

"Where have you been since?"

"On the move. I found a room for two nights, and I've slept rough since then. That's why I've come here. Mario told me to see you on Friday, but I didn't want to."

"Why not?" Monica asked.

"I don't know," Pedro said hesitantly. "I've only met you once, and I wasn't sure."

"I'm quite trustworthy, if that's what you mean," Monica said sharply.

"Of course, of course," Pedro said quickly. "That's not what I meant. I just find it hard to feel safe anywhere, that's all."

"So what changed your mind?"

"I ran out of money," he smiled, "and there are three days to go."

"Three days until what?"

"Until we see Ponti," Pedro explained. "After Michele was killed, Mario got in touch with Ponti. Apparently there's an operation planned, but nobody knows the details yet. Ponti said that Michele's death hasn't changed anything, and it's still going ahead. On Wednesday he'll meet us and give us our orders. I don't know if he needs me, but he wants me to come. You too, apparently."

Monica's face lit up with delight.

"Me?" she said. "Are you sure?"

"That's what Mario said. I don't know any more, except that we're to meet here on Wednesday afternoon."

"At last," Monica sighed. "If only you knew how long I've been waiting . . ."

Torres glanced at her in amusement.

"You make it sound as if he's proposed marriage to you."

"Nonsense," Monica blushed. "But—Ponti's never given me anything to do. Nothing important, anyway. I've felt so useless."

"Don't worry," Torres laughed. "I'm sure you'll get an important job. Wait and see."

"What about you?" Monica said. "Why are you with us? I'm sorry, I don't mean to sound hostile. I'm just curious. Chile seems so far away. Why should you want to get involved with us?"

"It's quite simple," Pedro said. "I want to go home. This is how I'm paying for my ticket."

Monica frowned.

"There must be easier ways," she said. "By coming to us, you've become involved with some of the most wanted men in Europe. Surely you don't have to go underground to return to Chile."

"That's what you think. In Europe I'm just another exile from Pinochet. At home

I'm a political criminal. Sure, I could settle down here and live legally. Thousands of people have done just that.

"But I want to go back and fight. Nobody wants to help a troublemaker. You see, to get home I need a false passport. Those aren't easy to find. The only people who could get me one are your friends."

"I understand," Monica said. "So is Ponti going to help?"

"He says he will. But I came at a bad time. Everybody's waiting for this operation, and Ponti won't do anything until it's over. That's why I offered to help. It might speed things up a bit. With Michele gone you're a man short, so Ponti might have some use for me after all."

"He'd be a fool to refuse you," Monica said. "You've probably got even more experience than he has."

Pedro shrugged modestly.

"Maybe," he said. "But this isn't the same as my country. We have very different enemies, even if we do want the same thing."

"You must tell me about Chile," Monica said. "I'd like to hear about what you've done. All I know about your country is what I've read."

Torres smiled sadly.

"It's a painful story" he said. "Very painful, and very long."

"I want to hear it, however painful it is," Monica said firmly. "And don't worry about time: you've got three days."

37

A KEY scraped into the lock and turned. Professor Scheib looked up from his magazine as Franco Ponti entered the room.

"Good afternoon, Professor," Ponti said. "How are you today?"

"Oh, the usual," Scheib replied. "Bored, depressed, irritated, that kind of thing. How about you?"

"Fine, fine," Ponti beamed.

"That's a shame," Scheib said. "Still, I live in hope."

"Hope of what?"

"I pass the time here with little fantasies about you. Sometimes you drown in boiling oil, sometimes you suffer tertiary syphilis. Depends on how extravagant I'm feeling."

"Never mind," Ponti laughed. "I think we can relieve the tedium for you today. We might even give you some new plots for your fantasies."

"What have you got in mind?"

Ponti gestured towards the door.

"This way, Professor. You will note that my friend Vito is holding an automatic. Please don't provoke him into using it."

Scheib walked out of his prison and glanced at Vito's Walther P38.

"Hello Vito," he said. "Have I told you how good your cooking is lately?"

Vito gave Ponti a puzzled glance.

"He's always abusing my cooking," Vito muttered.

"Not all the time," Scheib said. "When Vito's got a gun in his hand, I just love his meals."

Vito's lip curled in disgust.

"You make me throw up," he said.

"So it's mutual then?" Scheib grinned. "If you did something about the food, maybe neither of us would feel so lousy."

"That's enough, gentlemen," Ponti smiled. "It's time to give the professor a big surprise."

He went over to another door and unlocked it.

"Follow me, Professor. I think you'll like this."

Scheib followed Ponti inside.

"Well, damn me!" he exclaimed.

They were standing inside a small, fully equipped laboratory. The walls were lined with shiny white tiles, and a formica worktop ran the length of the room. There was an electric microscope, rows of slides, burettes, pipettes and flasks. A couple of bunsen burners lay beside an electronic balance, with a centrifuge and an incubation oven nearby. An extractor fan was fixed above the bunsen burners. Along the walls were rows of glass-fronted cabinets, containing labelled jars of acids, alkali and distilled water. At the far end of the room stood two gleaming white sinks.

"I'm rather proud of it," Ponti said. "There's very little you could do in a university lab which couldn't be accomplished here."

"No kidding?" Scheib said. "So what *do* you do here?"

Ponti sighed.

"It's a long story, so I hope you'll bear with me. This lab has been set up for just one purpose. I'd like to describe the task to you in detail. You don't have to comment, but I'd be grateful if you listened carefully."

Scheib blinked at Ponti in curiosity.

"So this is what it's all about," he said slowly. "This is why you bastards grabbed me, and not some other poor mug."

"Exactly," Ponti agreed.

"Forget it," Scheib said. "Just forget it. I don't know what you guys are planning, and I'm not sure I want to know. But if you think I'm going to lift one lousy finger in this lab for you, you've got it all wrong. You can shove the whole thing right up your—"

"Professor, please," Ponti broke in. "I have no intention of making you do anything. I don't need to. You see, I'm a trained microbiologist. As I said, you don't even need to comment on my work, let alone help. I just want you to understand what I'm doing, and to see the results. That's all. If you don't want to watch, I can't make you. It makes no difference to me. But it might prevent a great many painful deaths."

"How come?"

"To understand that, you must hear about my task."

Scheib's brow knotted in a frown.

"I suppose you'll kill me if I don't," he muttered.

"Not at all. As I promised you, we'll release you unharmed, no matter what happens. The choice is entirely yours."

Scheib shook his head in perplexity.

"I don't get it," he said. "Are you sure I just have to listen?"

"Quite sure."

"That's all?"

"That's all."

There was a long silence as Scheib struggled to make sense of what went on. Finally, he threw his hands up in resignation.

"Okay," he sighed. "I'll listen."

"Excellent," Ponti beamed. "Believe me, Professor, you won't regret this. Vito, would you mind bringing a chair for the professor? Bring one for yourself as well."

"You want me here?" Vito asked in surprise.

"Certainly," Ponti said. "For the last three months you've demanded to know what I'm doing. Now I'm about to explain."

"I'm no scientist," Vito said uneasily. "I won't understand . . ."

"Nonsense," Ponti smiled. "Scientists only make themselves obscure because they want to limit the membership of their comfortable little club. That's why they command such preposterously high salaries. I'll make sure you understand exactly what's going on. Bring in the chairs."

Vito did as he was asked, and Ponti began his story.

"Last August, I rented a small plot of uncultured land from a farmer. The land had lain fallow for a long time, and it was free of fertilizer and insecticide. Vito and I bought a sheep from the farmer. We slaughtered it, dismembered it, and buried it in six different parts of the field.

"The object of the exercise was to obtain a sample of a common anaerobic bacterium, frequently found in soil. These bacteria are fond of decomposing matter. I reasoned that if I allowed a couple of weeks and then took soil samples from each burial spot, at least one sample would yield the bacteria I wanted.

"I therefore returned to the field, and filled half a dozen buckets with soil from each spot. I filtered each soil sample by straining it through a large sieve, breaking up the bigger lumps of earth by hand, and pouring distilled water through the sieve afterwards."

He went to a cupboard and drew out a large tube of glass. At one end, the tube was sealed. Inside the glass was a ceramic plunger, fitted to a metal handle at the other end.

"For Vito's benefit," Ponti went on, "this is called a homogenizer. You put the crude liquid soil sample at the bottom of the tube, and insert the plunger. When you pull the handle, it draws up the liquid and grinds it between the plunger and the inner wall of the tube. This gives a finer, more even sample. Does this make sense, Vito?"

"Sure," Vito said.

"Splendid," Ponti beamed. "You must tell me if it doesn't. Anyway, having homogenized the sample, I was then in a position to extract my bacteria. To do this, we use a centrifuge."

He pointed to a metal object which resembled a hub-cap. "I'm sorry to bore you," Ponti said to Scheib, "but I feel I ought to explain to Vito what this does."

"Go ahead," Scheib said. "Just wake me up when it's over."

"It's really quite simple," Ponti went on. "You lie test tubes inside this machine, and switch on the motor. It spins round at great speed, sending the heavier contents of a solution to one end of the tube, while the lighter part remains at the top. This lighter portion is called the supernatant.

"The speed of the machine is variable, and you adjust it according to the weight of what you're trying to extract. I knew the weight of the bacteria I wanted, so by setting a certain speed, I could ensure that heavier, unwanted bacteria would be sent into the heavy mixture, while the bacteria I sought would remain in the supernatant.

"Having done this once, I discarded the heavy mixture and repeated the process three or four times. This gave me increasingly light solutions which would help to isolate the bacteria I required. Do you understand all this, Vito?"

"Yes," Vito said. "So this is what you've been doing while I've been working in the kitchen."

"Don't worry, Vito," Scheib said. "What you get up to in that kitchen is just as sinister."

"I thought you were just going to listen," Vito protested.

Ponti grinned.

"He only does it to upset you, Vito. I would advise you to confine your remarks to the subject of my work, Professor. Otherwise, Vito won't cook for you any more, and I will have to do it instead. You'd regret that."

"I'm sure I would," Scheib agreed. "Okay Vito, I won't say anything more about your cooking."

"Good," Ponti said. "Now, where were we? Oh yes; we had achieved the desired solution. The task now consisted of creating the right conditions for our bacteria to breed. Here we use something called a Petri dish."

He opened one of the wall cabinets and took out a flat perspex plate with a transparent cover.

"Agar is a yellow powder made from seaweed. Our bacteria seem to enjoy dining off the stuff, provided one or two other substances are added to it.

"To get our bacteria to form colonies, I lined the bottom of this Petri dish with a mixture of agar, animal blood, and a number of amino acids called cystine, leucine, lysine, glycine and proline. I then put a sample of our solution on top of this mixture, and covered the whole lot with another layer of agar."

"Hang on a minute," Scheib said. "That combination of amino acids sounds familiar."

"It ought to," Ponti said. "I took the instructions from one of your papers."

"Which one?"

"Guess," Ponti smiled. "Anyway, Vito, are you still with us?"

"I suppose so," Vito said. "But I don't see what all this is leading to."

"That makes two of us," Scheib said. "But I'm beginning to suspect."

"Don't worry," Ponti said. "All will become clear. You see why I put the solution in the dish? Good. Now, you will recall there were six original soil samples. From each of these six I made a number of solutions, and for each solution I made a number of Petri dish colonies.

"You see, the more samples we have, the greater is the probability of finding the bacteria we want. As you can see, even the most advanced microbiology involves a great deal of trial and error.

"Thus, we now have over a hundred Petri dishes. These were put in an incubation oven to stay in the kind of temperature our bacteria like best, around forty degrees centigrade. I kept them there for five days, studying each of them under the microscope at regular intervals.

"Eventually, I found what I wanted. A small colony had formed on one dish. I made a solution out of that colony and reinfected several other dishes. These went back into the incubator for a few more days, and then I repeated the process again and again. After about four weeks I had achieved a pure sample of the bacteria I wanted."

"Well, that's just great," Scheib said. "I'm truly impressed by all this. I mean, in all my career as a bacteriologist, I've only ever seen this done about eighty million times. You're amazing, Ponti, an undiscovered genius. Can I go home now?"

"I know you've seen this process before, Professor. It was your paper that taught me how to do it."

"Yeah," Scheib said. "I've been trying to recall which one it was. Can't remember for the life of me. Which bacterium have you isolated?"

"You mean you haven't guessed?"

"This might come as a great shock to you," Scheib said, "but there happen to be quite a few different bacteria. After forty years of messing around with them, you get kind of vague about—"

"Professor," Ponti protested, "I've had enough of your sarcasm today to last me a lifetime. The answer to your question is this: I have created a large and thriving colony of Clostridium Botulinum."

"Okay," Scheib said. "That's all I wanted to know . . ." He stopped and gazed at Ponti in surprise. "What did you say?"

"Clostridium Botulinum," Ponti repeated.

At once, Scheib lost his composure, and stared at Ponti's smiling face in horrified incredulity.

"You mad bastard," he breathed.

38

"ENZO was going to offer us a reply to Monica's theory," Wyman said.

"That's right," Enzo said pugnaciously. "Ready when you are."

Wyman smiled and exchanged places with his student.

"Right," Enzo said, as he sat down before the others. "Monica said that there is a lot of suffering and injustice, and it's all the fault of Capitalism. She thinks the only way you can stop this suffering is by throwing out Capitalism and getting rid of Democracy. She says we must do this by using terrorism.

"Monica admits this is going to cause suffering, but she justifies this using Reductionism. She says Reductionism supports her, because the aim is to reduce the total amount of suffering. Monica's terrorism is supposed to result in a world with much less suffering, and she says it's the only way to achieve this.

"But is it? If Monica's is the only way

to reduce suffering, she'd have a strong point. But she hasn't proved that. I don't agree that Capitalism is the source of all our troubles, but let's suppose it is. Is terrorism the only way to get rid of it? Surely we can remove it using peaceful, democratic means, if we wanted to. If we agreed that Capitalism had to go, we could vote to have everything nationalized. We could remove suffering by means which involved no suffering at all.

"Monica has to prove that this wouldn't work. She's got to show that you can't chuck out Capitalism by peaceful means. A Reductionist's main aim is to reduce suffering. If you give him a choice—either reduce suffering with peace or reduce suffering with war—he'll obviously take the peaceful option. Monica's got to convince him there is no such thing as a peaceful option."

"That's right," Paolo agreed. "A Reductionist isn't going to be a terrorist unless he's sure there's no alternative."

"Then we call him a freedom fighter," Giulio said cynically.

"Also," Enzo said, "Monica has abused one important Reductionist idea. The

Reductionist says we should give less weight to distributive justice: he's less concerned about who events belong to, and more concerned about how good they are. This is why it can be right that some people suffer, if the total sum of good events is increased. Monica needs that idea to justify the suffering of the people she wants to shoot and blow up.

"But she's taken it too far. The Reductionist gives less weight to distributive principles, but he doesn't give them no weight at all. There is still some case for saying that people shouldn't be made to suffer through no fault of their own."

Wyman listened with interest, glancing occasionally at Monica to see her reaction. She remained surprisingly impassive.

"Does anyone want to add to that?" he asked, and the others shook their heads. "Thank you, Enzo. That was very lucid. Perhaps Monica would like to reply?"

Monica shrugged.

"I don't have to 'prove' anything, Enzo," she said. "I've no more obligation to prove my beliefs than Enzo has to prove we can vote Capitalism out of existence.

Of course, he can't 'prove' his view, for the simple reason that it's wrong.

"I agree that if you could just vote out exploitation and suffering, it would be better than my way. But you can't. After all, if it were possible, we'd have done it by now, wouldn't we? And I do give some weight to distributive principles. People shouldn't be made to suffer through no fault of their own. Under Capitalism, they do suffer in this way all the time. I want to get rid of that."

"You used a Reductionist argument," Lucia said, "but a Reductionist doesn't have to agree with you, does he?"

"Of course not," Monica said. "He might agree with Enzo. The Reductionism isn't in dispute. We're arguing about something else. Enzo believes in Democracy, and peaceful solutions, and he offers a Reductionist argument for Democracy and peaceful solutions. I think Democracy is a joke, and that there's no such thing as a peaceful solution. So I stick to my Reductionist argument for popular revolution."

"But most people—most Reductionists

—would disagree with your argument, wouldn't they?" Lucia persisted.

"I'm sure they would," Monica said cheerfully. "So what?"

39

"ARE you sure it's them?" Hepburn asked.

"Quite sure," Castellano said.

He produced some colour photographs and put them on Hepburn's desk.

"As you can see," the Colonel went on, "even though they've been in the water for some days, there's no doubt about who they are."

Hepburn's face screwed up in distaste.

"Most unpleasant," he said. "So what happened to them?"

"At the moment, I can't say. We haven't yet heard from the forensic people. I would guess they were simply shot and thrown into the river afterwards. Apart from the bullet wounds, all the injuries appear to have been inflicted after death."

"But why throw them in the river?" Hepburn asked. "I thought the Red Brigades liked leaving corpses lying around on street corners with messages stuck to them."

"We can only guess," Castellano said. "I suspect that whoever killed them knew it would cause us the maximum embarrassment to dispose of them this way."

"They certainly knew what they were doing," Hepburn observed. "I still can't understand how our guys could have just walked into that. The Joneses were experienced men. You can't jump people like that."

"As I recall, Rawls was also experienced," Castellano said drily. "It didn't save him, either. Your people really must learn that lesson, Mr. Hepburn."

"I know, I know," Hepburn lamented. "Try telling them yourself; they won't listen to me. After we last spoke, I made a formal protest to the Director. I threatened to resign if this business wasn't cleared up."

"What did he say?"

"He said I was over-reacting. The insolent bastard practically accused me of being hysterical. Me! He said 'Take it easy, Julie. They're good men, Julie. They can handle the situation, Julie. Just relax, Julie.' Patronizing shit. You know, I hate being called Julie."

"But that was before the Jones men were killed. Surely they'll listen to you now."

"The hell they will," Hepburn said bitterly. "They'll just blame me for not giving them enough help."

A worried look appeared on Castellano's face.

"Does this mean that more agents will be sent out?"

Hepburn shook his head.

"I honestly don't know, Colonel. The trouble is, we have an administration in Washington that thinks it owns the world. They've got this idea fixed in their pea-sized brains that they can just crap all over any country they like without asking for permission.

"Sure, we've always been arrogant bastards, but it used to be different. When Kissinger wanted to play rough, he'd consult Bismarck, Machiavelli, or maybe Clausewitz. Nowadays, our foreign policy is inspired by John Wayne movies. If the President wants a few ideas, he puts on a video of *The Green Berets*, and his aides explain the difficult bits to him."

"Are you suggesting those agents were

sent here on orders from the White House?"

"No, Colonel. I'm just saying that if this is the attitude on Capitol Hill, what do you expect from the poor bastards who have to implement the policies? You have to make it clear to the guys at the top that you won't tolerate any more from them. If you do that, the message might get through to the lower orders."

"Such as your CIA Director?"

"Exactly," Hepburn said.

"What do you propose?"

"Straightforward blackmail. You should get your ambassador in Washington to deliver a formal complaint to the Secretary of State. Tell him you'll only cover up these deaths on one condition: that no more agents are sent out on covert operations in Rome connected with the Scheib kidnapping. Otherwise, you'll tell the world what's been happening, and propose a motion at the United Nations, or something like that."

"Would that work?"

"It might. Hasn't it occurred to you that they've been very quiet about Scheib? No publicity, no speeches. In America, they stopped newspaper coverage of Scheib about a week after he got kidnapped."

"Do you know why?" Castellano asked.

"Maybe," Hepburn said coyly. "But if I did, I couldn't pass it on. Now *that* should tell you something."

Castellano leaned back in his chair and smiled thoughtfully.

"Let me see," he said. "If you're not allowed to tell me about Scheib, that means he has direct bearing on US intelligence. Your people don't want his case publicized, because somebody might find out why he is so useful to you. If we were to make a public issue out of these latest deaths, people might want to know more about Scheib. The threat of this publicity might worry the Americans, even though we wouldn't know why."

"Well done, Colonel," Hepburn smiled. "I've taken the liberty of warning Washington that a formal protest might be under way from your people."

"A sensible move, Mr. Hepburn," Castellano said. "I will take the necessary steps straight away."

"Great," Hepburn said. "Let's hope it works."

Castellano got to his feet. As he shook hands with Hepburn, a thought occurred to him.

"There's just one thing . . ." he began.

"What's that?"

"Why are you so anxious to help us? Of course, I appreciate your co-operation very much, but I'm a little puzzled by it. You seem more sympathetic to us than to your own people. Why is that?"

"Two reasons, Colonel," Hepburn said. "Firstly, I want a quiet life. We have a well-ordered, efficient set-up here in Rome. I don't want it disrupted by hoodlums like Rawls and the Joneses."

"And the second reason?"

"The CIA is a great organization, Colonel. It suffers from one major problem: the people in charge of it. They're plumbers, Colonel, artisans. I really hate artisans."

40

"YOU have a lot of books," Pedro Torres said approvingly. He was looking at the well-stocked shelves in Monica's flat. "Marx, Proudhon, Lenin. Very impressive. I wish I'd read a tenth of all this. All these subjects I know nothing about: metaphysics, logic, political science."

"You must have read some of them," Monica said.

"A little," Pedro admitted. "Mainly Marx, but I've forgotten most of it."

"Weren't you a student?"

"Yes, a long time ago," Pedro smiled.

"What did you read?"

"Business Studies at Santiago, believe it or not. My father traded in copper, and he wanted me to be a good little capitalist like himself. I dropped out after a couple of years. Maybe I should have taken philosophy instead. It sounds more interesting."

"It is," Monica said. "It has a lot to offer us."

"Is that so?" Pedro said, as he sat down. "Can you give me an example?"

"I think we can build a new case for revolution," Monica said grandly, "based largely on the need to reduce the sum total of a country's suffering."

"That's new?" Pedro asked in surprise. "What do you think we're doing in Chile?"

"The same, of course," Monica said. "But there's always a problem. Declaring war on the State inevitably means creating casualties. In Chile, there's no real moral dilemma about that. But in Europe, people often claim we are increasing suffering for no good reason. I think we can persuade them by showing that we're aiming for a reduction of the *worst kinds* of suffering.

"The argument depends on our reconsidering what a person is. If we move away from the dogma of 'the Person' as a distinct metaphysical entity whose essence is defined in abstractions, and head towards the notion of mere interrelated physiological and psychological events, we can redefine . . ."

Monica tailed off in embarrassment, as

she saw the concussed expression on Pedro's face.

"I'm sorry," she said. "I'm not making any sense, am I?"

"Don't apologize," Pedro said. "I asked you to tell me, and it's my fault if I'm too ignorant to understand. Perhaps if you went a little slower . . ."

Monica shook her head.

"It doesn't matter," she said.

Pedro leaned over and took her hand.

"It *does* matter," he said firmly. "You wouldn't find it interesting if it were useless, would you? You know, four years ago, they banned philosophy in Chile. They ordered all the universities to dismantle their philosophy departments. The subject must be a threat to them, and if that's so it must be worthwhile. Don't feel ashamed because people like me can't understand what you're doing. *They* can; it worries *them*, and that's what counts."

Monica smiled.

"Thank you," she said softly. "But I feel such a fool."

"Why?"

"Talking about suffering in front of you. You must have seen so much of it . . ."

"Maybe," he said. "But it's nothing to be proud of. Since Pinochet took over, they've killed over thirty thousand people, and there are ten thousand more in prisons and concentration camps. They got rid of a lot of friends of mine, but I got away. That doesn't make me feel a better person."

Monica shook her head.

"You've got a real war to fight. By comparison, we're just playing games."

"You sound disillusioned," Pedro said. "Have you lost your faith already?"

"I don't know," she said. "It seems we're the only people in this country who understand, and even the people we're fighting for hate us. Usually I take pride in that, but sometimes it frightens me."

"But have you lost your faith?" Pedro persisted.

"I don't think so. I believe—no, I *know* we have to take up arms."

"So what's troubling you? Let me guess: it's Ponti, isn't it? You can't understand what he's doing, and you dislike being kept outside it."

"Of course I dislike it," Monica said. "What's the point of kidnapping someone if nobody understands why you've done it? Why hide your intentions? We're supposed to be at war with the State, but when Michele was killed, what did we do? Nothing. We just seem to be utensils in Franco Ponti's little intellectual games."

"Perhaps you're being unfair to Ponti," Pedro said.

"How?"

"We don't know what Ponti's plan is, but we can make some intelligent guesses. Ponti wants you to know nothing for now. That means if you were picked up by the police, you couldn't say anything. Right? Most importantly, you couldn't help them find Ponti himself. That probably means that Ponti himself is an important feature of his own plan; it may need a special skill which only he has."

"So why does he need us?" Monica said. "If he's that skilled, why doesn't he just fight his own war with the State? If he needs no help—"

"I didn't say that," Pedro broke in. "You should remember that different people have different talents. Yours is theory, mine is with guns. We're both needed at different times, but we still depend on each other. If Ponti's skills are needed most now, we should be happy to let him have priority."

"I understand," Monica said. "But I still resent his secrecy."

Pedro smiled.

"It's better to be ignorant than to be in prison. You said Ponti's never given you anything important to do. What have you done for him?"

"Nothing," Monica said uneasily. "I haven't done anything for him."

"What did you do with the other groups?"

"Other groups?"

"Well, I suppose you got your fighting experience with another column before you joined . . ."

There was no need to finish the sentence: Monica's crimson face answered the question for him.

"I've had no experience," she muttered.

"None at all?" he asked incredulously. "You've never used a gun?"

She shook her head.

"I'm sorry," he laughed. "You must think I'm very patronizing. I just thought . . ."

"I know," Monica said. "It's my fault. I should have explained."

"So how did you become a part of all this?"

Monica related her entry to revolutionary politics, and her friendship with Claudio Prando. She recounted how Prando introduced her to Mario Pagani, who had promised her membership of Ponti's column.

"We were simply friends, you see," Monica explained. "It was just a coincidence that Claudio knew Ponti. When he and Mario became sure they could trust me, they spoke to Ponti about it. Then Claudio died in a car accident, and I heard nothing for a while.

"Later, Mario found me and said that Ponti agreed to my joining, but only in reserve. He would let me know when Ponti needed me. I've run one or two small errands for Mario, but they weren't very significant."

It occurred to Pedro that, far from being "just a coincidence", Monica's introduction to Ponti's column was a classic piece of recruitment. He kept this thought to himself, however, and merely said:

"So you're still waiting for your baptism of fire?"

"Yes," she said. "You could say I'm still a virgin."

"Is that a fact?" Pedro said, looking at Monica with new interest.

She replied with a shy smile.

"What shall we talk about now?" she asked quietly.

41

"ANY luck with the Venuti girl?" Castellano said.

"Not really," Wyman sighed. "She still argues the case for revolution with all the experience and common sense one expects of a born theorist. If discretion is the sign of a practising terrorist, then we can discount Monica."

"I don't understand it," Castellano said. "That girl *must* be involved. The CIA men were convinced she was linked to Ponti. If they were wrong, why were they killed?"

"They were following up other leads, as well as Monica. Perhaps they stumbled across something else . . ."

"In that case," Castellano concluded, "she is of no further interest to us. Her friendship with Mario Pagani is purely fortuitous, as were her links with Claudio Prando. The fact that both these men led straight to Franco Ponti was just a happy coincidence. Do you believe that?"

"Of course not," Wyman said. "And nor do you. All the circumstantial evidence suggests that she's in it up to her neck."

"And there's our dilemma," Castellano said. "I still lack one solid piece of evidence to justify pulling her in. That girl can walk around with a T-shirt saying 'I'm a Terrorist', and she can pin signed photographs of Carlos the Jackal to her wall, but poor old Castellano mustn't go anywhere near her. If I gave her ten minutes of routine questioning, the people who pay me to protect them from terrorists would be the first to accuse me of jack-booted authoritarianism. Crazy, isn't it?"

"You'd achieve little by questioning her right now," Wyman observed. "I think she only has a minor role in Ponti's scheme of things."

"What do you mean?"

"According to your files, Ponti's fighting units are carefully structured affairs. Ponti plays Napoleon at the top, there are other people in the middle, and menials at the bottom. I can only suppose that Monica is one of the 'other ranks'—possibly just a reservist. That might explain why she appears to be both involved and inert at the same time."

"It's possible," Castellano nodded. "But it doesn't help us find Ponti, does it? I wonder why he's so quiet. After we shot Michele Rucci I expected some kind of reprisal. Not only did we kill his colleague, but we also uncovered a large cache of their weapons. You'd think Ponti would have something to say about that, wouldn't you?"

"What about Mario Pagani?" Wyman asked.

"Vanished," Castellano said. "There's no sign of him."

"If you'll forgive me," Wyman said, "this gives further credence to my theory about a plot. I know you disagree, but I'm still convinced Scheib was kidnapped as part of a larger plan. If that's true, it would explain Ponti's silence over Rucci's death."

"Why?"

"Suppose Ponti does have such a plan: it would explain why we've heard nothing more about Scheib since his abduction. Rucci's death might have been a blow to Ponti, but it need not have upset this plan.

If so, Ponti wouldn't want to be distracted from his main purpose by wasting time and energy on a few symbolic reprisals against the police.

"Conversely, if the raid *had* wrecked his plan, we'd know about it by now. Ponti would have taken revenge, and Scheib would probably have floated up in the Tiber alongside the CIA men."

"An interesting idea," Castellano said, "but I'm still not persuaded. The chances are that Scheib has already been killed, and we just haven't found the body yet. And if you're right, it means the raid on Rucci's flat was a waste of time—a side-show. Our findings there will probably tell us nothing."

"Precisely," Wyman agreed. "After all, what did you find there? A few arms and a dead terrorist. It doesn't bring you any nearer to Ponti, does it?"

Castellano picked up a typewritten inventory of the items found at Michele's flat.

"I suppose you're right," he grunted. "Two Walther P38 automatics. Seventy RGD-5 anti-personnel hand grenades. Assorted explosives, including some RDX.

A Skorpion VZ61 automatic pistol, and three cases of ammunition clips."

"Is any of that unusual?" Wyman asked.

"One hates to describe arms as boring," Castellano said, "but really, this is very tedious. All this material has been used by terrorists for years. Aldo Moro was killed with a Skorpion pistol in '78. The grenades were used by the Viet Cong, and Carlos had some when he raided the OPEC meeting in Vienna ten years ago. The P38 is the Red Brigades' favourite pistol: years ago they published a leaflet with the slogan 'Never Again Without A Gun', and the P38 is the gun they had in mind. I would recommend this inventory as a cure for insomnia."

"Was anything else found?"

Castellano read through the list and shook his head.

"Nothing of any interest. One of the arms cases contained a black rubbish bag. Inside it we found a couple of old overalls and a machete."

"A machete?"

"Yes. The overalls were covered in dirt and bloodstains. For a moment I had a vision of Professor Scheib being hacked to death by his captors, but it was a false alarm. The blood came from an animal, probably a sheep."

"Why would they want to kill a sheep? And why use a machete? That's a very crude way to slaughter an animal."

"Who knows?" Castellano shrugged. "I've given up trying to understand these people, Professor. For all I know, this could be evidence of a black magic rite. I wouldn't put it past them."

"But why use the machete?" Wyman persisted. "Why be so messy?"

"I suppose that's why they wore the overalls," Castellano said patiently. "It doesn't matter, does it?"

"I'm not sure," Wyman mused. "You say there were two sets of overalls?"

"That's right." Castellano looked at Wyman in amusement. "You're not suggesting these are of interest, are you?"

"I don't know," Wyman said thoughtfully. "But I think we'd be rash to ignore them."

Castellano collapsed in his chair and roared with laughter.

"Really, Professor," he bellowed.

"That's too much. Ponti runs a terrorist cell, not an abattoir. How do you start a revolution with a dead sheep?"

42

"HELLO," Ponti said, as he shook Pedro's hand. "I'm sorry we didn't meet earlier."

The two men looked at each other with interest, as Monica closed her front door behind them.

"Pedro's been looking forward to seeing you," Monica said.

"It's mutual," Ponti smiled. "And I'm sorry we couldn't help you straight away. If you'd come to us a few months earlier . . ."

"I understand," Pedro said. "And I'm grateful for what you've already done."

"You're still anxious to return to Chile?"

Pedro nodded.

"In that case," Ponti said, "you'll still need a new passport. I know a man in Paris who supplies these things to the *Action Directe* people. I'll be there in a couple of weeks, so I can get it then. Can you wait that long?"

"Sure," Pedro said. "Does this mean your operation will be finished by then?"

"It does," Ponti said. "I understand you'd like to help us."

"I'd like to pay my way," Pedro said. "And if it helps speed things up, then I'll be doing myself a favour as well."

"That's right," Ponti agreed. "You can take over Michele's job."

"So what's happening?" Monica said. "Are we all leaving?"

"It's a little complicated," Ponti said apologetically. "I'd like Pedro to come and stay at our HQ on the other side of town. You should come too, Monica, but there's a little task I'd like you to perform before you do that."

Monica's face lit up with excitement.

"What sort of a task?" she said.

"I'll tell you later, I don't want you to do this job for a few days yet, and until you've done it I'd like you to carry on as usual."

"You mean I should stay here?"

"Yes, and you should continue going to the university. It's only for another four or five days; after that you'll join us permanently."

"How much should I bring from here?"

"As little as possible," Ponti said. "In fact, I'd prefer you to bring nothing. Come along with us to the HQ this afternoon. You can buy whatever you need over there—clothes, toiletries, and so on. After you've done that you can come back here. I'll explain why when I brief you for the job."

"Okay," Monica said brightly.

They left her flat and got into Ponti's car outside. During the trip, Ponti asked Pedro about his work for MIR. Torres was impressed by Ponti's detailed understanding of events in Chile. After about twenty-five minutes, Ponti stopped the car outside a four-storey house in Pietralata, on the eastern outskirts of Rome.

"Welcome to my miserable home," Ponti said, with the mock humility of an Eastern potentate. "The top two floors are ours, and the lower storeys belong to a businessman who lives in Milan. He only comes here twice a year, and he thinks it's beneath his dignity to rent out the rooms. I'm not complaining."

They went upstairs, and Ponti showed

them around his headquarters. The rooms were comfortably furnished, with little decoration. Ponti had no use for flowers, paintings, or any of the usual domestic adornments.

"There are a couple of other rooms I'll show you tomorrow," he said. "One is a laboratory, and the other is a small compartment containing our guest."

"You mean the American?" Monica said.

Ponti nodded.

"He's quite comfortable, of course, but he's completely shut off. You can only get into his room through a hidden door in the hallway. It's locked on both sides and soundproofed."

"In case of a raid?" Pedro asked.

"Exactly. If, by some mischance, the police burst in, they'd never find him."

"Is it that secure?" Monica asked.

"I worked from the same design our colleagues used in the Via Fani. It was quite successful then, as I recall."

Aldo Moro's kidnappers imprisoned him in a house on the Via Fani, in Monte Mario. After Moro's body was found in a Roman street, the police were unable to discover where he had been held. Seven years later, a captured Brigadist finally revealed the location. Without that confession, Moro's prison might never have been discovered.

"How is Scheib coping?" Monica asked.

"As well as you'd expect," Ponti said. "We give him everything he wants, except his freedom. Not surprisingly, he's a little frustrated. It doesn't matter."

Ponti sat down, and he invited the others to do the same.

"Now you're with us," he said to Pedro, "there might be a little difficulty about space. We've got four single beds. That's enough for you, me, Vito and Mario, who's joining us tomorrow. When Monica comes to stay, there'll be a small problem. Would you mind taking the floor . . ."

He trailed off as he noticed Pedro and Monica exchanging uncomfortable glances.

"At least," Ponti said, "I assume there is a problem. Maybe I'm wrong."

"You are," Pedro murmured.

Ponti burst into laughter.

"Very well," he said. "Problem solved. But let me make one thing clear: it won't interfere with anything. If I see one sign of marital difficulty, I'll put you in separate rooms. Is that clear?"

"You . . . don't mind?" Monica said.

"As long as it has no bearing on our job, I couldn't give a damn. In fact, Monica, I'll even let you spend the night here. But you'll go back tomorrow, and you mustn't return here until you've finished that little job for me."

"When will that be, exactly?"

"Let me see . . . today's Wednesday. Have you any plans for next Monday?"

"I have a lecture in the morning, that's all."

"Do you want to go?"

"If there's nothing else happening," Monica said. "The course is extremely useful . . ."

"Ah yes," Ponti said. "Our liberal friend, Professor Wyman. Mario's told me about this. You're very taken with him, aren't you?"

"I suppose I am," Monica said.

Ponti smiled cynically.

"This is the fellow who lets you preach armed revolution, isn't it? Very chic, I must say."

Monica stared at him coldly.

"Is something wrong with that?" she said.

"No, not at all," Ponti said. "But from what I hear, he's more interested to hear your views than to teach his own."

"What are you driving at?"

"There are different ways of getting someone to talk," Ponti said. "Those CIA men took one approach; a very crude one. There are more sophisticated methods. Maybe your friend Wyman . . ."

"Rubbish," Monica snapped. "You don't know what you're talking about."

Ponti shrugged.

"We'll see," he said mysteriously.

43

DR. SALUSTRI'S forensic laboratory was a tidy, well-ordered place. The walls and floor were lined with clean white marble, and the benches were spotless. The prevailing odour was of disinfectant, with just a hint of formaldehyde.

Salustri himself was a jolly little man with pebble glasses and a permanent smile. He showed Wyman and Colonel Castellano into his laboratory and shook their hands.

"Nice to see you again, Colonel," he beamed. "I'm afraid I haven't had the pleasure of . . ."

"This is Professor Wyman from the university," Castellano explained. "He's helping with our investigations."

"Delighted to meet you," Salustri said. "Now, I know the Colonel likes a glass of Sambuca when he comes here. Can I offer you the same?"

"That would be marvellous, thank you," Wyman said.

Salustri opened a cupboard and poured out three glasses of the anisette.

"I've finished my report," he said, as he gave them their drinks. "Nothing very spectacular. Quite simply, the two men were shot at close range and dumped in the river a couple of hours later. Apart from the bullet wounds, all the other injuries are post-mortem."

He motioned them over to the other end of the laboratory, where the bloodless, ravaged remains of Jones A. and Jones P. were laid out on marble slabs. There was crude, erratic stitching across their abdomens, and cardboard labels were fastened to their ankles.

"There are no complications," Salustri added. "It was a very tidy killing."

"They don't look very tidy," Wyman remarked.

"That's all post-mortem," Salustri said, waving his hand. "All the lacerations were caused by contact with underwater obstacles. The green stains on the abdomens are caused by the gut bacteria breaking down the haemoglobin. Immersion usually slows down putrefaction, but not here. The Tiber's a dirty old river, and things rot quickly in it."

"So I see," Castellano said drily. "How long do you think they were under water?"

"About two days," Salustri said. "Much longer and their own mothers wouldn't have recognized them. You see, the putrefactive bacteria work their way along the veins, causing a dark marbling effect. You can see the start of that here, on their legs.

"Also, the body fat turns into a kind of wax called adipocere, and things tend to get a bit shapeless after that. In certain conditions, all you're left with is a skeleton with a lot of foul-smelling sludge clinging to it."

Wyman smiled feebly.

"That's fascinating," he said, though he didn't put much enthusiasm into it. "I understand why you give your guests a glass of Sambuca, Doctor. They need it."

"I'm sorry, Professor," Salustri laughed. "The Colonel has seen a lot of this sort of thing. I assumed you were also in the business, so to speak."

"I'm afraid not," Wyman said weakly.

"Professor Wyman is a philosopher," Castellano said.

"A slightly bilious philosopher," Wyman added.

"Oh dear," Salustri sympathized. "Would you like some fresh air?"

"No thank you. I'm sure another glass of your excellent Sambuca will do the trick . . ."

"But of course," Salustri said, and he went back to his cupboard for the Sambuca. "A philosopher, eh? A fascinating subject. I read Plato's *Phaedo* once. Marvellous book. I was particularly taken with the ending."

"You mean Socrates' death?" Wyman said.

"Yes, most absorbing. I've read it again a number of times."

"It was a very moving end," Wyman agreed.

"Moving? Oh, yes, I suppose it was. That's not what I meant. It was the poison that interested me. Fascinating stuff, hemlock. First your legs go numb, then your lower torso, and by the time it reaches your heart—*arrivederci*. A very *civilized* way to poison someone, don't you think?"

"Civilized?" Wyman gasped.

"Yes," Salustri said. "If you consider what people do nowadays, the Athenians had a lot to be said for them. You should see some of the cases of poisoning we get here: people who drink hydrochloric acid, carbolic, any old rubbish. You get people who drink Lysol, and they turn up here with half their head dissolved after throwing it all up again. Other people overdose on barbiturates and send most of their stomach pouring back out of their faces. Most uncivilized."

"Yes," Wyman shuddered. "I—I suppose it is."

"You'd better stop there, Doctor," Castellano laughed. "I don't think it helps the Professor feel any better. What about the bullet wounds on our American friends? Have you identified them?"

"Of course," Salustri said. "They were caused by nine-millimetre Parabellum cartridges belonging to one of the P38 pistols found in Rucci's flat. These gentlemen were shot at a range of seven or eight feet."

"Not at point-blank range?" Wyman asked.

"Not quite."

"Had they been tied up first?"

"There's no sign of that," Salustri said. "In fact, there's no evidence of any kind of struggle."

Wyman and Castellano exchanged glances.

"How curious," Wyman muttered.

"Were there any other clues?" Castellano asked.

"Just one," Salustri grinned. "It's the *pièce de résistance*. Inside the nostril of one man and the ear of the other, I found traces of sawdust."

"Sawdust?"

"Yes. It matches the sawdust in the packing cases at Rucci's flat."

"Do you think that's where these men were killed?"

"It's possible," Salustri said. "I had a look around that flat yesterday evening. There were traces of blood inside two of the packing cases matching the blood-types of these men. I would guess they were taken to the river inside those cases.

"But there were no similar stains elsewhere in the flat. The only blood I could find outside those packing cases belonged to Rucci."

Castellano glanced at Wyman again.

"Let me suggest something," he said. "Suppose the arms were originally kept somewhere else. These men stumbled across them and were shot. Their bodies were put inside the cases and dumped. The arms were then put back in the cases, and the whole consignment was taken to Rucci's apartment for safe keeping. Is that possible?"

Salustri paused for thought.

"Maybe," he said slowly. "It would certainly be consistent with the forensic evidence. Where do you think those arms were kept in the first place?"

Castellano threw up his hands and sighed.

"If only I knew, Doctor. If only I knew."

44

"GOOD morning, professor," Ponti said with quite unnecessary cheerfulness, as Vito escorted Professor Scheib into the laboratory. "And how are you feeling today?"

"No better for seeing you," Scheib grunted.

"Let me introduce you to some more of my colleagues," Ponti grinned. "This is Mario, and this is Monica, who only joined us recently. Pedro is a guest of ours from Chile."

Scheib gazed morosely at his new acquaintances.

"I'd like to say it's a pleasure meeting you," he said. "But I'd be lying."

"The Professor has an unusual sense of humour," Ponti explained. "I think he's a little irritated by his captivity, and I can't say I blame him. Never mind, Professor. In ten days, you'll be a free man."

Scheib's eyebrows rose inquiringly.

"Oh yeah? So what's happening in ten days?"

"That's why I've brought you all here," Ponti replied. "You see Professor, you're not the only one who's complained about my secrecy. Even these people don't understand why we've kidnapped you, and what I have in mind. Today I'm going to change all that."

"I'm glad to hear it," Mario said, and Monica nodded in agreement. Pedro Torres remained silent.

"Young people are so impatient," Ponti sighed. "I'm afraid you'll have to bear with me a little longer before I can give you a full explanation.

"The whole point of this plan concerns an experiment I've been working on for the last four months. I've been describing this experiment to the Professor.

"Four days ago, I recounted my preparatory work to him. This consisted of a fairly routine task: the isolation of a common anaerobic bacterium called Clostridium Botulinum. There's a sample of it under that microscope over there, and I'd like you all to take a look at it. First, Professor Scheib."

He motioned the American over to the microscope, and Scheib peered into it.

"Yes," Scheib said reluctantly. "No mistaking them. Sporulating rods, four to six microns long, one micron across. Four to eight peritrichal flagella. Swollen subterminal spores. That's type A Botulinum, you crazy sonofabitch."

"What is it?" Monica asked.

Scheib looked up at her and grimaced.

"Death on a Petri dish, honey. These are some of the most dangerous bacteria on this planet. Ever heard of botulism? These are the little bastards that cause it."

He left the microscope, and stepped aside for the others. When everybody had taken a look, Mario asked:

"What's the point of all this?"

"A good question, sonny," Scheib said. "I've been asking myself the same thing."

"I gave the Professor an account of how I isolated this strain," Ponti said. "Now I'm going to explain what I did with it. That should answer your question."

He pointed to a flask on the worktop.

"That contains a medium for the bacteria. It consists of something called pancreatic digest of casein, which is obtained by extracting enzymes from the pancreas of an animal and cultivating them in milk protein. The medium also contains some yeast and glucose.

"I took two millilitres of our Botulinum sample and added it to ten millilitres of our medium. It went into the incubation oven for twenty-four hours at thirty-seven degrees centigrade. After that, I put this into another litre of our medium, and gave it another four days in the oven. Does this make sense?"

He looked around, and was pleased to see that everyone was nodding.

"Good," he said. "The rest is quite straightforward. I added a little sulphuric acid to our culture, and put it in the centrifuge. After spinning it, I threw away the supernatant and diluted the culture with water. When the temperature came down to four degrees, I repeated the process, and added a millilitre of calcium chloride.

"I then filtered this sample through fluted paper at room temperature, and put it back in the centrifuge. The supernatant was discarded again, and this time I added a little hydrochloric acid. I spun it once again, and added some ethanoic acid. I then let it stand in the freezer for twenty-four hours at minus five degrees.

"The next day, I put it back in the centrifuge, and added a few crystals of ammonium sulphate. One more session with the centrifuge gave me what I required—pure crystals of type A toxin."

Professor Scheib turned an interesting shade of puce. He tried to say something, but could only emit a dismayed croak.

"The Professor is highly flattered," Ponti explained. "You see, the instructions for all this work came from his own writings."

He took a couple of surgical masks from a cabinet, and gave one to the American.

"I'd be grateful if you'd all step back," Ponti said. "I'd like to show the crystal to the Professor. It's so concentrated, you could accidentally breathe some in if you were too close."

They shuffled back to the other end of the laboratory, as Ponti and Scheib put on their masks. Ponti then put on some gloves, and he opened a special cabinet containing a single black plastic flask. He unscrewed the lid, and tilted the flask gently towards the American.

"You see?" Ponti said. "A perfect sample: amber-coloured, heavily viscous. You have no doubt that this is Botulinum toxin?"

"No doubt," Scheib said gloomily. "Do me a favour, Ponti: drink it all in one. It would make my day."

Ponti laughed, and put the flask away.

"I still don't understand," Pedro frowned. "What exactly have you achieved?"

"Tell them, Professor," Ponti grinned.

"Type A Botulinum toxin," Scheib said hoarsely. "He isolated some poisonous bacteria, right? Now he's extracted the poison from the bacteria themselves, and he's achieved a pure, concentrated sample of it. That's what the semi-liquid gunge in the flask is; they're known as toxin crystals. This lunatic has got a sample of the most poisonous substance known to man."

"What does it do?" Vito asked.

"It literally gets on your nerves," Scheib said. "When your brain wants your muscles to do something, it sends impulses down your motor nerves. Botulism interferes with the conduction of these impulses: it paralyses the terminal twigs of the nerves, and suddenly you lose control of your muscles.

"If you swallow it, the major symptoms start about eighteen hours later. You get double vision, vomiting, and constipation. You have difficulty talking, you can't swallow properly, and soon your throat becomes paralysed. After a day of this agony, you should die, but it might take as long as a week. I wouldn't recommend it."

"Thank you," Ponti said. "Though I don't suppose that would impress our cynical young audience here. Ever since nuclear weapons arrived, people have grown terribly blasé about other forms of mass destruction. By comparison with missiles, a poison seems so *pedestrian*, doesn't it? If only they knew."

"Knew what?" Mario asked.

"If it were a choice between the risk of nuclear strike and that stuff," Scheib said, "I'd take the nuke every time."

"Just how powerful is it?" Mario asked.

"What's the population of Rome?" Ponti said. "Just under three million, isn't it? Let's suppose it were five million—a nice round figure. The theoretical dose of botulism required to kill five million people is 3.23 times 10^{-4} grammes—that's three *ten thousandths* of a gramme. If you wanted to kill them by putting it in their water supply, you'd need more, of course, because the water would dilute the poison.

"That's why I propose to put sixty grammes into Rome's water supply."

45

"WE appear to have a choice," Wyman said to his students. "On the one hand, you can use Reductionism in an argument for a popular revolution. This is what Monica has done.

"On the other hand, you can use Reductionism as Enzo has done, in an argument for reducing suffering by peaceful, democratic means.

"Most people take Enzo's view. Monica isn't troubled by this, presumably because she feels that most people are deluded about what Democracy is."

The students listened keenly to Wyman's reply. All but one hoped that Wyman would somehow deliver the *coup de grâce* to Monica's argument.

"You will remember," Wyman went on, "that I said we should give minority views a further hearing. The argument here is not about what our ultimate aim should be. We said our general aim was to ensure that for all people, things went as well as possible. Nobody has disputed that.

"However, we *are* in disagreement about two other things: what causes suffering, and what we should do about it. Monica insists that 'Capitalism' is chiefly responsible for suffering. She will appeal to certain facts to back her view. Enzo will disagree, and he will point to other facts to support his own position.

"There are a couple of points I'd like to make to Monica, before we head for any sort of conclusion. Firstly, is it not true that there have been many cases where overthrowing Democracy increased suffering, but none where it reduced it?"

There was a long expectant silence as Monica pondered this remark.

"Yes," she admitted finally. "That's quite true. But I don't think it affects what I've said. Just because something never worked before, that doesn't prove it won't work in the future."

"So you accept that you have no historical evidence to support your case?"

"I suppose not," Monica said. "But that doesn't disprove my argument, does it?"

"No, it doesn't," Wyman agreed. "It

just makes it less plausible to the rest of us. I don't expect you're worried by that, though."

"I'm afraid not," Monica grinned.

"My second point is this; your argument is entirely justified on the grounds of its consequences. The reason you argue for violent revolution—terrorism, Enzo says—is because you think the violence and suffering are justified by the benefits we will ultimately enjoy. You defend violent actions by appealing to their happy consequences."

"That's right," Monica agreed.

"In that case," Wyman said, "you have an unusual argument. For most people to be persuaded by a moral argument, they normally require more than just an appeal to its consequences. They would want something else besides. They might also believe it is wrong to inflict great harm on anyone, even if this did reduce the overall suffering in the long run."

"If that's what most people believe," Monica said calmly, "then most people are wrong."

"But you may never be able to persuade those people with your argument."

"I don't really want to." Monica said. "I don't want to persuade everybody. It only needs a few people to believe what I say."

Suddenly Wyman remembered the words of Colonel Castellano: *You'll know about it if she ever becomes actively involved. The first sign will be a sudden reluctance to make fresh converts.*

"I see," Wyman nodded. "Does everyone follow this? It's most important. All of you disagree with Monica's theory, not because you can disprove it, but because you think it's implausible, and because you prefer an alternative theory.

"Monica is saying that just because it's implausible doesn't mean it's wrong. You might have persuaded yourselves that she's wrong, but you can't persuade *her* of that. She believes her own theory, and that's what matters to her. Presumably, she would now feel justified in committing the acts of violence she's described. Is that correct, Monica?"

"Perfectly correct," Monica said.

"Hold on," Paolo broke in. "She feels justified in putting her own views into practice. But we can also feel justified in acting out our convictions, and that means locking up people like Monica."

"Of course," Monica said quietly. "But that's not the point, is it? There are plenty of people in prison who got there by holding my view. That hasn't stopped others taking their place. You can't imprison an idea."

Wyman looked at Monica and smiled sadly.

"Thank you," he said.

"What for?"

"I've often wondered how it happens; how a perfectly intelligent person can reason their way into a position like yours. Now I know."

46

"COME in," Castellano said, as Soldani entered the office. "Take a seat."

The young officer sat down and noted the scowl on his chief's face. He had seen it before, and he knew it could mean two things: dyspepsia or displeasure.

There was a long silence, as the Colonel gazed out of his window.

"Is something the matter, sir?" Soldani finally ventured.

The Colonel ignored him and continued to look out of the window.

"It's funny how one gets used to certain things," he said at last. "There was a small crucifix on a wall in my home, and I'd never noticed it. The other day, I could have sworn something had changed in the house, but I didn't know what it was. I asked the wife, and she mentioned the crucifix. She broke it while she was cleaning, and it was put away. I was never aware of having the thing until it was gone. Odd, isn't it?"

"Yes," Soldani gasped. "Most peculiar."

He wondered if the Ponti business had finally taken its toll of his chief.

"The point I'm making," Castellano went on, "is that we often grow unconsciously accustomed to certain things. When they're changed, we get uncomfortable, and we don't know why. I've had this feeling for about two weeks now."

"Here or at home?" Soldani asked.

"Here, Soldani. Here. Something's been missing, and I've only just realized what it was."

"I'm glad to hear it, sir," Soldani said. "You must be feeling a lot better."

"Not really," Castellano said heavily. "In fact, I feel slightly worse."

Soldani frowned.

"I'm sorry, sir. You'll have to explain . . ."

"With pleasure," Castellano said courteously. "Remember October 31? Nineteen days ago. On that day, a certain cine camera in a certain street filmed certain people. One of them was called Monica

Venuti, and the other one was called Mario Pagani. Remember them?"

"Of course," Soldani said. "That was why we decided to tail Pagani."

"Exactly. We tailed Pagani. Or, more correctly, you tailed Pagani. He led you to Michele Rucci, and he in turn led you to the flat in the Trastevere. We had a shoot-out, and Rucci died. Pagani has vanished again. No more leads, no more terrorists. Isn't that right, Soldani?"

"Unfortunately, that's so," Soldani agreed.

"And we've tried everything, haven't we?"

"Of course," Soldani said, though he became increasingly uncomfortable.

Castellano moved away from the window and looked directly into Soldani's face.

"Oh no, we haven't," Castellano said. "We've forgotten something. That certain cine camera, remember?"

"Oh, God," Soldani breathed. He finally understood.

"What were your orders? Do you remember?"

"I had to change the film twice every day and get it processed."

Castellano nodded grimly.

"That's right. And you obeyed your orders scrupulously until October 31. What happened after that?"

"I forgot . . . I mean, I did replace the films, until four or five days later. After Rucci died, I stopped."

"Is that so?" Castellano said. "And why did you stop?"

"It seemed a waste of time," Soldani gasped. "I mean, the lead had dried up. There was no point in pursuing that, was there . . . ?"

"In other words," Castellano sighed, "you used your initiative. That was a foolish thing to do, Soldani. Very foolish."

He sat down behind his desk and lit a cigarette.

"Let's get this absolutely clear: after October 31, you didn't present me with any more stills, but you did continue to replace the films for another five days. Is that right?"

Soldani nodded miserably.

"What happened to these later films?"

"I gave them in to the processing

people," Soldani said. "They're around somewhere."

"And why didn't you give the stills to me?"

Soldani acquired a sudden fascination for his own shoelaces.

"I don't really know," he mumbled. "I suppose I forgot. It didn't seem terribly important at the time. We were chasing Pagani and Rucci, and that had nothing to do with the later films."

Castellano gazed at him incredulously.

"I suppose you never thought to ask for my opinion," he said. "After all, I'm just the man in charge around here."

Soldani shrugged and continued to scrutinize his shoelaces.

"Very well," Castellano said quietly. "Here are some new orders for you. Find those stills and bring them to me. If they're not on my desk within an hour, I'll tear your liver out. Can you understand that, or does it leave too much scope for personal initiative?"

"I—I understand," Soldani said, getting to his feet.

Castellano took a long hard look at Soldani and frowned.

“Tell me,” he said, “what made you join the Carabinieri?”

“I wanted to be a priest,” Soldani explained, “but they said I wasn’t smart enough, so I decided to do this instead. Is something the matter, sir?”

“No,” Castellano gasped. It was his turn to be at a loss for words. “No, that will be all.”

Soldani went out, leaving his chief to make frantic mental calculations about the cost of setting up a pleasant little restaurant in a quiet corner of the city.

47

A COUPLE of hours after the lecture ended, Monica returned to her flat. The time had come to do the "little task" Ponti had promised her. He had briefed her carefully, and she now realized that his casual demeanour cloaked a scrupulous passion for detail.

Bring nothing with you, he had said. *You're leaving for good, but they mustn't be sure of that. Leave your passport behind—that will confuse them. Don't even bring your toothbrush. Keep them guessing*. Monica felt a twinge of sadness as she gazed at her room. She would miss her books most of all.

She put her lecture notes into a desk drawer and left the flat. Ponti wasn't certain they would raid the place, but it seemed likely. She stepped out into the street and paused before walking off. Her instructions gave Monica a new awareness, and it did not make her feel more comfortable. Nothing had really changed in the

Via della Vetrina: the old Piaggio van was still parked there, and the usual motorcycles slouched casually against the wall. There was also a saloon car Monica had not seen before, a white Lancia, but it was empty and harmless. Nevertheless, she felt glad to be leaving. She walked away quickly towards the river.

A few minutes later she reached the Piazza Augusto Imperatore. She stood at a bus stop on the south side. Across the road was a shiny modern building which housed the *Ara Pacis Augustae*, the monumental altar built by Augustus to lend holiness to his dictatorship.

As Monica glanced at the entrance to the building, a car drove past her and stopped at the far end of the square. With a slight thrill, she realized it was the white Lancia she'd seen outside her flat.

Or at least, she thought it was the same car. Lancias are as common in Rome as Renaults in Paris. She cursed her own nervousness, but cursed herself again for failing to note the number of the car. Well, next time she would have no doubt: it was a Rome number plate with the numbers 29666H.

"What if I'm followed?" she had asked Ponti. *Expect it*, was the reply. *But don't worry, they can't touch you. You're doing nothing wrong, so just behave normally*.

A couple of minutes later her bus arrived, a 913 heading over the Tiber and north-east. She got on and fed her ticket into the machine. The Lancia was still there, and it remained stationary as the bus moved off. She sighed with relief, and felt slightly ashamed of her apprehension.

The bus drove over the river and through the Piazza Cavour, past the Castel Sant'Angelo. As usual, the roads were jammed by frenzied motorists. The bus got as far as the Piazza del Risorgimento and stopped. There was a thirty-second pause as more passengers got on. An aged jaywalker brought the line of traffic to a halt by hobbling through the maelstrom of hooting cars.

Monica glanced to her left and saw the walls of the Vatican, with the dome of St. Peter's a quarter of a mile to the south. She turned around in her seat and looked down on the traffic behind her.

Her bus lurched forward again, and her eyes fell on one of the drivers, a young man with slicked-back hair and a pair of reflecting sunglasses. He was driving a white Lancia, registration number 29666H.

Just behave normally. And how do I do that, Monica thought, when I'm feeling anything but normal? The bus swung up into the Via Leone IV and took a sharp left on to the Via Andrea Doria. The Lancia was out of sight, but was it gone?

The answer was no. The bus turned into the Viale delle Medaglie d'Oro, a long tree-lined road surrounded by shops and hotels. The Lancia was now a hundred yards behind her, still following on. As the bus drove north, the shops gave way to apartment blocks and private houses. The gap with the Lancia widened. After a few minutes, the bus turned on to the Via Trionfale, and the Lancia was out of sight once more.

She was now in Monte Mario, a pleasant suburb of Rome, and it was time to get off. She left the bus and looked back down the road. The Lancia had not yet caught up with her, so she crossed over to a garage on the corner of the Via della Pineta Sacchetti. This is a long steep road which curls back down into the western outskirts of the city. She walked down it for about thirty yards, and stopped.

Behind a tall grey fence stood a gleaming white building, one storey high and sixty feet wide. Adjoining the rear of the building was a taller, flat-roofed construction which resembled a school gymnasium. A bronze plaque explained that this was the Pineta Sacchetti water purification station, belonging to the ACEA, Rome's water board.

She drew a small automatic camera from her handbag and followed Ponti's instructions. The building is too wide to fit in one shot, so take several: start at the left of the building and work across. When you've done that, take a few shots of the perimeter. What sort of fencing has it got? Is there barbed wire at the top? Is there a gap anywhere? We need to know.

She took a series of photographs and walked away from the entrance. *Don't look around you, and if anyone calls out, say nothing. Walk a little further down the road; on your right is a small street called the Via Pestalozzi. Go into it and turn right again. This takes you to the back of the waterworks complex.*

Ponti's directions were faultless. Behind another iron gate stood the rear of the flat-roofed "gymnasium". It was faced in blue-painted metal, and a row of large white cylinders led out of it. Look out for the row of drums; they're the horizontal pressure filters for the water supply. Keep photographing until the film runs out. Walk back the way you came, on to the Via Trionfale. You can go back by bus or train—it's up to you.

She took her last photograph and turned round. A man walked away from her, in the direction she had come from. Had he been watching her? She hesitated, then decided to catch him up. He walked up the Via della Pineta Sacchetti with long strides—not a casual walk, Monica thought. If only he'd turn round, and I could see his face . . .

She kept about ten yards behind him until he reached the top of the hill and the Via Trionfale. He turned the left corner, and Monica quickened her pace. She arrived at the turning and stopped. In front of her was the garage she had passed on the way to the waterworks. There was no one in sight.

Someone started a car engine and drove out of the car park. Monica caught a glimpse of his face as he left the garage and drove back towards central Rome. He wore reflecting sunglasses and drove a white Lancia, registration number 29666H.

48

"HE'S still not in," Wyman said, as he put the phone down.

Margaret Wyman put a cup of espresso beside her husband, and sat down opposite him.

"Who isn't?" she said.

"Colonel Castellano," Wyman said. "I've been trying to speak to him for the last hour, but nobody can find him. He's got to find Monica—arrest her if necessary."

"What's happened?" Margaret said.

"Nothing—yet."

"I don't understand."

"She's become active," Wyman said. "I'm sure of it. Until now, we had no reason to believe that Monica was anything more than a member of the Red Brigades Appreciation Society. This morning she changed my mind."

"What did she do?"

"Nothing. She stopped proselytizing,

and withdrew. If you don't agree with her, too bad: that was her message today."

"I thought Monica was anxious to make new converts," Margaret said.

"She was," Wyman said, "but that's finished, and I know what it means. If only I could get hold of Castellano."

"Would that do any good?" Margaret said quietly.

Wyman blinked curiously at his wife.

"What does that mean?" he asked.

"Michael, has it occurred to you that Colonel Castellano is a complete incompetent? That poor American was abducted in September, and he's still nowhere near finding him. The Colonel doesn't even know what Franco Ponti looks like, much less where he's operating from."

"I'm quite aware of the Colonel's limitations," Wyman sighed. "As far as he's concerned, the issue is simple: an American was kidnapped, and other Americans have been killed. The kidnappers made an impossible demand, so their hostage is probably dead. That's why this investigation has been maddeningly slow."

"But you don't agree?"

"Of course not," Wyman said. "If

Scheib had been killed, his body would have reappeared by now. In fact, our terrorists have behaved oddly from the very beginning. Their public response to the CIA investigation has been strangely muted. One of their number was killed, and nothing was done about it. There wasn't even a statement. Why not?

"There can only be one explanation: the kidnapping is leading up to something, and rather than risk having his plot revealed, Ponti is maintaining absolute secrecy. Unfortunately the Colonel doesn't agree with me."

"Why on earth not?" Margaret asked. "After all, he's got plenty of experience with terrorists."

"Because he doesn't want to agree," Wyman said. "It's easier to take his line: it involves less work. If you regard the kidnapping and the killing of the CIA men as finished episodes, you are left with a straightforward objective: find Ponti. The urgency of that task is dictated by how much of a nuisance Ponti makes of himself. Ponti's column is very quiet at present, *ergo* there is no rush."

"But that's dreadful," Margaret

exclaimed. "Ponti is a wanted criminal: if he has killed Professor Scheib, that's all the more reason for finding him."

"The Colonel is thinking in terms of practicality, not justice," Wyman said. "In his own slow-moving way, the Colonel is a very rational creature. After all, no Italians have been killed have they? Except, of course, for Rucci, and he was one of the forces of evil."

Margaret frowned.

"I still think it's dreadful," she said. "And you don't agree with him either."

"True," Wyman admitted. "But for different reasons. I'm positive Scheib is still alive and, unlike the Colonel, I believe that Ponti's silence is designed to feed our complacency. As for Monica, I think—"

The phone rang, and Wyman answered it.

"Hello?"

"Professor Wyman? It's Castellano speaking."

"Thank heavens you phoned," Wyman exclaimed. "Colonel, you must take Monica in for questioning. I'm now sure that—"

"We have a warrant out for her arrest,"

Castellano said. "You know where she lives, don't you?"

"The Via della Vetrina," Wyman said. "But I'm not sure—"

"Number six, second floor. That's where I am now. Perhaps you'd like to get over here."

"What's happened?"

"A great deal. I suggest you come and see for yourself."

"I understand," Wyman said. "I'll be along in about fifteen minutes."

"Excellent," Castellano said, and hung up.

Wyman replaced the receiver and gave his wife a wry smile.

"I wonder if we haven't done the Colonel an injustice," he said.

49

"IF there's a patron saint of terrorists," Castellano remarked, "I hate to think how many candles Ponti has put before his altar."

Monica's armchair sagged beneath his unusual bulk, as he exhaled large quantities of cigarette smoke and gloom. Uniformed Carabinieri were searching the flat, examining the stairway and questioning Monica's neighbours. Outside the building, armed policemen slouched casually against their cars. The Via della Vetrina was suffering from an overdose of law and order.

"What's happened?" Wyman asked.

"Just about everything," Castellano said wearily. "And we've missed it. When did you last see her?"

"This morning," Wyman said. "She attended my lecture: that's why I was trying to call you. Her tone changed quite markedly . . . What has she done?"

Castellano ignored the question and drew some photographs from his pocket.

"Remember the camera we put outside this flat? After Rucci died, that imbecile Soldani remembered to reload the films for a couple of days, but he neglected to have them processed. After that he forgot them altogether.

"I remembered the camera this morning. The first thing I did was to put one of my men in a car outside this flat. I then called Soldani, tore a strip off him, and got the last films processed.

"While we were waiting for those stills, Monica returned from your lecture. She went away again almost immediately, and our man followed her. She went by bus to Monte Mario and took some photographs of the waterworks there."

"I beg your pardon?" Wyman said.

"The Rome waterworks is on Monte Mario," Castellano explained, "on the Via della Pineta Sacchetti. Apparently she went up to the front and rear entrances and took photographs of it."

"So what did your man do?"

"That's the tragedy of it," Castellano said. "There's no law against taking snapshots of public utilities. He couldn't arrest her, and my orders were simply to watch Monica's flat, so he decided to report back to me.

"Of course, this was before our films were processed. If I'd known about those, I'd have told him to stay with her at all costs. That idiot Soldani: in more civilized times he would have been drowned at birth."

He gave the photographs to Wyman.

"They're in order," he said. "The first one was taken on November 5 at 5 p.m. Remember those men? In case you've never seen a door lock being picked, that's how it's done."

"Of course," Wyman said. "That's Jones A. and Jones P."

"Keep going," Castellano said. "The next one shows Monica returning home at 5.30. The one after that was taken twenty minutes later."

"Monica's landlord," Wyman said. "What's his name again?"

"Gennaro. After he went in, nobody else appeared until 7.05. That's the next photograph. The man going in is Vito Maresca, Ponti's closest associate. You can see the bumper of his car in the corner of the photograph. At least, I think it's a car. One of the boys thinks it's a van, which is more likely under the circumstances."

Wyman moved on to the next picture.

"My word," he exclaimed. "What's going on here? Those crates look familiar."

"They ought to," Castellano said. "They're the ones we found at Rucci's flat. Note that Gennaro is helping Maresca carry them out. Do you notice anything strange about him?"

Wyman removed his glasses and stared carefully at the photograph.

"He appears to have changed somehow," he muttered, and he compared it with the earlier photo of the landlord. "His face is different—it's longer and thinner. He looks younger as well. Most peculiar."

"Let me offer you an explanation for all this," Castellano said. "At five o'clock Jones A. and Jones P. broke into the flat, expecting to surprise Monica when she returned. Half an hour later, the girl appeared. We can only guess at what they did, but I suspect they were only at the threatening stage when salvation arrived in the form of Monica's landlord.

"The forensic evidence tells us what happened next; Gennaro took the CIA men by surprise and shot them from a range of a few feet. Of course, there were now a couple of bodies to dispose of, so he phoned for help. At five past seven, Maresca arrived, and they took the Jones men out in these packing cases."

"It would make sense," Wyman nodded. "And it would also explain the conundrum about Michele Rucci's flat. We now know where those arms really belonged, and why they had to be moved. But I'm still baffled by this landlord of Monica's.

"When Gennaro appeared in the first photographs, you told me he was senile and deaf. Are we to take it that this old man is a member of Ponti's column?"

Castellano smiled sourly.

"Yes," he said. "But I think you've missed the point."

He produced another photograph and showed it to Wyman.

"This one is about eighteen years old. Compare it with Gennaro."

Wyman held the photographs together.

"It's odd. In the first photo he bears little resemblance to the old picture, but in the second you can see Gennaro is the same man—good God, he's Franco Ponti!"

Castellano nodded gloomily.

"In all these years, we never dreamed he was anything more than just an old idiot."

"But how did he do it?" Wyman said disbelievingly. "He seems to be able to add twenty years to his age at will."

"It's easy," Castellano said. "All you need is a set of dentures. With no teeth in your mouth, you look much older. If you also dye your hair white, nobody will believe your real age."

"I see," Wyman said. "And so this is the man we're looking for. Well, at least we know what he looks like."

Castellano lit another cigarette and shrugged.

"It helps," he agreed. "And I've got a team of people contacting every manufacturer and supplier of dentures in Italy. It might work."

"What about Monica?"

"She hasn't come back from this

morning's outing," Castellano said. "And I have a feeling she's not coming back here."

"Why not?"

"Just a suspicion. She's taken nothing with her—even her passport's still here. But that may just be to confuse us. After all, if she's gone underground, she won't need any of these things."

"I wondered what had happened," Wyman said. "She was so laconic this morning, as if the work didn't really matter any more. Now we know."

"The talking's stopped," Castellano said. "Monica has joined the doers. I don't know why she took these photographs this morning, but I'm taking no chances. I've posted four of my men on permanent guard at the waterworks, and Monica is now a wanted person."

Wyman looked around Monica's room and sighed.

"What a terrible waste," he said quietly.

50

"WHAT time is it?" Monica asked.

"Half-past twelve," Pedro said. "I think everyone's gone to sleep."

"Franco's awake," she said. "He's still messing around in his laboratory. You know, he reminds me of the mad professors in those old films."

She giggled at the mental image she had conjured, and Pedro put his arm round her.

"So," he said. "You've finally got what you wanted. You've gone underground. Do you like it?"

"Yes," Monica said uneasily. "But . . ."

"Second thoughts?"

"Not at all," she said quickly. "I'm just trying to get used to not being a student any more. It's very strange."

"Did your studies mean that much to you?"

"Yes," she said. "I'm convinced I made

some sort of breakthrough. With a little more time . . ."

Her voice trailed off as Ponti entered the room. He carried a tray, which bore a flask of water and three glasses.

"Hello, Franco," Monica said.

"Good evening," Ponti said smoothly. "Would you like to join me for a nightcap?"

"It looks like water," Pedro said.

"It is," Ponti said. "Good, clean tap water. I thought it would be appropriate, under the circumstances. This could be one of your last opportunities to taste ordinary Roman water for many years. Forever, perhaps."

He filled the glasses and gave one each to Monica and Pedro.

"I posted a letter to the Carabinieri today," he said, as he sat down. "And I sent copies to a couple of newspapers. They should arrive tomorrow, or the day after."

"What did it say?" Pedro asked.

"It's our final ultimatum. If they don't release all our colleagues from prison, we'll destroy Rome's entire supply of drinking water. It's neat, precise and unambiguous. I was rather proud of it."

"They won't let anyone out of gaol," Monica said.

"Of course not," Ponti laughed. "And I'd be disappointed if they did."

"Can it be done?" Pedro asked. "Can you really poison all of Rome's water?"

"Easily," Ponti said.

"What's going to happen when you've done it?" Monica said.

"There'll be panic," Ponti said genially. "Complete hysteria. They'll flee from Rome in their thousands. No one will have the faintest idea how to handle the crisis. Who knows? There might even be a spot of rioting."

"And that's the aim?"

"Of course, I got this idea years ago, but Curcio always vetoed it. I had to wait for all the old leadership to be imprisoned before I could start work."

He put his glass down and lit a cigarette.

"They were so myopic," he sighed. "We wasted so many years with small operations, because everyone thought in terms of barricades and bullets. And where did it get them? The best thing we ever did was kill Aldo Moro, but that wasn't enough. There should have been a hundred Aldo Moros, and they should all have died at once."

"Think big," Pedro grinned.

"Definitely," Ponti agreed. "We're supposed to be the pioneers, the people who set the example and lead the rest. That's why I've always argued for the big strike, but everyone else was too scared.

"You see, the faith people have in their governments—even bad governments—largely rests on their belief that governments somehow protect them. It's an evil lie, of course, but I'm amazed by how many people believe it. They have to be shown the State isn't nearly as powerful as they assume.

"That's the beauty of this plan: in one stroke we can undermine popular faith in the leadership, and show just how weak the State really is. Any imbecile can then draw the right conclusion: that the leaders can be overthrown easily."

"Some people will be killed, of course," Pedro said. "How many, do you think?"

Ponti shrugged.

"It depends on the authorities. In

theory, nobody should die. Given the massive incompetence of our leaders, hundreds might be poisoned."

"Can you be sure things will go the way you want?" Monica asked.

"Definitely," Ponti said. "After all, if governments can't even be trusted to supply a basic necessity like safe water, then the very notion of government becomes questionable, doesn't it?"

He raised his glass in a mock toast.

"Cheers," he said.

51

THE Ministry of Defence is an ornate, chocolate-brown palace on the Via Venti Settembre. On the morning of November 20, Wyman's taxi stopped outside its main archway, and a bored sentry examined his papers. He was shown up to a conference room on the fourth floor.

Beneath a dense cloud of tobacco smoke, about twenty people were seated around a massive marble table. Castellano stood up to greet Wyman.

"Professor, thank you for coming. Let me introduce the others. This is Commissioner D'Amico of the police; Doctor Virno of the ACEA; Signor Leone from the City Hall. The other gentlemen represent the various ministries affected by this threat."

He quickly introduced the civil servants, as Wyman took his place at the table.

"Professor Wyman works at the university," Castellano explained. "He has helped with our investigations for some time. One of his students is on our list of suspects, and he has special knowledge of the circumstances of this case."

The Colonel opened his file and drew out the ultimatum from Ponti.

"Let me remind you of the threat: 'Our original demand for the release of our comrades was ignored. We repeat that demand, with this added threat: if our colleagues are not released within seventy-two hours, we will destroy Rome's supply of drinking water.' He then lists the colleagues he wants freed; it's the same list we received when the American was kidnapped.

"We must first consider how seriously we should regard this threat. We have some knowledge of Ponti, and I believe such a plan is entirely in character. There is no question of releasing the prisoners, so I would recommend that we take this ultimatum at its face value. Does anyone disagree?"

The others shook their heads.

"Very well," Castellano said. "In that case we must establish what Ponti intends to do. If Dr. Virno would explain how our water supply reaches Rome, we night get an idea of how Ponti could tamper with it."

He sat down again, and Dr. Virno got to his feet. He was a frail man in his mid-thirties, with a nervous expression that was entirely forgivable under the circumstances.

"In a way, we are quite fortunate," Virno began. "This man tells us he will wreck our supply of drinking water. Rome's water comes in from a number of sources, and if he doesn't specify which supply he's after, we'd have to worry about them all.

"In fact, domestic water only comes in from one source; this is what Ponti means by the term 'drinking water'. It's sent to all houses, hotels and offices, and every domestic tap pours water from this source. The other sources supply water for industrial purposes, so we can discount those.

"As I say, drinking water comes from one place: Lake Bracciano. The lake occupies the crater of an extinct volcano, and it's fed by underground streams from its surrounding hills. The water is sent directly to Rome by subterranean pipes.

"When the water arrives at the city, it's purified at the Pineta Sacchetti waterworks on Monte Mario. We filter it, check the pH level, and send it directly to the city's buildings."

He sat down.

"Thank you," Castellano said. "I take it there are only two places where Ponti can damage the supply—Lake Bracciano and Monte Mario."

"That's right," Virno agreed. "Otherwise, he'd have to go for the main supply pipes. They're buried very deep, and it would be virtually impossible for a small group of people to get at them."

"I understand," Castellano said. "So this prompts two questions: which of the locations will they choose, and how will they try to affect the supply?"

"We can rule out Bracciano," Virno said. "It's too big, and the pipes are too inaccessible at that point. The inflow pipes are sunk about 100 metres below the surface of the lake. Unless this Ponti is an expert diver—"

"He's not," Castellano broke in. "So we'll assume he's going for the waterworks on Monte Mario. We have evidence to support this; one of Ponti's protégés was seen taking photographs of the waterworks two days ago.

"I believe Ponti intends to destroy the waterworks using explosives. I already have men guarding the building, and I hope to extend the security arrangements there. I'd be grateful if the police could help us in this: I'd like to divert the traffic from the surrounding roads and set up a series of checkpoints."

Commissioner D'Amico nodded gravely.

"That should be no problem," he said.

"Why do you think Ponti's going to use explosives?" Wyman asked.

"I can't see any other way," Castellano said. "The building will be completely isolated, and Ponti must expect that. I believe he plans to bombard it from a distance.

"For example, he might have got his hands on a portable rocket launcher. The RPG-7 has a maximum range of about half a kilometre. But if he wanted to launch an accurate full-scale attack, he'd have to come much closer.

"There's also the possibility of an aerial assault, in which something is dropped from a light aircraft. We're keeping an eye on all the airports, including private airfields."

One of the civil servants looked up in astonishment.

"Could he really do all this?"

"It's all happened before," Castellano said. "Either here or elsewhere in Europe. I'm simply going by the precedents that Ponti's friends have set over the past fifteen years. If you want case histories, I'll be happy to let you have them . . ."

"No thank you," the civil servant replied hastily. "I'm sure you're right."

"Let's ignore the precedents for a moment," Wyman suggested. "Have you thought about the possibility of Ponti trying to poison the water?"

"I have," Castellano said. "Ponti's worked as a biochemist, so it's a genuine possibility. But to use poison, he'd have to get into the waterworks itself. How would he do that?"

"What about the lake?" Wyman said. "Why doesn't he just throw poison into Bracciano?"

Dr. Virno found this idea quite amusing.

"Professor, have you ever been to Bracciano? It's huge: over nine kilometres across at its widest point, and 160 metres deep. It contains many millions of litres of water. Anything you dumped into the lake would simply disperse. To ensure the water was contaminated, you'd need to bring poison in several truckloads."

"But suppose he did," Wyman persisted.

"We'd catch him first," Castellano said. "There's an airfield at Vigna di Valle, on the lower shore of Bracciano, and the area's constantly patrolled from there. If the operation were that large, it would be clearly visible from above."

"Besides," Virno added, "we'd spot most poisons at the water station. Our machines keep a permanent watch on the pH level—that's the ratio of acids and alkali in the water. So if he threw in a strong acid, for example, we'd know about it long before it could harm anyone.

"But even if he threw in a barrel of hydrochloric acid, it would still dilute to the point of harmlessness. The sheer quantity of water would always defeat him."

"What about mercury, or something radioactive?" Wyman asked.

"Those would also show up at the waterworks," Vimo said. "It's impossible: Ponti would need a poison that had a harmless pH level, one that couldn't be filtered out of water, and one that is so strong he could poison all of Lake Bracciano with so tiny a quantity that no one would notice him doing it. There's no such thing."

"I think that answers your question, Professor," Castellano said. "We will assume that Ponti is aiming for the waterworks on Monte Mario, and we'll expect some kind of explosive attack.

"I have prepared a draft plan for your attention, with some ideas for safeguarding the site. Perhaps we can now discuss those."

52

"AND that's it," Ponti said. "You'll now appreciate my desire for absolute secrecy over the last few months. It's not a complicated plan, but the simplest schemes are prone to the simplest error, and I couldn't take any risks."

He put out his cigarette and looked inquiringly at his accomplices.

"I'll run through it again quickly, just to make sure. Vito will leave tonight with the van, and he'll take the bulk of our weapons to the farm house in Piedmont. We will stay here, and for the next three days we'll do nothing—absolutely nothing.

"On Sunday, the rest of us will leave. In the morning, Monica and I will take Professor Scheib in the Fiat, and we'll dump the poison. In the afternoon, Mario and Pedro will take the rest of the arms north in the Lancia. We'll meet on Sunday night in Piedmont. Are there any questions?"

"When will we cross the border?" Mario asked.

"A day or two later. You, Monica and Pedro still need false papers. With luck, Vito will have got hold of them by the time we join him. Is something wrong, Monica?"

"Are you sure it will work?" she asked. "It all sounds so . . . straightforward."

"It is straightforward," Ponti said. "That's precisely why it's going to work."

"But . . . are you sure the poison is strong enough to take effect? There's so little of it."

"You heard Professor Scheib," Ponti smiled. "It's the most poisonous substance known to man. Thanks to our politicians and the advertising industry, superlatives don't mean much any more. But that's what our poison is."

He picked up a newspaper and smiled at the front page.

"Complacent cretins," he said cheerfully. "They've put half the army around the Monte Mario waterworks, and they're saying there's no cause for alarm. They've got no idea: nothing can stop that toxin once it's in the water."

"Is there no cure?" Monica asked.

"You can inoculate against it," Ponti said. "Our friend Scheib used to manufacture anti-toxins for just that purpose. But that's only a preventative measure. Otherwise, once you've taken botulism into your system nothing can cure you."

"So it's indestructible?"

"Of course not," Ponti said impatiently. "The toxin is a protein, so it's relatively fragile. It won't survive boiling or extreme cold. But how do you boil millions of gallons of water? Or freeze them, for that matter?"

"What about the waterworks? Won't they do something there?"

"No," Ponti said emphatically. "A waterworks can only filter water and maintain the right pH level. You can't filter out botulism. You *could* destroy it by radically changing the ratio of acids and alkali, but doing so would still leave the water undrinkable."

"But that isn't your real worry, is it Monica? I think you're suffering from a twinge of conscience; a vague concern about 'innocent victims'. Isn't that so?"

Monica shrugged.

"I thought so," Ponti said. "I suspected our friend Wyman might have infected you with his liberal opinions. Interesting fellow, Professor Wyman. I was so taken with him that I had Vito make some inquiries."

"Yes," Vito said. "I had a word with our contact at the Russian embassy. I bet you didn't know that Wyman used to work for MI6."

"Who's that?" Mario asked.

"British Intelligence," Vito said. "He was once stationed in their Rome office. I'm told he has a lot of friends in the security business. Castellano, for example."

"A colonel in the Carabinieri," Ponti explained. "The man in charge of the Scheib investigation. Wyman's been using you, Monica."

"Wyman knows nothing," Monica said loudly. "He can't . . ."

"You think so?" Ponti said calmly. "He knows you're with us. I wonder what else he found out."

Monica fell into stunned silence.

"Never mind," Ponti said. "We'll just

have to repay him for his interest. Pedro, I'm sure you'd like to help us here."

"What do you have in mind?" Pedro asked.

"On Sunday, you can make a small detour. Load up the car, as planned. But instead of leaving Rome at once, you and Mario can pay a quick visit to Professor Wyman."

"Sure," Pedro said.

"Put a silencer on your gun," Ponti advised. "This had better be an informal execution. After that, leave Rome immediately."

Pedro nodded calmly.

"No problem," he said.

53

THE sentry examined Castellano's papers. Not surprisingly, they were in order. He waved the car through, and the Colonel drove down to the waterworks.

He parked outside the main gates and got out of his car. Under the circumstances, Castellano had thought it best to wear his uniform. He was already regretting the decision: the trousers bit mercilessly into his plentiful gut, and the jacket felt at least three sizes too small.

Soldani spotted the arrival of his chief, and strolled up to greet him.

"Good evening, sir."

"Hello Soldani," Castellano said. "How's it going?"

"Fine," Soldani said. "Everyone's in place. As you can see, we've blocked off the Via Aurelia and the lower end of the Pineta Sacchetti. The traffic police say they're having no problem in diverting motorists."

"That's because it's late evening," Castellano grunted. "Wait till tomorrow. It'll be chaos then. What about the local residents?"

"They're taking it very well. We've checked every building and given them all special passes. We found nothing unusual."

"Good," Castellano said.

He looked around him with some satisfaction. The area was deluged by police activity. Blue Carabinieri vans were parked beside white police cars. Patrols of armed policemen calmly examined the streets, checking every parked vehicle and questioning pedestrians.

Castellano jerked his thumb at the waterworks.

"What's happening in there?"

"We've vetted all the staff," Soldani said. "They're all OK, but we're still searching them as they enter the building."

The Colonel nodded in approval.

"Ponti gave us seventy-two hours, but he didn't specify when the clock was supposed to start. I'm assuming that the deadline falls three days after he posted the letter—that'll be Saturday the 23rd."

"Two days from now."

"Right. From tomorrow morning I'll have the area patrolled regularly by helicopter."

"The residents won't be pleased."

The Colonel shrugged.

"It's better than dying of thirst," he said.

Soldani frowned.

"I don't understand it, sir," he said. "This area's like Fort Knox. How can Ponti expect to get inside that building?"

Castellano lit a cigarette.

"Christ knows, Soldani," he said. "How do you get inside the mind of a lunatic? I'm a soldier, not a psychiatrist."

He blew out a long stream of smoke and tossed his spent match on to the pavement.

54

"WHAT'S the matter?" Pedro asked softly.

"Nothing," Monica said.

"In that case, why are you still awake?"

He turned and put his arm around her.

"You're worried about something," he said. "Tell me."

Monica shook her head, and Pedro put the light on. "Why are you crying?"

"I'm not," Monica said stubbornly.

He drew his hand gently across her face, and held it before her. She could see a single teardrop glisten on his finger.

"In that case, what do you call this?" Pedro smiled.

Monica shrugged.

"All right, so I'm crying. I don't know why."

"Tell me," Pedro repeated.

"I don't understand," she muttered. "What did he mean . . . ?"

"Who are you talking about?"

"Professor Wyman. The last thing he

said to me was 'I've often wondered how a perfectly intelligent person could reason their way into a position like yours; now I know.' What does that mean, Pedro?"

"What it says," Pedro replied. "He thinks you have to be stupid or crazy to think the way you do."

"No," Monica said. "He wasn't being sarcastic. He even thanked me for it."

Pedro grinned.

"Forget about it," he said. "After tomorrow, Wyman won't be a problem for anyone."

"You'll really do it?" Monica asked.

"Of course," Pedro said calmly. "He's working with the police, isn't he?"

Monica frowned in confusion.

"Can it really be that simple?" she said. "Wyman's a cop—cops are the enemy—we kill all cops—let's kill Wyman. Is it really that simple?"

"Of course it is," Pedro laughed. "Why are you looking for complications?"

"I don't know . . ."

"Well let me tell you. You trusted Wyman. You thought he was all right. Now he's betrayed you, and you don't want to believe it. That's why you're worrying."

"Is that it?" Monica said. "That also sounds too simple."

"You're hesitating," Pedro observed. "You should never do that."

"'He who hesitates is lost'," Monica quoted. "So I'm lost. Help me."

She buried her face in Pedro's arms and sobbed gently. For a long while, silence reigned in their room.

"It's half-past four," Pedro said at last. "You should try to get some sleep. You're leaving early tomorrow, remember?"

Monica said nothing. Pedro slowly lifted her head away from his chest. She had cried herself to sleep. He put Monica back on her own side of the bed, and looked calmly at her face. It was some time before he put the light out again.

55

THE village of Bracciano lies nearly forty kilometres northwest of Rome. It spreads across a hill almost half way up the western shore of the lake which bears its name. Its most famous attraction is the Castle of the Orsini, a colossal structure built in the latter half of the fifteenth century, whose ivy-covered towers are clearly seen from the opposite shore, over eight kilometres away. In the summer, tourists descend on Bracciano in their hundreds. In late November, however, it is virtually deserted.

Early on Sunday morning, Franco Ponti took Monica and Professor Scheib up to the lake in his yellow Fiat. He handcuffed Scheib to the front passenger seat, and asked Monica to keep an eye on him from the back. If the American was pleased to leave his prison, he kept the fact well hidden. Scheib gazed morosely ahead of him and ignored Ponti's cheerful conversation.

They drove through the village and went down the series of hairpin bends leading to the shore of the lake. It was a sunny morning, and the pure blue water threw back sharp, clean reflections of the surrounding hills. There was no one in sight. Ponti parked the car by a small jetty, where a collection of boats bobbed languidly at their moorings. He opened the glove compartment and took out a gun, which he gave to Monica.

"I'll be back in a minute," Ponti said to Scheib. "If you make a sound, Monica will kill you. Understand?"

Scheib nodded miserably and said nothing. Ponti got out of the car and opened the boot. He drew out a canvas grip, shut the boot, and strolled over to a nearby house.

A man appeared at the door, and they chatted for a few minutes. They walked over to the jetty, and Ponti was shown a powerful four-seater speedboat. He nodded, and gave some money to the other man, who gave him the keys to the boat.

The owner returned to his home, and Ponti went back to the car.

"All in order," he said brightly. "Let's go for a spin, shall we?"

He unlocked Scheib's handcuffs and took the gun back from Monica.

"The warning still stands," he said. "Make any noise and you'll be shot. And don't think about escaping."

They went over to the jetty and took their places in the boat. This time, Scheib sat with Monica in the back, and the canvas grip was tied to the seat beside Ponti. The engine roared into life, and Ponti guided the boat out towards the centre of the lake.

When they had moved out half a kilometre, Ponti turned the boat to starboard, and headed in a south-easterly direction. After about fifteen minutes, they were a kilometre away from the lower shore. Ponti slowed the boat down and switched off the engine.

"What a lovely morning," he declared. "The village over there is called Anguillara-Sabazia. You'll find a charming mediaeval palace there, if you ever pass through. Unfortunately, we don't have time to see it today."

He opened the grip and took out some surgical masks and gloves.

"There's not much breeze," he said, "but we don't want to take any silly risks, do we?"

When they had taken this precaution, Ponti took out the sealed flask of toxic crystal.

"Take it," he said to Monica. "Don't worry, it's quite safe while it's sealed."

With a little apprehension, Monica took the flask from Ponti's hands.

"Watch carefully, Professor," Ponti said, "and don't try anything. Now, Monica, unscrew the lid and hold the flask over the side. It won't spill until you tip it."

"Must I?" Monica said. "Why don't you?"

"You answer your own question by hesitating," Ponti said. "The others would think it a privilege."

Monica nodded and removed the lid from the flask. She stretched her arm out, so the flask was held a couple of feet above the surface of the water."

"Don't do it, kid," Scheib murmured.

"Be quiet," Ponti snapped. "Tilt the

flask, Monica—gently, so it doesn't splash too hard."

Monica looked first at Ponti, and then at the imploring expression on Scheib's face. She tilted the flask, and watched the amber dollops of poison plop into the water.

"Now throw away the flask," Ponti commanded.

Monica hurled away the container with all her strength, and slumped back in her seat.

"Well done," Ponti smiled. "The inflow pipes begin about a hundred metres below us. The toxin dissolves quite easily, but I'll help it on its way by churning up the water. On full throttle, this boat should disrupt the water nicely."

He turned to Scheib.

"Perhaps you now understand your part in all this," he said.

"All I understand," Scheib said wearily, "is that you are a homicidal lunatic. I guess this is where you kill me."

"Quite the opposite," Ponti grinned. "We are going back to Bracciano. When we return to the car, I will blindfold you so you won't know where we're heading.

Tonight I will release you. You'll be free to go."

Scheib frowned, and then his eyes widened as the answer hit him.

"Of course," he exclaimed. "I'm the perfect witness!"

"Precisely," Ponti said. "After all, I could send the police a detailed account of what I've done, explaining how I made the poison. Why should I bother? You've seen the procedure, you examined the bacteria, and you're acquainted with the toxin. They might not take my word for what I've done, but they'll have to believe you."

"And that's why you kidnapped me?" Scheib said.

"Exactly."

"The only reason?"

"Why else? Of course, I'm not going to let you go until I'm sure the water reaches Rome. It travels at about one metre per second, so in twelve hours it will be through the waterworks and into the system. At that point I'll release you. I suggest you get in touch with a gentleman called Castellano; he's a colonel in the Carabinieri, and he'll be delighted to hear from you."

Ponti turned on the engine, and the boat moved away, accelerating swiftly. He swung it round and opened the throttle, shattering the stillness of the lake. For about fifteen minutes the boat whirled round in ever-widening circles, until the entire stretch of water was white with foam. Having satisfied himself that he could do no more, Ponti resumed a direct course for Bracciano.

56

LATE on Sunday afternoon, Wyman sat at home ploughing through the last of Professor Scheib's published work. It was a depressing task, made all the more wearisome by his mounting conviction that he was too late.

The publications did not boast the most stimulating titles: "The Journal of Bacteriology", "The Journal of Biological Chemistry", "Proceedings of the Society for Experimental Biology", and so on. Scheib's essays were equally uninviting. Wyman's next task was to read something called "A Revised Procedure for the Isolation of Type A Clostridium Botulinum Toxin".

Wyman had no idea what the difference was between Type A Clostridium Botulinum toxin and any other type. He wasn't too clear about what Clostridium Botulinum was, either. Nevertheless, the word "toxin" caught his eye, and he began to read the article. After a page and a half, he realized that none of it meant anything to him: too much reader knowledge was assumed. But the word "Botulinum" had a familiar ring, so he referred to a dictionary of biological terms.

The entry began soberly enough: "Botulism was first positively observed in Germany in 1758. The causative bacterium was isolated by van Ermengem in 1896 . . ." After a while, the entry grew more interesting: "Botulinum toxin is unique in that it is not destroyed by the digestive enzymes of the gastrointestinal tract, and hence is effective when taken orally."

It was a paragraph further down that made Wyman gasp in astonishment: "It is the most potent bacterial toxin known; the guinea pig MLD can be as small as $1 \times 10-^{6}$ millilitres of broth culture. In general, 1 milligramme of Botulinum toxin will kill 1,200,000 guinea pigs. Humans are only slightly more resistant to the toxin than guinea pigs, and they in turn are more susceptible to its effects than mice, rats and dogs."

Wyman paused for reflection. One milligramme could kill over a million guinea pigs. The population of Rome was 2.8 million. Even assuming that humans were twice as resistant as guinea pigs, one would still only need seven or eight milligrammes. Of course, this was only the theoretical dose. Wyman understood that far more would be needed to infect an entire water supply. But the true quantity would still probably run to under a kilogramme.

Wyman noted that the bacteria were commonly found in soil, and thrived on decomposing matter. He recalled the bizarre find at Rucci's flat: the overalls and machete, probably used in killing a sheep. A messy way of doing it, he thought, but the best way to ensure rapid decomposition.

He looked back at his own notes about Ponti. The two main questions were still unanswered: *4. Why does Ponti need Scheib?*, and *5. What could Scheib do for Ponti?*.Wyman had assumed this meant an advanced, specialist piece of work. He now realized it could mean something far simpler: Scheib could watch, understand, and tell the world.

Suddenly, the plan became clear to him.

Ponti had deliberately sent Monica to photograph the waterworks in broad daylight, assuming she would be spotted. The waterworks were purely a red herring: despite Dr. Virno's confidence, Ponti *could* poison Lake Bracciano, and nobody would notice him doing it. "You'd need to bring your poison in truckloads," Virno had said. He hadn't thought of the sheer power of the Botulinum toxin.

Wyman went over to the phone and dialled an emergency number Castellano had given him.

"Hello?" he said. "Is Colonel Castellano there? . . . In that case, how can I find him? . . . It's Professor Wyman . . . I understand, but this is extremely urgent . . . he'll be at the Ministry in one hour? Are you sure of that? . . . Good. If you hear from him before then, tell him I'll be waiting there for him . . . Yes, it's vital that I see him at once . . . Thank you."

He put the phone down and donned his jacket. It was just possible that something could be done, provided they acted swiftly. He went downstairs, and out into the street.

Two men were sitting in a Lancia

parked outside the front door. As Wyman left the apartment, one of them got out of the car and called his name. Wyman turned round in surprise, and stared at the smiling face of Pedro Torres.

"Hello, Professor," Pedro smiled. "Can we offer you a lift."

There was a pistol in Pedro's hand, and Wyman supposed that Pedro knew how to use it.

"Why not?" he shrugged.

57

THE Aeroporto dell'Urbe lies well to the north of Rome, on the Via Salaria. It is a small airfield, in no way rivalling the main airports of Fiumicino and Ciampino. At ten-thirty on Sunday evening, an army helicopter landed there, carrying a special passenger.

A number of Carabinieri were waiting to greet the aircraft. Among them was Colonel Castellano. The helicopter touched down, its door opened, and out came the bulky figure of Professor Theodore Scheib. He was somewhat agitated.

"For Christ's sake!" he bawled out. "Don't any of you imbeciles speak English?"

"It's all right, Professor," Castellano said soothingly. "Tell us what's wrong."

The Professor had been found on a roadside just north of Bologna. He was highly agitated, and of all his confused babble, the police could only understand the words "Colonel Castellano, Rome

Carabinieri". This was enough to get him flown back to Rome, but the cause of his hysteria remained unclear.

"I tried to tell those stupid shit-heads in Bologna, but no one listened. Are you Castellano? Then for the love of God, shut off that water supply!"

"Calm down, Professor," Castellano said. "Just tell us what's the matter."

Professor Scheib did not calm down. He exploded.

"That mad idiot Ponti has just thrown sixty grammes of Botulinum toxin into your drinking water, that's what's the matter."

"What does that mean?"

"It means you're going to die, you bloody cretin!" the Professor shrieked. "He's derived a toxin from Clostridium Botulinum. That's the most powerful bacterial poison on this planet, and Ponti's put sixty grammes of it into Lake Bracciano."

Castellano was not impressed.

"Sixty grammes? That doesn't sound very much—"

"You don't realize how strong it is," Scheib panted. "Sixty grammes will kill everybody in Rome, no trouble. That's why Ponti kidnapped me. He knows I understand that toxin."

Castellano scratched his head in bewilderment.

"Are you sure about this, Professor?"

"Of course I'm sure!" Scheib howled. "Listen, Colonel, Ponti got the recipe from one of my own papers. I saw the bacteria under the microscope. I saw the toxin. I saw it being thrown in the lake. You've got to stop the water supply!"

At last Castellano understood.

"My God," he said slowly. "Is there a cure?"

"No," Scheib said. "You can immunize against it, but it's too late for that. Jesus, Colonel, what are you hanging around for?"

Castellano rapped out a string of orders to some of his men, and they ran back to their cars. One officer barked a series of messages into his radio, and the others drove off to central Rome. The Colonel turned to Soldani and grimaced.

"So Wyman was right after all," he mused. "He was convinced Ponti's plot depended on this man. Perhaps that's why he tried to see me earlier on. Is there still no word?"

"He's vanished without trace," Soldani replied. "Apparently his wife's distraught."

"I'm not surprised," Castellano said grimly. He glanced at the frantic figure of Professor Scheib. "But from the sound of it, that's the least of our worries. Come with me, Professor."

58

ROME was in chaos. Within an hour of Professor Scheib's return, the Monte Mario waterworks was shut down and the news was made public. Late-night television programmes were interrupted by newsflashes asking people not to use tap water, and to remain calm. The Prime Minister made a hurried appearance to insist that the situation was under control, but few people were convinced.

At first, the police issued their warning from loudhailers on vans, but this soon became impossible. The streets quickly became jammed by motorists struggling to leave the city. The GRA, Rome's orbital motorway, was clogged with hooting, static cars. Helicopters chattered over the city, reporting the mayhem to the helpless traffic police. All the phone lines out of Rome were engaged. The Pope added his voice to those urging calm, but his entreaties had little effect. The bars sold out of all their supplies of bottled mineral water, and then a new rumour suggested that these were also contaminated. People began to present themselves at the hospitals, with real or imaginary ailments.

An emergency committee was swiftly convened at the Ministry of Defence. Its clamorous confusion echoed the panic on the streets outside.

"I still don't believe it, Colonel," Dr. Virno said. "From what we've seen, it's not possible that—"

"It's not only possible," Castellano snapped. "It's happened. Professor Scheib didn't dream all this."

The unhappy American was seated a few feet away from the Colonel, emitting clouds of anxious cigar smoke. An interpreter had been summoned to allow Scheib to take part in the meeting.

"Listen Colonel," Virno insisted, "we have taken several dozen samples of water from Bracciano and Monte Mario. We've put them through a detailed analysis, and they're all clear. There isn't the remotest trace of botulism in any of them."

"Try using a microscope," Scheib suggested. "It helps."

"Very funny, Professor," Virno said. "But just think about this: the first symptoms of a poisoned lake are the dead fish which float to the surface. So far, nothing has appeared. We even found a live fish forty minutes ago."

"What about the casualties?" someone said. "People are already being taken to the hospitals."

"Yes," Virno agreed, "and not one of them has so far shown any symptoms of botulism. Not one. Whenever you get scares like this, collective hypochondria sets in."

Professor Scheib brought his fist down on the table.

"Listen, buddy," he expostulated, "I saw that poison go in. I know about that stuff. What do you think I've been doing for the last forty years, playing with myself or something?"

There was a pause as the interpreter struggled for an acceptable translation.

"Then why is there no evidence?" Virno replied.

"You've got the bloody evidence," Scheib roared. "Me! I keep telling you, I saw the poison go in—"

He was interrupted as the doors of the conference room flew apart, and a breathless, dishevelled figure ran in.

"Professor Wyman!" Castellano exclaimed.

"It's all right," Wyman panted. "Panic over."

"What's happened?"

Wyman ignored the question, and produced a scrap of paper, which he gave to the astonished Colonel.

"This is the address of a farm in Piedmont," he explained. "If you send your people there, you should find Franco Ponti and his cronies. I suggest you waste no time: they're planning to leave the country soon."

His eyes fell on the American.

"Professor Scheib," he said quickly. "What happens if you boil a sample of Botulinum toxin for thirty minutes?"

"You neutralize it . . . it'll just go inert."

"Good," Wyman said. "In that case, your worries are over. Unbeknown to Ponti or yourself, the toxin was boiled before it went into Bracciano. The poison's harmless."

Castellano stood up and pulled a chair over for Wyman.

"Perhaps you'd better start at the beginning," he said.

59

THE Rebibbia Prison is a top-security establishment in Rome's Ponte Mammolo district. Suspected terrorists are held in its G8 wing when they await trial. If convicted, they are moved on to special prisons such as Asinara, or Favignana, an island off Trapani in Sicily.

On the morning of November 30, Wyman was shown into the visiting room at G8. He found himself in a sealed cubicle, with Monica seated on the other side of a pane of bullet-proof glass. They talked using phones on either side of the booth.

"Are you well?" Wyman asked.

"Okay, I suppose," Monica said indifferently. "How's Margaret?"

"She's fine," Wyman said.

"They were going to kill you, you know."

"So I heard," Wyman said drily.

"What happened?"

Wyman blinked in surprise.

"You mean they haven't told you?"

"They tell us nothing," Monica said. "It helps break our morale. I've seen none of the others, and you're the first visitor I've had."

"What about your father?"

"He's disowned me," Monica grinned. "He sent me a long, nasty letter saying that I've let him down, that I've made my mother ill—you can guess the rest."

"He'll get over it," Wyman said. "Parents usually do. But I'm surprised no one's told you about what happened."

Monica shook her head.

"I still don't know how the operation went wrong. They surrounded the farm house in Piedmont, we were taken away in separate vans, and that was that. We didn't get a chance to put up a fight. Mario and Pedro never even made it to Piedmont. I suppose they were caught first."

"Yes," Wyman replied. "It was something like that. The poison was harmless, you know. It was boiled beforehand."

Monica's surprise quickly gave way to laughter.

"He *boiled* it? So Ponti never meant to poison Rome. It was all a hoax. My God."

Wyman began to speak, but checked himself. After a pause, he said:

"Did you really mean to do that? Did you really want to poison all of Rome?"

"It was panic we were after," Monica explained. "Only a few people would have died, and we'd have brought the authorities to their knees."

"For a short while you succeeded," Wyman observed. "They wouldn't have coped. I think the casualties would have run to more than just a few people."

Monica shrugged.

"It would have been worth it," she said simply.

"Do you think so?" Wyman asked incredulously. "Do you really think so?"

"Of course," Monica said calmly. "You know my views, Professor. You went to enough trouble to make me state them. Isn't that what they asked you to do?"

"What do you mean?"

"Wasn't that entire course of lectures designed to get me to admit I believe in armed revolution?"

"Not quite," Wyman said. "Personal

Identity was on the syllabus for this term, and I was due to give the lectures. But after Professor Scheib was kidnapped, you became a police suspect. They needed to know if you were directly involved in Ponti's column, and therefore a clue to Scheib's whereabouts, or whether you were merely a sympathetic acquaintance."

"So what did you tell them?"

"What I saw. You argued brilliantly for your views, but you were too frank to be an activist. People who campaign vigorously for revolution often betray a lingering belief that populations can be persuaded rather than coerced, even if they argue for the exact opposite. A terrorist has abandoned that belief, by definition of what he is. Something more was needed to tip the scales, and make you do the things you preached."

"Maybe it was," Monica said. "But it's too late to worry about that now. You know, if that's the only reason why you talked about Personal Identity, you were wasting your time. You should have just asked me: I'd have told you freely enough."

"No," Wyman disagreed. "You could

have told me what you believed, but you couldn't have explained how you came to believe it. Your theory showed me how an educated, intelligent person can reason their way into beliefs the rest of us find abhorrent."

"But you can't disprove my theory, can you?" Monica said triumphantly. "My use of Reductionism still stands. Sure, Enzo had his peaceful, democratic alternative, and the rest of them preferred that. But he couldn't refute what I had to say. Can you?"

"Probably not," Wyman conceded. "But that's not to say it can't be done. One day, we might be able to strangle that idea at birth."

"That's what you'd have to do," Monica agreed, "strangle the idea. You can always put us in places like this, but as long as the idea's still alive, there'll always be someone to take our place."

She laughed sadly.

"It's funny how all this started with Personal Identity. 'What is a person?', you asked. I never thought we'd finish off that discussion in a prison. Well, if it's any consolation to you, Professor, you've made a Reductionist out of me."

"Have I?" Wyman asked in surprise.

"Yes. I believe that people are no more than the events which make them up. There's no extra ingredient. And I believe everything which follows on from that, right up to my own argument for revolution."

"Is that so?" Wyman smiled. "You really believe you know what a person is?"

Monica nodded.

"In that case," Wyman said, "let me tell you a quick story about Personal Identity —one person's identity, to be precise.

"Once upon a time there was a Chilean refugee called Pedro Torres. He said he wanted to go home, but he needed help to do so. A column of the Red Brigades checked up on his identity, and Pedro got an excellent set of references. Even the Russian embassy gave him their seal of approval.

"So the Red Brigades gave Pedro their protection, and admitted him to their inner sanctum. Then they told him about their plot to poison Rome."

Monica lost her composure.

"No," she said hoarsely. "It's impossible . . ."

"Unfortunately," Wyman went on, "they were misinformed about Pedro's identity. He wasn't a Chilean freedom fighter. He was an American, working for the Central Intelligence Agency. It is known as a 'deep cover operation', I believe. In fact, the American's cover was so deep that he was completely beyond contact.

"On the night before the Red Brigades were due to poison Rome, when everyone else was asleep, Pedro boiled the toxin on a stove for half an hour or so. That completely destroyed the poison.

"The next day, he was supposed to kill me, but of course he didn't. The man with him didn't know he was an American, and he didn't find out until the very last minute, when Pedro overpowered him and set me free. I went to tell everyone the happy news, and we all lived reasonably happily ever after. What do you make of that, Monica?"

"Pedro," Monica said lamely. "So it was him . . ."

Wyman nodded.

"What's his real name?" Monica asked.

"Does it matter?"

"No," Monica said, wiping her eyes. "It doesn't matter at all."

Epilogue

ANATOLI BULGAKOV sat patiently in a departure lounge at London's Heathrow Airport. He looked up to see a familiar figure with tinted spectacles and grey crew-cut hair.

"Hello Rawls," he grinned. "You look quite absurd."

"It's the hair dye," Rawls explained, as he put his bag down. "With grey hair, I even *feel* older."

"So your disguise worked, then?"

"Sure," Rawls said, and he sat down beside the Major. "I took a couple of days to get used to the contact-lenses, but after that I had no problems."

"What did you think of our urban revolutionaries?"

"Bloody amateurs," Rawls said. "They couldn't get anything right. A blind man could have seen that car was booby-trapped: you could smell almonds a mile away."

"When plastic explosives sweat in warm climates they give off a powerful aroma of almonds."

"You handled it very well," Bulgakov observed.

"Piece of cake," Rawls said nonchalantly. "I took the explosive off the exhaust pipe before I drove away, and when I got to the park I stuck it in the cigarette lighter on the dashboard. That gave me a couple of seconds to get out before the fun started."

"I suppose your employers are delighted with you: the man who saved Rome, and so forth."

"Like hell," Rawls said. "They don't know whether to give me a medal or fire me. I guess they'll probably do both. 'An unwarranted abuse of personal initiative', Hepburn called it. Can you believe that guy?"

"But Scheib got back safely, didn't he?"

"Their minds don't work like that, Bulgakov. Now they know that Ponti was going to release Scheib anyway, nobody gives a damn about my risking my neck to save him."

"How very irritating for you," Bulgakov sympathized. "But surely they're impressed by how you destroyed the poison. If you hadn't done that . . ."

"Rome would be one big morgue by now," Rawls said. "Sure, they're happy about that, in a grouchy kind of way."

"Extraordinary," Bulgakov exclaimed. "If this is the American reward for success, what is your country's prize for failure?"

Rawls grinned.

"My old man used to say 'Failure is an un-American word.' Smug sonofabitch."

"Never mind," Bulgakov laughed. "You have my admiration, if no one else's. So what is the plan for today?"

"We're going straight to Langley, like we agreed. I told them you kept to your side of the deal and identified me as Pedro Torres. You'll formalize your defection, they'll debrief you, and you'll go to live in a nice house on the West Coast. Doesn't it make you want to sing and shout?"

A nasal female voice requested the passengers to move to the boarding area. As they got up and collected their hand-luggage, a thought occurred to Bulgakov.

"Tell me something. That girl you were investigating—Monica Venuti. What is she like?"

"I don't really know," Rawls shrugged. "A typical over-educated nut. I couldn't understand half her conversation. You know, even when I slept with her, the pillow talk was about philosophy: Personal Identity, whatever that means. What a screwball!"

Rawls shook his head in disgust as they went off to board their plane.

Acknowledgements

I AM grateful to a number of people for the help I received in preparing and writing this book. In Rome, I received valuable advice from Dottoressa Emma Marconcini, as well as Ingeniere Nelli of the *Comune di Roma*, and Ingeniere Paglia of the ACEA. Dawn Keneally's expertise with Roman map-sellers also proved to be a valuable asset.

Simon Knight, formerly of Chelsea College, London, patiently explained to me the preparation of the Clostridium Botulinum toxin. If my account of this process omits any vital steps, the fault is entirely mine.

My final typescript benefited greatly from David Cook's scrutiny, and Rob Jameson plucked out some of its more excruciating howlers. Were it not for Pilot Software Ltd, of 32 Rathbone Place,

London W1, this book would probably have been written with a quill.

My greatest debt of thanks is to Dr. Derek Parfit of All Souls College, Oxford. The theory of Personal Identity used in this story is a weak and vulgar relative of the brilliant family of ideas set out in his book *Reasons and Persons*. I am grateful to Dr. Parfit for his thoughtful reply to my questions, and I hope he can endure the gross unprofessionalism of Michael Wyman without suffering more than a passing shudder.

We hope this Large Print edition gives you the pleasure and enjoyment we ourselves experienced in its publication.

There are now more than 2,000 titles available in this ULVERSCROFT Large print Series. Ask to see a Selection at your nearest library.

The Publisher will be delighted to send you, free of charge, upon request a complete and up-to-date list of all titles available.

Ulverscroft Large Print Books Ltd.
The Green, Bradgate Road
Anstey
Leicestershire
LE7 7FU
England

GUIDE
TO THE COLOUR CODING
OF
ULVERSCROFT BOOKS

Many of our readers have written to us expressing their appreciation for the way in which our colour coding has assisted them in selecting the Ulverscroft books of their choice.

To remind everyone of our colour coding—this is as follows:

BLACK COVERS
Mysteries

★

BLUE COVERS
Romances

★

RED COVERS
Adventure Suspense and General Fiction

★

ORANGE COVERS
Westerns

★

GREEN COVERS
Non-Fiction

MYSTERY TITLES
in the
Ulverscroft Large Print Series

Henrietta Who?	*Catherine Aird*
Slight Mourning	*Catherine Aird*
The China Governess	*Margery Allingham*
Coroner's Pidgin	*Margery Allingham*
Crime at Black Dudley	*Margery Allingham*
Look to the Lady	*Margery Allingham*
More Work for the Undertaker	*Margery Allingham*
Death in the Channel	*J. R. L. Anderson*
Death in the City	*J. R. L. Anderson*
Death on the Rocks	*J. R. L. Anderson*
A Sprig of Sea Lavender	*J. R. L. Anderson*
Death of a Poison-Tongue	*Josephine Bell*
Murder Adrift	*George Bellairs*
Strangers Among the Dead	*George Bellairs*
The Case of the Abominable Snowman	*Nicholas Blake*
The Widow's Cruise	*Nicholas Blake*
The Brides of Friedberg	*Gwendoline Butler*
Murder By Proxy	*Harry Carmichael*
Post Mortem	*Harry Carmichael*
Suicide Clause	*Harry Carmichael*
After the Funeral	*Agatha Christie*
The Body in the Library	*Agatha Christie*

A Caribbean Mystery	*Agatha Christie*
Curtain	*Agatha Christie*
The Hound of Death	*Agatha Christie*
The Labours of Hercules	*Agatha Christie*
Murder on the Orient Express	*Agatha Christie*
The Mystery of the Blue Train	*Agatha Christie*
Parker Pyne Investigates	*Agatha Christie*
Peril at End House	*Agatha Christie*
Sleeping Murder	*Agatha Christie*
Sparkling Cyanide	*Agatha Christie*
They Came to Baghdad	*Agatha Christie*
Third Girl	*Agatha Christie*
The Thirteen Problems	*Agatha Christie*
The Black Spiders	*John Creasey*
Death in the Trees	*John Creasey*
The Mark of the Crescent	*John Creasey*
Quarrel with Murder	*John Creasey*
Two for Inspector West	*John Creasey*
His Last Bow	*Sir Arthur Conan Doyle*
The Valley of Fear	*Sir Arthur Conan Doyle*
Dead to the World	*Francis Durbridge*
My Wife Melissa	*Francis Durbridge*
Alive and Dead	*Elizabeth Ferrars*
Breath of Suspicion	*Elizabeth Ferrars*
Drowned Rat	*Elizabeth Ferrars*
Foot in the Grave	*Elizabeth Ferrars*

Murders Anonymous	*Elizabeth Ferrars*
Don't Whistle 'Macbeth'	*David Fletcher*
A Calculated Risk	*Rae Foley*
The Slippery Step	*Rae Foley*
This Woman Wanted	*Rae Foley*
Home to Roost	*Andrew Garve*
The Forgotten Story	*Winston Graham*
Take My Life	*Winston Graham*
At High Risk	*Palma Harcourt*
Dance for Diplomats	*Palma Harcourt*
Count-Down	*Hartley Howard*
The Appleby File	*Michael Innes*
A Connoisseur's Case	*Michael Innes*
Deadline for a Dream	*Bill Knox*
Death Department	*Bill Knox*
Hellspout	*Bill Knox*
The Taste of Proof	*Bill Knox*
The Affacombe Affair	*Elizabeth Lemarchand*
Let or Hindrance	*Elizabeth Lemarchand*
Unhappy Returns	*Elizabeth Lemarchand*
Waxwork	*Peter Lovesey*
Gideon's Drive	*J. J. Marric*
Gideon's Force	*J. J. Marric*
Gideon's Press	*J. J. Marric*
City of Gold and Shadows	*Ellis Peters*
Death to the Landlords!	*Ellis Peters*
Find a Crooked Sixpence	*Estelle Thompson*
A Mischief Past	*Estelle Thompson*

Three Women in the House	*Estelle Thompson*
Bushranger of the Skies	*Arthur Upfield*
Cake in the Hat Box	*Arthur Upfield*
Madman's Bend	*Arthur Upfield*
Tallant for Disaster	*Andrew York*
Tallant for Trouble	*Andrew York*
Cast for Death	*Margaret Yorke*

FICTION TITLES
in the
Ulverscroft Large Print Series

The Onedin Line: The High Seas
Cyril Abraham
The Onedin Line: The Iron Ships
Cyril Abraham
The Onedin Line: The Shipmaster
Cyril Abraham
The Onedin Line: The Trade Winds
Cyril Abraham
The Enemy *Desmond Bagley*
Flyaway *Desmond Bagley*
The Master Idol *Anthony Burton*
The Navigators *Anthony Burton*
A Place to Stand *Anthony Burton*
The Doomsday Carrier *Victor Canning*
The Cinder Path *Catherine Cookson*
The Girl *Catherine Cookson*
The Invisible Cord *Catherine Cookson*
Life and Mary Ann *Catherine Cookson*
Maggie Rowan *Catherine Cookson*
Marriage and Mary Ann *Catherine Cookson*
Mary Ann's Angels *Catherine Cookson*
All Over the Town *R. F. Delderfield*
Jamaica Inn *Daphne du Maurier*
My Cousin Rachel *Daphne du Maurier*

Enquiry	*Dick Francis*
Flying Finish	*Dick Francis*
Forfeit	*Dick Francis*
High Stakes	*Dick Francis*
In The Frame	*Dick Francis*
Knock Down	*Dick Francis*
Risk	*Dick Francis*
Band of Brothers	*Ernest K. Gann*
Twilight For The Gods	*Ernest K. Gann*
Army of Shadows	*John Harris*
The Claws of Mercy	*John Harris*
Getaway	*John Harris*
Winter Quarry	*Paul Henissart*
East of Desolation	*Jack Higgins*
In the Hour Before Midnight	*Jack Higgins*
Night Judgement at Sinos	*Jack Higgins*
Wrath of the Lion	*Jack Higgins*
Air Bridge	*Hammond Innes*
A Cleft of Stars	*Geoffrey Jenkins*
A Grue of Ice	*Geoffrey Jenkins*
Beloved Exiles	*Agnes Newton Keith*
Passport to Peril	*James Leasor*
Goodbye California	*Alistair MacLean*
South By Java Head	*Alistair MacLean*
All Other Perils	*Robert MacLeod*
Dragonship	*Robert MacLeod*
A Killing in Malta	*Robert MacLeod*
A Property in Cyprus	*Robert MacLeod*

By Command of the Viceroy	*Duncan MacNeil*
The Deceivers	*John Masters*
Nightrunners of Bengal	*John Masters*
Emily of New Moon	*L. M. Montgomery*
The '44 Vintage	*Anthony Price*
High Water	*Douglas Reeman*
Rendezvous-South Atlantic	*Douglas Reeman*
Summer Lightning	*Judith Richards*
Louise	*Sarah Shears*
Louise's Daughters	*Sarah Shears*
Louise's Inheritance	*Sarah Shears*
Beyond the Black Stump	*Nevil Shute*
The Healer	*Frank G. Slaughter*
Sword and Scalpel	*Frank G. Slaughter*
Tomorrow's Miracle	*Frank G. Slaughter*
The Burden	*Mary Westmacott*
A Daughter's a Daughter	*Mary Westmacott*
Giant's Bread	*Mary Westmacott*
The Rose and the Yew Tree	*Mary Westmacott*
Every Man a King	*Anne Worboys*
The Serpent and the Staff	*Frank Yerby*